THE FIRES OF BIRTH

TIME ALLEYS
BOOK 3

J.A. ENFIELD

WAYZGOOSE PRESS

Edited by Dorothy Zemach

Cover art by Morgen Witt

ISBN: 978-1-961953-26-0

Printed in the United States of America

CONTENTS

1. The Time Before Him   1
2. Christmas Present   18
3. Unfamiliar Hues   37
4. Longshanks   59
5. The Rumness Begins   72
6. The Need for Puppetry   87
7. Nonsensical Eyeballs   107
8. Rhymes with Cotton   132
9. Famed Shuttler   152
10. The Pointed Corners   170
11. The Time to Act   199
12. Red for Arteries   219
13. A Qualming Alley   247
14. The Shroud Falls   264
15. The Sight of Home   281
     Epilogue   301

For Magda, who worried about these kids.

1

THE TIME BEFORE HIM

Much of London was bustling with Christmas preparations, but the prosperous streets of Mayfair remained as calm and quiet as always. In the misty gloaming, hearth fires glowed from the tall windows of the stately homes lining Grosvenor Square, lending an emotional warmth to cold streets just starting to turn white with the snow that had been falling in flurries since noon.

Alison called a halt to the Squad's patrol on the pavement in front of a house bright with newly added white brick. She, Leech, Dolly, and Mick looked at one another for a moment before collectively shrugging to indicate that they had completed their task, even though they had nothing to show for it. Although Leech had felt a couple stirrings, there hadn't been any sign that any time alleys had opened recently or that any would open soon.

The lack of alley phenomena was pleasant because it made patrol more a brisk walk through festive London than yet another shift on a job that Mick would have to do daily until he either lost his alley sight or graduated from the Forsyth Institute. And Mick had the best alley sight at the Institute, meaning that he was extremely unlikely ever to lose it, much less before graduation. It was also a blessing that patrol was the only work he had that day. Michaelmas term had ended recently, so Mick and the rest of the Squad didn't have to worry about schoolwork until the new year. But time alleys, by their very nature, didn't care about the normal passage of time, much less anybody's term schedule or Christmas errands, so the Squad and the other Institute patrol teams were still out in full force, scouring the sequences for signs that time was misbehaving.

Although the need to patrol never changed, there had been a lot of changes at the Institute in the two-plus months since Mick had helped prevent the Realignment, which would have made it possible for some alley rats to travel backward through time at will, instead of the usual way: only accidentally and only once. For starters, the Squad was now a greet team, promoted from being a street team. So, out on patrol, they not only had more flexibility, they had more information, including being able to discreetly send and receive updates via the Institute's secret telegraph network. As the team's thane, Alison had also been allowed to broaden her network of non-alley rat informants beyond bribing the local constable with baked potatoes and sweet plums. She couldn't mention time travel to such informants, of course, but she could tell them any cover story she wanted, as long as Miss North or Mr. Victor signed off on it and as long as Chris Biggs, Mick's friend and one of the Project's spymasters, knew about it.

One of Alison's first new informants had been Tips, her friend from back when they had been homeless together on London's streets. A few years older than Alison, Tips was now a refined girl, basically a woman by Victorian standards. She had only a year or two left in her studies at the School for Orphans of the Empire, which she attended with her and Alison's other friends from the streets, Hoot and Gristle. Mick wasn't sure where the nicknames "Hoot" and "Gristle" came from, but "Tips" came from "fingertips." While living on the streets, Tips had often used her nimble fingertips to steal valuables from pockets, stalls, stores, and anywhere else the owner looked away at the wrong time. Mick wondered if Tips still stole things. He figured it must be harder now that she was so pretty that people were always watching her. But probably most of them weren't focused on her fingertips.

Another, bigger change was that it was harder to know whom to trust. Mick trusted Alison, Leech, and Dolly, of course. And he trusted Gail Atkinson, recently promoted to don, and Chris Biggs, Miss Emmet, Miss North, and a few others. But beyond that, he wasn't sure whose intentions were good or whose discretion was reliable. The Realignment clearly had been backed by powerful people and interests, but their identities remained hidden. The most obvious culprit had been the Earl of Harrowgrave, a ruthless, power-hungry man with vast wealth and a dark reputation. But Lord Harrowgrave wasn't the Realignment's only backer, and he might not even have been the main one. Within hours after the Realignment's failure, Lord Harrowgrave had been mysteriously murdered. Soon afterward, Chris, Mick, and a handful of other "Palladians" had learned that Catherine Collins, the young woman who had done most of Lord Harrowgrave's legwork for the Realignment, had probably been working for a different powerful aristocrat, Lady Penbrook, at least as much as for Lord Harrowgrave.

Mick and the Squad had met Lady Penbrook when they

were attending the Institute's version of summer school at Demeter Academy, a sort of school-farm-workshop far south of the river in Peckham. Through her influence, Mick and Alison had eventually been introduced to the Undertaking, a group of alley rats stealthily trying to chip away at some of Victorian England's dumbest and cruelest inequities. Mick had found Lady Penbrook too intimidating to like, but he had admired her, as had Alison and many others. It had been a painful, frightening shock to learn that Lady Penbrook probably had been trying to cause the Realignment rather than working with the rest of the Undertaking to prevent it. And that had been the reason the Palladians had formed their own small, secret group —even key people in the Undertaking couldn't always be trusted.

Of course, it wasn't absolutely certain that Lady Penbrook had been involved with the Realignment, and if she had been, nobody except her and possibly Catherine Collins knew why. Everything was confusing and shrouded in secrecy.

Still, it sure looked like Lady Penbrook had been involved, and it was hard to think of a *good* reason for that. Lord Harrowgrave had taken his motivations to the tomb, but it was a safe bet that he had thought the Realignment would make him even richer and more powerful. Catherine Collins' motives—and loyalties—were unclear, and nobody could find her to ask her. She had disappeared the day the Realignment failed, and not even Chris had been able to find her. And Chris could find anybody, at least anybody in London.

Mick had his own reasons for wanting to find Catherine Collins, starting with the fact that despite now being a decade older than he was, she was almost surely his sister Emilia, whom he had last seen when she was a baby and he had gotten pulled into the time alley that brought him from 2024 Chicago to 1853 London.

"Are you quite all right, Gunner?" Alison asked, the fretful vertical line between her blue eyes deepened by the frown taking over her long, narrow face.

Mick wondered what had been showing in his expression. He nodded.

"Only, you don't look at all well," Alison said.

"I'm well enough," Mick said. He couldn't talk to them about Catherine Collins because he hadn't told anybody that she was his sister. Every day that went by made him both more desperate to tell someone and more afraid to tell anyone.

"Yet you look like you've just seen Marley's ghost," Leech said, his bright green eyes alert with interest.

The Tory Six boys' prefect, Mr. Braddock, had been reading *A Christmas Carol* to the Sixers each night in his newly deep voice, and he was a surprisingly good actor. He'd made Marley's ghost sound legitimately spooky.

Mick noticed that Dolly's rounded face was also wearing an even more worried expression than usual. Clearly, his friends were going to keep asking him questions unless he came up with an explanation. He realized that he could get away with telling them the truth. Well, *a* truth, even if it wasn't the truth that was bothering him at the moment. "Well," he said, trying with partial success to maintain a high-class London accent that matched the neighborhood, "we're really close to Lady Penbrook's townhouse. It makes me anxious."

Leech and Dolly opened their mouths slightly in surprise as they consulted their mental maps of London. Alison's expression relaxed, without, of course, showing any surprise. Alison had survived on the streets of London for years as a small child.

She always knew where she was and what was around her, and she obviously hadn't forgotten that Lady Penbrook's townhouse was nearby.

After the initial surprise, Leech's face hardened. "Perhaps we should pay her ladyship a call," he said, in a perfect upper-class London accent. "Perhaps we might offer her a gift in remembrance of Owl." His voice reverted to his actual Irish accent. "A firebomb, maybe."

"Leech," Alison said sharply, "don't talk rubbish. You and Dolly both promised never to tell another soul that we suspect Lady Penbrook was involved in the Realignment, did you not?"

"We most definitely did," Dolly said.

Palladians weren't supposed to unnecessarily share information, even with each other, but Mick had gotten permission to tell the Squad enough about Lady Penbrook and the Realignment so that they would know, and could avoid, the biggest risks. But knowing that Lady Penbrook had probably helped cause the fight over the Realignment that had gotten their friend Owl killed had filled Leech with a burning fury. Mick suspected that Dolly's and Alison's anger, like his own, was burning just as hot but with the fires mostly screened from view.

"And telling Lady Penbrook of that suspicion would be telling another soul, would it not?" Alison asked.

"It most definitely would," Dolly said.

Leech remained silent, his face tight.

"Leech?" Alison prompted.

"She got Owl killed," Leech said.

"You gave your word, Leigh Charles," Alison said. "You are our friend, you are our teammate, and you gave your word."

Leech threw his arms forward slightly and sighed, now more frustrated than angry. "I'll keep my word. But she got Owl killed."

"We don't know that," Alison said, "not to a certainty. And even if she did—*especially* if she did—she would still be a powerful and ruthless person not to be trifled with. If she is guilty, at the moment there is nothing we can do to punish her. Accusing her to her face now would simply allow her to cover her traces and strengthen her defenses."

"It isn't right," Leech grumbled.

"No, it isn't," Alison agreed.

"Leech," Dolly interjected, "you know that if Lady Penbrook is responsible for what happened on the Hungerford Bridge, she's almost certainly responsible for Lord Harrowgrave's murder as well."

This was something that Chris had pointed out to Mick, but Dolly had figured it out on her own before he could warn her and the rest of the Squad.

Leech nodded grudgingly.

"And Lord Harrowgrave was a powerful man. Physically powerful too, they say. According to the broadsheets, he was locked safely in offices that he had hired, his minions all about him. Yet someone stabbed him in the neck and strolled away, unseen and scot-free. Given all that, *perhaps*, just perhaps, it would be unwise to announce ourselves as her enemy, wouldn't you think?"

Leech shrugged, not conceding the point aloud but not able to dispute it.

That was another thing that had changed since they had helped to prevent the Realignment. Dolly was more … relentless, maybe. She had always been willing to argue with Leech, but now she was more willing—and more able—to shut their arguments down. She even did it sometimes to Mick and Alison. Mick wasn't sure why she had changed. Maybe it was Owl's death. Maybe it was losing the "Collapsers," the eight brave young men and women who had risked their lives taking a one-way trip to 1767 to stop the Realignment. She'd certainly been spending a lot of time trying to learn whether the Collapsers had survived that trip. Whatever the reason, Mick hoped she was okay.

"Besides," Alison said, "there are at least two Eyes watching us at the moment. Or, better said, watching the square. And there must certainly be others watching Lady Penbrook's townhouse. We've no way of knowing whether those Eyes are in her service. For that matter, *they* likely have no way of knowing. It's a most difficult situation."

Mick caught Alison's gaze, and she flicked her eyes to each of the Eyes surveilling the square. Mick winced. He'd spotted the teenage girl in the ragged coat, but he'd taken the middle-aged gentleman with the tremendous sideburns for a prosperous resident of the neighborhood, not for a street spy. Thanks to Alison, compared to most kids at the Institute, Mick had excellent street sight. But compared to Alison herself, he was still pretty clueless.

Leech sighed heavily. "Very well," he said, slipping back into his posh English accent. "We shan't see if Lady Penbrook is at home to callers. Should we instead pop in at Lady Grenville's to enroll you fine ladies?"

Alison and Dolly rolled their eyes, and Leech grinned at them. Like the Institute, Lady Grenville's Academy was part of the Project, a large collection of loosely connected and sometimes feuding alley rats and their organizations. Lady Grenville's had the reputation of being a place where young women with bad grades or bad alley sight went to learn how to be respectable wives to men of high position. Alison and Dolly used its name to scare each other into studying harder.

After squabbling a bit over what to do next, they decided to wander back to the Institute by a route that would take them past street-sellers with coffee (for Leech) and roasted chestnuts and baked potatoes (for everyone). Mick thought about making up an excuse to meet them back at the Institute so that he could detour south to Belgravia to see if Catherine Collins had emerged from hiding. But there was no reason to think she had, and surely the dons at the Eaton Square Outpost would be keeping an eye on her Belgravia rooms, which were just across the square from the outpost. For that matter, surely Chris would be keeping an Eye (or two) on the rooms as well. Besides, many of the same reasons it would be dumb and potentially dangerous to confront Lady Penbrook also applied to Catherine Collins. Mick might know she was his sister, but she didn't. She didn't know she was *anybody's* sister. And maybe she wouldn't care even if she did know. So, reluctantly, Mick let go of the idea and tried to keep his thoughts from showing on his face.

Later that night, Mick and the Squad clustered together with the rest of the Sixers in the warmth and light of one of Tory Six's big common room fireplaces to listen to Mr. Braddock read the last stave of *A Christmas Carol.* Some of the older students tried to pretend they were too cool for Ebeneezer Scrooge and that they were only there so the fire would protect them from the wintry airs stalking the Institute, but Mick could tell most of them were enjoying it as much as the younger kids.

The Squad was enjoying it too. They were all sitting at their accustomed table, where their faces flickered in the firelight. As usual, Leech was smiling and outwardly relaxed, his eyes wide with interest beneath his heavy, rectangular forehead. Alison's and Dolly's good cheer was more subtle but obvious now that Mick knew them so well, testified to by the absence of their usual faint frowns. Especially in the English winter, all his friends' faces were pale enough that they picked up a faint orange shine from the fire, and their eyes glowed brighter than could be explained by the light of fire and lamp. That glow marked them as alley rats with very good alley sight. Well, it marked them to Mick, anyway. He didn't know of anybody else who could see the alley rat glow in people's eyes.

Overall, Mick was enjoying it too, although his emotions were messy. For starters, it was a weird scene. The story had been written in 1843, so it was only about as old as the kids listening to it, though it had been written a century or more before any of them were born. Mick had always enjoyed the Scrooge story. His mom and dad had read it to him at Christmastime when he was little, and they'd all watched the movies together, sometimes two or three versions on the same day. His dad had liked an old black and white version. His mom and her sisters, Tía Verónica and Tía Julieta, had all liked the Muppets version, and his Uncle Dan had liked the one where the Ghost of Christmas Present wore a tutu and kicked Scrooge in the crotch.

So, on one hand, listening to Mr. Braddock reading the story filled Mick with happy memories of being a little kid. On the other hand, it also reminded him that, like all his torymates and, for that matter, like all the students at the Institute, he had been born far, far in the future. For Mick, remembering his Christmases Past meant remembering Victorian London's Christmases Future, which forced him to remember that his world was at least as weird as Scrooge's world of ghosts and spirits. In Mick's world, time travel was inexplicable but real. In Mick's world, one day Scrooge's story had been published a couple centuries earlier and Mick could stream a dozen movie versions of it. But then, somehow, the next day it was 1853 and Scrooge's story was only ten years old and its author was still alive.

For that matter, Mick had passed the offices of the story's publishers many dozens of times since dropping in 1853, sometimes patrolling on foot for time alleys, sometimes clunking through the city in a wagon with Chris while she checked in with the secretive Eyes who spied on most of London for her, sometimes just out walking with his friends. So he knew those offices were real and that real editors worked there. He knew that all of 1853 London was real, including its millions of inhabitants and all its smokes, smells, and clamors. But sometimes he couldn't quite believe it, couldn't totally accept that he had dropped from the twenty-first century into a time when people read novels by oil lamp because nobody had electricity.

Mr. Braddock was reading the part about Scrooge waking up after the Ghost of Christmas Future had given him a horrifying vision of his own lonely death. It contained a line describing how Scrooge could change that future if he lived a better life: "the time before him was his own." In 1853 London, which soon would be 1854 London, "before" was a slippery word. For

Scrooge, in that instant, "before" meant "ahead of." But of course it could also mean "earlier than." And for Mick, the future was before him in both ways—both far, far ahead of him and something that had already happened. Being both shouldn't be possible. And yet, there it was.

Or there it would be.

Or something like that.

As he often did, Mick wondered about his friends' former lives. At the Institute and, indeed, throughout the Project that ran the Institute, alley rats weren't supposed to talk about their futures, in case talking about the future could change the future. They weren't even supposed to talk in ways that came from the future, or to do anything else that wasn't normal in 1853. Anything that noticeably came from the future was a "conspicuous anachronism," or "connan" for short, and Mick had spent his first few months at the Institute getting scolded for connans that he'd had no idea were connans. Nobody knew if you could really change the future just by talking about it, much less how to tell whether a particular connan was harmless or a dangerous, unforgivable "mortal anachronism" that might radically change the future. Still, a lot of smart people thought there was a real risk and that everybody needed to protect the future with silence.

Mick was starting to wonder if the silence was also supposed to protect everyone's feelings. Where Mick came from, people like Tía Julieta were always saying you had to talk about your trauma to fix your trauma, but that definitely was *not* how they rolled in Victorian London. If your trauma was physical, Victorians either would tell you to stiffen your upper lip or would throw some weird, possibly deadly, "remedy" at it. Victorians sprinkled opium into everything like 2024 Americans with pumpkin spice. Except that 2024 Americans didn't use pumpkin spice to keep babies quiet.

As far as Mick could tell, if your trauma was psychological, Victorians would throw silence at it—a heavy, invisible blanket of This Will Not Be Discussed. The theory seemed to be that what you didn't mention couldn't hurt you. Even at the Institute, where nobody had actually been born a Victorian, a lot of people used the blanket of silence to tuck themselves in at night. That had become really clear a couple months earlier when Owl had died helping to prevent the Realignment. After Owl's funeral, people almost never mentioned him. It drove Mick crazy.

Mr. Braddock got to the end of the story, when Tiny Tim didn't die, and Mick saw his friends' faces grow sad as they remembered Owl. He could feel his own face doing the same.

"Do you suppose villains like Scrooge ever truly repent?" Alison asked the group.

Mick suspected Alison was thinking about Lady Penbrook, but he found himself wondering about Catherine Collins (Emilia!) instead. He'd been doing so since he'd found Swaggy Bear while he and Chris had been searching Catherine Collins' rooms in Belgravia. Swaggy Bear was the lumpy, barf-orange teddy bear Tía Julieta had made for Emilia, and Mick had recognized it immediately, even before finding "J" and "E" stitched into its ears. He'd realized that Catherine Collins had always seemed familiar because she looked so much like photographs of their mom when their mom had been about the same age. That meant that, somehow, Emilia and her teddy bear had gotten pulled into Mick's time alley. But something strange must have happened in the alley because she'd ended up in 1833, not with him in 1853, which was why she was now a decade older than he was instead of a decade younger. Something similar had happened to Alison and her brother, though Alison and her brother had only ended up a couple years apart. And, of course, Alison's brother had died in the time alley.

Catherine Collins didn't recognize Mick as her brother, of course. She had dropped into the past as a baby, so the only thing she could know about her old life was what the greet team had recorded about finding her. Mick had convinced Miss Emmet to show him the relevant log entry, which said almost nothing. Shortly after noon on December 28, 1833, Catherine Collins had been found as an infant on Union Street near Clarendon Square (about a mile and a half north of Mick's drop site). There had been "no marks of identity about her person," and "her dress and swaddle" had been in "customary derangement." The log also said that she had arrived "possessed of one poppet of the animal sort & naught else."

The "poppet of the animal sort" had to be Swaggy Bear, which, if Dolly's theory was right, had survived the time alley because Tía Julieta had made it with all-natural fibers. Mick thought it was a good theory. Dolly was definitely right that alley rats tended to arrive without other kinds of materials on them—no fancy wicking fabrics or stretchy fabrics, no glasses, no braces, and so on.

In any case, Catherine Collins had no way of knowing that she was his sister. But then, maybe she wasn't, not really. His sister had been a one-year-old gurgling and giggling in the crib next to Mick's bed at Uncle Dan's place on a sweaty August night in 2024 Chicago. In Mick's mind, Emilia was someone whose life would continue forward from that night. Sure, she'd grow up. But she'd grow up in the twenty-first century and, if he could get back there soon enough, she'd always be way younger than him. Catherine Collins, on the other hand, was a twenty-one-year-old woman who had been old enough for kindergarten when Queen Victoria took the throne.

Since the day he'd fallen bruised and exhausted out of his time alley, Mick had been trying to figure out how to get back to his baby sister and the rest of his life. But now his baby sister was in the past and older than he was, and her baby version probably wasn't even still there, whatever "still" and "there" meant. Under normal conditions, time alleys didn't stay open long, so she had probably gotten dragged into the alley right after he had. Could he somehow stop her from getting pulled into the alley? Stop *himself* from getting pulled in? Even if he could, should he? Messing with the alleys that way was exactly the sort of thing that killed innocent people, just like Cassandra Halliwell, Lord Harrowgrave, and, probably, Lady Penbrook had already done. The thought of one more dead kid falling out a time alley made him want to barf.

On the other hand, Catherine Collins might turn out to be pretty dangerous herself. She possibly saw alleys even better than Mick, and she definitely could do things with alleys better than anybody at the Institute. And she'd been willing to use her talents to endanger the future, either to benefit Lord Harrow-grave or Lady Penbrook, or both. Maybe she'd been part of getting all those kids killed in the first place. Maybe he had a duty to stop her, and maybe that meant making sure that baby Emilia never got into the time alley that had turned her into grown-up Catherine Collins.

These were all familiar thoughts, ones that had twisted and tortured his brain countless times ever since he'd realized Catherine Collins was his sister. And they always led him to think what he was thinking now: he needed to talk to her. He needed to see if any part of her somehow recognized him as the older brother who had dangled Swaggy Bear over her crib and read her Squirrel Girl comics when she got fussy in the middle of the night. If he could do that, maybe he'd know what to do next.

But he had no idea how to find her. Well, at least not until her December 28 drop anniversary. A lot of rats went to visit the spots where their time alleys had dumped them into the past, especially on their drop anniversaries, and she might be one of them.

Yet again, he wondered if he should tell somebody that Catherine Collins was his sister. Maybe the Squad. Maybe Chris, or Gail, or Miss Emmet. He could really use some advice. But he couldn't bring himself to tell anyone. He was afraid that they might think he was guilty by association. Or that they would realize how desperately he wanted to talk to her and would forbid him from doing it because, well, forbidding him made sense.

Mick felt a slap on his shoulder. Leech.

Mick realized that Alison, Leech, and Dolly were all staring at him. He wondered how long he'd been spacing out.

"Have you just been visited by the Ghosts of Christmas?" Leech asked him. "Are you only now returning from the realm of spectral visions?"

"Close enough," Mick said.

Mick caught Alison's eye. It was obvious she had questions for him. But to his relief, she didn't ask them and instead changed the topic of conversation to some gossip about Mr. Victor. Mick felt a rush of gratitude toward her, a rush that, to his surprise, spread out to basically everybody in the room. He was grateful to be warm, to have enough to eat, and to have friends. A lot of kids in a lot of centuries never got any of that, much less all of it at once. He couldn't stop wanting to get back to his real home, and he couldn't stop wondering if Catherine Collins was his sister, his enemy, or both. But he tried to put those worries and wonderings at the back of his mind for a bit.

2

CHRISTMAS PRESENT

Like all the students, the Squad exchanged presents on Christmas Eve. Nobody had time or money for anything fancy, but they had done the best they could. Alison had painted them pretty watercolor miniatures of time alleys they had seen while patrolling together. But only the happy ones—nothing associated with echo phantasms or dead kids. Dolly gave everyone little printed illustrations of the Midlands countryside because she found them "soothing in moments of distress." Leech gave everyone boiled sweets, and Mick gave everyone their favorite street-seller goodies, including spice cakes from Mayor Cakes for Dolly. Even though the gifts were simple little things, they all teared up and pretended they hadn't. Partly, they were all glad to have such good friends. And partly, Mick was pretty sure, they were missing loved ones far away in the future or, as with Alison's brother and Owl, forever in the past.

On Christmas morning after breakfast, all students not assigned to the skeleton Christmas patrols gathered in the

Great Hall for caroling. Under the cheerful supervision of the Vicar, the youngest children were on the ground floor, gathered around both the enormous tree at the center of the hall and the student choir beside it. Mr. Phillips was leading the choir with a broad grin on his face. A lot of kids made fun of Mr. Phillips for teaching music instead of something related to time alleys, but he had grown on Mick. Partly that was because he'd protected Mick from somebody trying to bury a knife in Mick, but partly Mick just appreciated that Mr. Phillips loved teaching music so much.

The children not in the choir were gathered at the railings encircling the Great Hall on each floor, getting older as the floors went up. The Squad was on the English second floor (American third). The professors were scattered on every floor, staring menacingly at kids who misbehaved. There had been some rude lyrics wafting from the top floor while the choir sang "Coventry Carol," but the floor had gone silent as a tomb when Mr. Victor appeared at the railing, glaring.

Many of the students, including Mick, were dressed in the Institute's uniform, the "instisuit," but many were dressed in their respectable outside clothes so that they could attend Christmas services after caroling. Leech was among them, ready for Mass at St. Clare's. Alison was also dressed up, but not for church. If she and Dolly attended services, they usually attended the Vicar's services in the Institute chapel. Alison was dressed up to visit her friends at Orphans, but only *after* her friends finished sitting through the lengthy and, Alison said, painfully boring High Church Mass at Christ Church.

That morning, most of the singing had come from the choir while the other students listened, more or less respectfully. But the Vicar was making everybody, even the professors, sing the last few carols together. Mick had worried that the carols would turn out to be more Victorian lore that everybody knew but him. Fortunately, a lot of the Christmas carols he'd learned as a twenty-first-century kid were carols that Victorian kids sang too. He got through "God Rest Ye Merry Gentlemen" and "O Come All Ye Faithful" without embarrassing himself. By "Joy to the World," he was actually enjoying himself, though mostly that was because he got to listen to Dolly, who turned out to have a beautiful—and powerful—singing voice.

As Alison took her leave, she told Mick that Miss Emmet wanted to see him in her office. Neither of them knew why Miss Emmet would want to see him on Christmas. Mick navigated the crowded main hallways and dusty back corridors until reaching the library's rear door. It was locked, of course, but he tugged on the bell pull. Soon, the heavy door opened with gentle creaking to reveal Miss Emmet's cheerful, round face. "Merry Christmas, Mr. Gunn."

"Merry Christmas, Miss Emmet," he said as she closed and locked the door behind him.

Mick wanted to ask why she'd summoned him, but she made non-stop small talk until they were in her office with the door closed. Mick was caught off-guard when he looked around. Miss Emmet's office was always crowded with half the books in the universe, but that day it was also crowded with Chris, Miss North, and Mr. Victor.

Along with her usual conspiratorial half-grin, Chris was wearing the sort of suit one might expect to find on a skilled tradesman attending Christmas Mass. Miss Emmet and Mr. Victor wore their usual somber gray woolens and alert, grim expressions. Miss North was a slender woman with slender features who made Mick think of scalpels, and Mr. Victor was a broad-shouldered, solid-waisted man who made Mick think of daggers.

Mick squeezed himself into the last remaining seat, a wobbly stool that usually served as a plant stand for the only plant in Miss Emmet's office, a valiant fern that always looked like it was dying but somehow continued to survive.

Mick figured that this had to be about Palladian business. Miss North's and Mr. Victor's offices were both bigger and easier to get to than Miss Emmet's. If this had been about school business, it would have made more sense to meet in either of their offices. Miss Emmet's office's only real advantage was being much harder to spy on.

Chris said, "We've asked you here to discuss Catherine Collins."

Mick tried to keep his face neutral.

"Doubtless this detail escaped your attention," Chris said, "but Miss Collins' drop anniversary is the twenty-eighth of December."

Her tone made clear that everybody in the room knew that detail had *not* escaped Mick's attention.

"And no doubt it also escaped the attention of Miss March, Miss Tee, and Mr. Charles," Miss Emmet said with equal irony.

Mick knew his best course was to keep quiet, which wasn't hard. It was intimidating to be ganged up on by adults, especially this particular gang.

"It's really for the best that it escaped your attention," Chris said. "If you had remembered it, you might have thought it worthwhile to visit Miss Collins' drop site to see if she returned there to commemorate the anniversary, as so many alley rats do."

"Which," Miss Emmet said, "might have jeopardized *our* plan to do that very thing."

"So you and your friends must avoid Miss Collins' drop site," Mr. Victor said. "If you do not, it could be disastrous."

Mick nodded, trying to look as innocent as possible. "I'll let the others know," he said.

"See that you do, Mr. Gunn," Miss North said. "And, to be clear, *none* of you is to go near Miss Collins' drop site—not on the day of her drop anniversary itself, not before."

"It is," Mr. Victor said, leaning forward slightly, "quite important, Mr. Gunn."

Mick nodded but found them all still staring at him intently. "I understand," he added.

The stares relaxed slightly.

"Well, if you fine folk of the palace don't need anything further from your humble servant...?" Chris asked, rising to her feet.

Mr. Victor snorted with amusement.

"I'll take Gunner with me, shall I?" Chris asked.

"Thank you, Chris," Miss North said. She nodded to Mick. "And thank you, Mr. Gunn. Merry Christmas to you both."

"Merry Christmas," Mick said before squeezing through everyone to follow Chris out of the office.

"Grab your coat and meet me at the garden gate, Gunner," Chris said. "Let's take a Christmas constitutional and discuss fortune and philosophy, what?"

Mick knew Chris well enough to understand that she was telling him not to talk about any Palladian business until they were outside. He jogged to his room, threw on his outdoor clothes and coat, and trotted downstairs, out to the garden gate. Since the cooks and scullions were on Christmas holiday, Chris locked and unlocked the pedestrian gate herself, somehow, as usual, magically having the correct key to hand.

Mick wondered if they would be walking, taking a cab, or doing something more exotic. Chris had once told him that she occasionally traveled across London by hopping on and off moving trains, but she might just have been messing with him. She liked to mix truth with fiction to see how he responded.

That day, at least, there were no moving trains. Squinting slightly against the unusually bright sunlight of a clear, cold day, they made their way to Tottenham Court Road, where Chris paused at the intersection, which was busy despite the holiday. "I'm perversely tempted to escort you directly to the site in question," she said, slightly emphasizing "the site in question" to make clear that she was avoiding names, which Mick took as a reminder that they might be overheard. *"I'm dreadfully sorry, darlings,"* Chris continued in a fancy accent, *"do you mean, we shouldn't have gone? Oh, I do wish you had said something earlier."*

Mick laughed. Miss North and the others really had been leaning hard into telling him not to go to Catherine Collins' drop site. He asked, "This isn't one of those things where they tell me I shouldn't do something so often that I'm supposed to realize that they actually want me to do it, is it?"

Chris grinned. "It *very* much is not, young sir. They meant every word. As," she said, staring seriously at him, "do I."

They were now at the heart of Museum Cluster. By habit, Mick was alert for alley signs and phenomena, but so far the time alleys were also taking Christmas off.

After they had strolled in silence for a while, Mick asked, "Why?"

"Why should you do as your elders instruct?" Chris asked. "Why, because you're a dutiful and obedient child, naturally."

Mick grinned at that. "I won't go to the place," he said, trying to stick with his rich kid London accent, even though it made him feel like a doofus. "And I'll tell the others not to do it either."

Saying it out loud, he realized that he meant it. He wasn't going to defy instructions just because he wanted to see his sister again. A lot of adults, especially in Victorian London, liked to tell everybody what to do, especially kids. For those adults, being obeyed was the point, not making sense. But Miss North and the others tried to make sense. And Mick had learned that the adult Palladians often knew more than they could safely tell him—and that if he didn't accept that, he could cause problems. Maybe even get people hurt or killed.

Still, he was pretty sure that sometimes they could have told him more and that the extra information might have helped him *avoid* problems. "I simply wish to understand better," he explained, trying to sound primly Victorian.

"A noble motive, young man. A noble motive. I'm afraid there's nothing I can say as to their reasons for wanting you to keep away, beyond the obvious fact that they are attempting to make plans and very sensibly don't want you complicating those plans." She held up a finger to prevent protest. "However, I can say that, were I in their place, I would lay down the same prohibition, especially as to you and the young headmistress," she said, using her personal nickname for Alison. "Recall that during the recent unpleasantness"—meaning during the fight over the Realignment—"the young lady under discussion tugged you a few feet toward the railing while you were unconscious. So far as I can tell, it was simply to leave you in a safer spot, a point in her favor. In any event, she would surely recognize you, and very possibly the young headmistress, who also was conspicuous during those events."

Mick felt dumb for not having thought of that. He knew that Catherine Collins had pulled him to safety on the bridge, but he hadn't really realized that meant she would recognize him. He'd been too busy wondering whether that good deed might mean that she was a good person even though she was working for bad people.

"What's more," Chris said, "I must assume that our friends making the plans are likely aware that children such as your-selves would be somewhat beyond their customary routes at the site in question."

Mick tried to decipher that as they walked along the southern edge of Russell Square, past the enormous statue of the Duke of Bedford and his sheep. Eventually, he concluded that Chris' point was that Catherine Collins' drop site was a half mile or so north of the Institute's usual patrol sequences. Mick tried to remember who patrolled that area. There wasn't a dons' outpost nearby, but St. George's School, the boys' version of Lady Grenville's Academy, was pretty close. Were there dons stationed at St. George's? The Project did seem to quietly smuggle people back and forth between different schools. Mr. Victor had taught at Orphans when Mick's friend Ward had briefly been a student there, and Alison said that her friends at Orphans had told her that for months Miss Emmet had been visiting Orphans once or twice a week for some reason.

Mick tried to focus on the topic at hand. The main point, of course, was that Catherine Collins had spent fifteen years or so at the Institute before transferring to Lady Grenville's. She'd almost certainly be able to spot Institute students and would wonder why they had strayed so far from the Institute into an area that didn't have much time alley activity.

"That has sense, I suppose," Mick said, trying to maintain his fancy English accent and diction. "Where are we going?"

"No particular destination. I merely thought you might wish to escape the palace for a short spell."

Mick snorted politely to let Chris know he wasn't buying it. Although he *was* glad to get out of the Institute, especially on a sunny day, he didn't for a minute believe that Chris had simply wanted his company on a stroll.

Chris raised her eyebrows at him, the picture of casual innocence.

Soon, they were walking by Lincoln's Inn. As they passed the Portugal lookout, Chris exchanged a complicated set of signs with the grubby Eye in charge of the lookout but didn't stop to chat.

Not long after that, they reached St. Clement Danes. There was probably a Christmas Mass underway inside the church, but the little yard on the Pickett Street side was quiet and nearly empty. Chris led him to a spot beside the tall iron fence as far as possible from other people.

"I truly did think you might wish to escape the palace for a moment or two," Chris said.

Mick knew there was more than that and waited her out.

She smiled as the silence stretched out. "Good lad," she said. "Yes, I also wanted to warn you to be cautious. I imagine Miss Emmet and the others have said much of this to you since the fracas on the bridge." She jutted her chin in the general direction of the Hungerford Bridge. "And I know you're far from foolish. You're one of the most sober-minded chaps of your age I've encountered, and I don't know whether to praise or pity you for it. But the great lady who has commanded so much of our attention and curiosity of late—"

That had to be Lady Penbrook, Mick thought, a little surprised that Chris was still speaking in code in this isolated spot.

"That lady is an immensely clever and patient woman. Her plans, her thoughts, her everything, are layered one upon another like an onion wrapped with ruffled petticoats, and one can never be sure that one has reached the core. I have known the Eye at the Portugal lookout whom I just now greeted for nearly five years, and I cannot say with any confidence whether she is loyal to me. She may be loyal to the lady and know it. She may serve the lady but think herself still loyal to me. And whether loyalty even matters when every Eye makes their reports and those reports are transmitted along the chain to old Mr. Bly—" She paused for a second with her eyebrows raised.

Oh, right, Mick thought. Not "old Mr. Bly" but "Old Pye," the street where the Project had its headquarters. He nodded to show he understood.

"And the lady has quite enchanted Mr. Bly. He'll tell her anything for a kind word. Or perhaps the reports that should go to Mr. Bly are altered or simply sent to her instead, and only the lady ever gets the true picture. Loyalty may not much matter in such circumstances."

Mick nodded.

Chris sighed. "I fear I'm wandering from my course. The main point I wish to make is that the lady is powerful, subtle, and, it would seem, capable of great ruthlessness. And she is aware of you. Likely also of the young headmistress, perhaps even of your friends. But most assuredly of you. Your role in the … unpleasantness on the bridge may not have been entirely

clear to the lady or her lieutenants. We have certainly endeav-
ored to ensure that your full contribution remains unknown to
Mr. Bly, the lady, and the rest. But something of what you did,
of what you can see, I'm afraid that is very much known. And
that assuredly makes you of interest to the lady."

She raised her eyebrows at him to make sure he was listening. He nodded.

She sighed thoughtfully, choosing her next words. "As to
what that might mean for you, I cannot say. Perhaps nothing.
But perhaps something quite important. As someone who is
also of interest to the lady, I must tell you that being of interest
to her can be demanding. And uncertain. For example, the lady
certainly knows that I went to great lengths to thwart her plans
on the bridge. But I haven't any idea whether she knows that I
know they were *her* plans, or whether instead I continue to
blame only ... the other."

Mick nodded to show that he knew she meant Lord
Harrowgrave.

"My situation is," Chris continued, "rich in complications.
My labors often require me to visit her domains. They sometimes require me to provide the lady with certain information,
often in person. Which allows her to scrutinize me closely."

Mick didn't envy Chris. The few times he had spoken with
Lady Penbrook, she had given him the impression that she
could read his mind like a book. A baby book with easy words
and big pictures.

Which was another reason not to go charging after Lady
Penbrook like Leech wanted. She'd probably learn too much
from him even if he didn't open his mouth. Maybe the same
thing would happen if he tried to talk to Catherine Collins, but
he didn't want to think about that.

"At the moment," Chris said, "we have one another stale-mated. The lady may well suspect that I suspect her. But I haven't denounced her, and nobody has made any move against her. Indeed, with ... the other ... dead, she's taken on a more active role with Mr. Bly, taken power that was once the other's, and no obstacles have been placed before her. So she may think that, even if I suspect her, I approve of her actions. She may think that I disapprove of her actions but that she can sway me to her side. She may think any number of things. And so for the moment, outwardly we proceed just as always. And if I seem unusually nervous, or she seems especially close-lipped, well, there are many explanations."

"So, I should stay off her rad— should avoid her attention?" Mick asked.

"If you can do so without behaving unnaturally," Chris said. "But, as you know, she prefers to receive certain information from those most directly involved, as you very much have been. Nobody would be surprised were she to put questions to you about recent matters of interest, and she would regard it as suspicious if you were simply to refuse to speak with her." She paused. "If you are summoned to her, let the right person know immediately. If possible, let several of the right people know. We shall guide you."

Mick nodded.

"I am keenly conscious," Chris said, "that the most effective way to convince a child that something is unimportant is to have an adult say with great solemnity that it is important. And yet..." Her lips twitched with a small smile.

"It's important," Mick said. "I understand."

They stood silently for a moment, turning to look through the iron bars of the fence at the unusually sparse Christmas traffic clattering by on either side of the church. Even on a quiet day, there was a reliable stream of wagons, hansoms, broughams, cabriolets, and growlers. There was even a pair of young men swaying in their expensive saddles in a way suggesting that their holiday spirits came from the flasks in their hands rather than from Father Christmas. Those riders had been slowly circling the church since before Mick and Chris had arrived. Mick had wondered briefly whether they were somehow trying to eavesdrop on him and Chris, but they were too far away to hear anything, especially because their erratic weaving through traffic was generating angry shouts.

"One expects that their families are attending Mass behind us," Chris said.

"Really?" Mick asked.

"If not, it's a waste of a rather good drunken spectacle," Chris said.

Mick looked at the drunken young men disappearing from sight behind the church. In Victorian London, everybody warned you to look out for all the desperate poor people with knives and grudges against the world. And it was a useful warning. But there should have been more warnings to look out for the rich. Real danger lurked inside people who were convinced that they had big piles of money because God wanted it that way, when actually they—or probably their great-grandparents —had simply stolen the money from all the desperate poor people, leaving them with nothing but knives and grudges. The rich didn't need jobs, so they had lots of time to pass laws to give themselves tax breaks or chunks of India and Ireland. Or plot to use time travel to take over the world.

Mick knew it was hypocritical of him to be so irritated by rich English people since it was basically their money paying for the Institute, and the Institute gave him a safer, cleaner, and healthier home than almost all the other kids in London. But, then, some of those same rich people were getting kids killed. So he wasn't exactly going to send them Christmas cards.

Chris and Mick stood quietly for a while. Then Mick surprised himself by saying, "Since I'm down here, maybe I'll go to the bridge, you know, where Owl... I'd just like to ... be there for a bit. Would you maybe come with me?"

"I'd be pleased to accompany you, Gunner."

Mick was grateful for that.

On the way, Chris stopped to buy nuts. She got into a long argument with the young vendor about whether he'd over-charged her a half farthing, which led to a couple minutes of ye olde insults before Chris finally admitted she might theoreti-cally be wrong and walked away, still muttering. Mick was impressed by Chris' ability to subtly change her accent and voice so that she sounded like a working-class male Londoner with just a bit of education and polish. He was also impressed with both her and the vendor's acting ability—it had all been fake. The street-seller's eyes had a faint alley rat glow, which almost surely meant he worked for the Project, possibly as an Eye. Mick assumed there had been a coded message buried in their argument.

As they strolled the short distance to the bridge, Mick asked quietly, "Is it all right for us to walk around together? I mean, since you don't know who's watching and who to trust?"

Chris looked at him carefully. "It's impossible to be certain what is safe. Or advisable." After a short pause, she said, "But stopping a familiar thing can provoke suspicion, and you and I have been seen together for months."

"And visiting the bridge, where Owl died?"

"Perfectly above-board, I should think," Chris answered as they reached the nearly empty Hungerford Market. "Unless you wish to confess that you have some secret reason for bringing me here..." She left it hanging.

Mick shook his head.

"Well, then, on a day to honor our Lord and Savior, you wish to remember a friend whom He holds in His embrace. A motive as laudable as it is unremarkable."

As they stepped onto the bridge, Mick wondered if Chris actually believed that Owl was in Heaven with God. Much like Lady Penbrook, Chris was wrapped in so many layers of charm, irony, and jokes that it was hard to tell what she believed. In some ways, the same was true of all Victorians. The church bells of London sounded every quarter hour, and none of them precisely agreed on the time, so sometimes it seemed as if they rang all day and all night. So the city sure *sounded* like its residents believed in God and Heaven. But many Londoners still ignored the poor and cheated at business and knifed each other in alleyways, so the ceaseless clangor of church bells didn't prove that Londoners believed in God and Heaven. It just proved that they wanted you to think they did.

Mick looked down at the Thames as they walked. Despite its faintly sparkling surface, the water was especially brown, suggesting that the tides were even stronger or messier than usual. Probably that, as much as Christmas, was why there were so few small boats upon the river, though there were plenty of low-slung steamboats panting in both directions. Or maybe not. For Mick, the Thames was Victorian London in a nutshell. Each day, he understood it better, and each day, he accepted a bit more that he'd never fully understand it.

This was his first time setting foot on the bridge since Owl had died, and memories of the fight over the Realignment came rushing back. He remembered creeping up the stairs inside the south pillar and waiting nervously just inside the pillar door until something went wrong with the alley that Catherine Collins and her partner August Blake had stepped into. Dizzy and suffering as the result of the alley's sickness, Mick had staggered across the bridge in time to watch the dons realize that, to stop the Realignment, they had to do more than make a few adjustments in the alley. They had to destroy the alley thread and all the threads tied to it utterly, causing the Collapse and stranding themselves in 1767. Or getting killed in the effort.

He remembered all the dons volunteering to take that journey, including Miss Mitchell, and he remembered Miss Jennings' stealing Mr. Victor's brass knuckles to break Miss Mitchell's ribs so that she could take Miss Mitchell's place and spare her from traveling even further into the past—a past in which Miss Mitchell would have spent her life a Black woman before the abolition of slavery in the British Empire. He remembered staggering far enough to partially escape the shock wave that had knocked out all the alley rats on the bridge when the alley closed and then waking up with Catherine Collins putting something soft under his head.

Later that day, Chris had told Mick that Owl had been killed while Catherine Collins was hovering over Mick, which was when Mick realized that he'd seen Catherine Collins' horrified expression as she'd watched one of Lord Harrowgrave's thugs throw Owl off the bridge. Mick remembered getting to his feet in time to see everyone on the bridge staring over the railing except for Chris, who had sprinted to the door leading down into the north pillar. He later learned she'd been trying to get to Owl before he drowned. But Owl's head had apparently hit the bridge railing on the way down, and he probably hadn't still been alive when he hit the water. He definitely hadn't been when Chris pulled him out of the river.

Mick became aware that he'd been walking through the day of Owl's death without really noticing the present. Fortunately, the bridge wasn't nearly as crowded as it would have been most sunny Sunday afternoons. They were about a third of the way across, and Mick realized that they must be pretty close to where Owl had gone over the railing.

He turned to Chris. "Where?" he asked. "Did it— did Owl..."

Chris turned to scan the bridge, frowning with concentration and maybe sadness. "There," she said, pointing.

Not wanting to go but not able to stop, Mick trudged over to the spot. He scanned the railing, looking for some trace of what had happened. Blood, chipped stone, a memorial plaque. But there was nothing except the bridge's stolid weight brooding over the Thames' sullen surging and swirling.

"He attacked that enormous man to protect Alison without any hesitation," Chris said, placing a hand on Mick's shoulder from behind. "We can be sad and angry that he died, naturally. But we should also admire his decency and his bravery." She withdrew her hand and then said hesitantly, "Words of any kind can seem an insult to the dead. Sometimes I fear we haven't any right to speak of those who can no longer speak for themselves."

Mick nodded. He agreed with both thoughts. On one hand, Owl had been brave and good, and Mick didn't want to forget that or to stop talking about Owl and his virtues. On the other hand, sometimes talking about Owl now that he was dead seemed unfair somehow, as if even the kindest, most honest words were more dirt shoveled onto Owl's coffin. Mick wondered if others felt that way too. Maybe that was why nobody talked about Owl.

Mick was faintly surprised to realize that he didn't feel much. Not sorrow, not anger. Mostly just numbness. He stood for a while longer, looking at the complicated waters below. Eventually, the light faded as London's usual clouds slid back across the sun. Without looking at Chris, Mick turned back toward the north bank.

Reaching land, he passed through the Hungerford Market and kept walking without thinking about where he was going. It wasn't until he turned onto Long Acre that he realized he was heading back to his own drop site, an alleyway not far from Drury Lane. Once there, he stared at the cobblestones and rats and listened to the church bells and hoofbeats, which had seemed alien then but felt normal now. Owl had been with him when he'd visited this spot with the Squad, the only other time Mick had been there since he'd dropped. Mick remembered being so disappointed that there hadn't been even the faintest hint of alley activity. It had felt like proof that he'd never get back to his real life.

It still felt that way, but it was also a reminder that, even in the past, some things drifted into a more distant past. Owl was doing that now, no longer moving on the same tides as the living. His life, his memory, were drawing away like a steamboat panting into a fog bank—the boat and even its smoke fading from reach and then from sight.

In that moment, Mick could have forgiven Lord Harrowgrave and Lady Penbrook if he'd thought they had been risking lives and meddling with alleys to fix some terrible loss, to raise tall sails to the winds of time to follow a fragile little boat into the fog and tug it back to safety.

But Lord Harrowgrave and Lady Penbrook weren't rescuers. No, they captained great ships that capsized little boats in their wakes.

"I'll take you back to the Institute, shall I?" Chris asked him.

Mick stood and nodded, unable to speak. They were halfway there before he realized that he once again felt a lot of things, including the tears running down his cheeks.

3

UNFAMILIAR HUES

With only a few days left until Epiphany term started in late January, Mick was trying to figure out whether he was an idiot who had gotten himself into deep trouble or an idiot who might get away with it.

His predicament had snuck up on him. Catherine Collins' December 28 drop date had come and gone uneventfully. As promised, Mick and the others had gone nowhere near her drop site. Although Chris said that Catherine Collins hadn't shown up, Mick spent most of the following week, including New Year's Eve, being grumpily convinced that she had managed to sneak there undetected. He still felt that the Palladians should have let him keep watch because she couldn't have concealed her burningly bright alley rat eyes from him.

Then, a few days into the new year, Gail Atkinson had been waiting for him near the Institute as the Squad finished patrol, and she took Mick on a walk to inform him that Catherine Collins had reappeared the night before, attending a boring but respectable lecture in boring but respectable company at the Ladies Society for Moral Advancement. Catherine Collins had pretended that she'd spent the months since the Realignment's failure with relatives in the country (relatives she didn't actually have). She had given every indication that all was well with her, except being sad about Lord Harrowgrave's death.

As Gail told it, Catherine Collins was pretending to be as mystified by the murder as all the other members of the Ladies Society, most of whom agreed that it must have been some dirty fiend from some dirty neighborhood, or possibly some dirty foreign fiend from some dirty foreign part. In any case, many of the members of the Ladies Society were quite indignant that the police had not caught the murderer and hanged him by the neck until dead. To Gail's amusement, although Lord Harrowgrave had no children, there was a distant cousin who might have a claim to the earldom, and many of the ladies had been quite interested in whether the cousin was in search of a wife. Reluctantly, however, most had concluded he was not, in that he was a notorious woman-hater. "A fault all too common in six-year-old boys," Gail deadpanned.

With that, Gail took her leave of him. It had been pleasant, even reassuring, to have a real conversation with her. During the previous term, she had been pressed into service as a don because the Institute had lost seven dons preventing the Realignment. Along with a few other students, she'd had to take her sorting exams unusually early, without any real prepa-ration. Having passed with top marks, she was learning how to be a don with less time and less training than usual. Mick was sure she was nailing it, but he missed having her as the thane of his greet team, when he'd gotten to see her almost every day.

Now he was lucky to exchange waves with her across the Great Hall once a week.

After Gail had left, Mick had followed his feet until realizing they were taking him to Catherine Collins' Belgravia rooms. And that turned out to be how he'd put himself in his current, very stupid predicament.

For a couple weeks, whenever he could, he lurked close enough to see Catherine Collins' building but far enough away he wouldn't be easily seen. He'd caught a few glimpses of her entering by the front door and arranging the drapes in her parlor window, but she had at least one other door and seemed to be using it often. Although he didn't think she'd spotted him, her frequent and unpredictable use of the back door suggested that she thought somebody was watching her.

Indeed, somebody *was* watching her. A lot of somebodies. During his week of surveillance, Mick spotted a half-dozen Eyes and recognized two dons from the Eaton Square Outpost. At first, he'd worried that an Eye or a don would report him to Chris or the Institute and he'd get yelled at. But that didn't happen.

Finally, that afternoon, he had some good luck when he spotted Catherine Collins leaving her building. She was alone and wearing a plain dress that allowed her to move quite briskly for someone wearing a corset. Being alone and in a plain dress was unusual for a woman of her station, but Mick supposed she didn't have much choice if she wanted to do some sneaking. It was hard to be sneaky with a couple of servants and a few cousins tagging along, especially if your dress weighed more than you did.

Watching both Catherine Collins and the pair of Eyes shadowing her, Mick followed her for a while until bad luck burst from the shrubbery lining St. James's Park in the form of a mute swan. The swan had a big wingspan and apparently believed Mick had insulted its mother. Wings half-raised, it skidded to a stop right in front of Mick, snaked its neck a few times, hissed, and thrust its snapping beak at him.

Mick skipped backward, narrowly dodging the swan's beak. He backed away slowly, but the swan closed the gap, flapping its huge wings a few times. When the swan's beak whipped toward him again, Mick whirled and ran up Great George Street. The swan gave chase for ten or fifteen yards before turning and waddling smugly back toward the park.

Watching the swan disappear into some bushes, Mick tried to take stock. He figured Catherine Collins must have seen at least some of the ridiculous encounter. Most of the other people nearby definitely had. Nobody sniggered quite like Londoners in top hats and fancy bonnets.

By the time Mick got back to the path around the park, Catherine Collins and the Eyes tailing her had vanished. Dejected and embarrassed, he started walking back to the Institute, taking Hay Market, hoping the street's riot and color would cheer him up.

As he was crossing Piccadilly, a woman's voice with a thick Cockney accent said, "Oy, tiddy yob, you're right lucky I don't have the Beefeaters on you for assaultin' 'er Majesty's birds, y'are."

The young woman who appeared at his elbow didn't match her voice. For a half second, he thought it was Catherine Collins, but only because they were both brunettes wearing plain but respectable dresses. Then his brain caught up to his eyes. "Tips?" he asked.

"Greetings, Mr. Gunn," she said in a well-bred accent that matched her appearance.

"Greetings," he said, trying to use his own fancy London accent. Partly because of all the Institute rules and partly because Alison didn't want Tips and her other non-time-traveling "arrow" friends to think she was crazy, Alison couldn't tell them about time travel, which meant that she had to avoid giving them details about where her Institute friends came from and, for that matter, most of what happened at the Institute. So it made sense for Mick to try to blend in with the way he talked. "What a happy surprise," he added.

"Not half so surprising as that swan, I'll wager," she said.

He laughed despite himself.

They turned onto the graceful curve of Regent Street Quadrant. Mick liked the Quadrant. It was broad and elegant, but also a fun mix of styles, like the architects had built it using leftover materials from a bunch of fancy but very different neighborhoods.

Keeping to the pavements and the colonnades to avoid the busy traffic clattering along the streets, they let the Quadrant turn them gently north as they walked, but only until reaching a quiet street, where Tips nudged him toward a deep archway leading to a closed store.

"There we are," Tips said, still using her cultured accent while straightening the cream-colored gloves covering her from fingertip to elbow. "I think you'll find that you wish to tell Poppy what you were about when Tsar Swan invaded the Danubian Principalities back there."

"Poppy" was the name Alison's friends had given her when they all lived together on the streets. "Why?" Mick asked, careful to sound curious rather than confrontational.

Tips smiled blandly. "No secretary in Whitehall keeps secrets half so close as our Poppy. So I often haven't any idea *why* she wishes to know certain things. But I do know her, and I often know *which* things she wishes to know."

Mick nodded hesitantly. He really didn't want to tell Alison about following Catherine Collins. Telling Alison would probably mean telling the Palladians, which would get him a lot of grumpy adult faces and demands to explain himself. And then he'd have to admit that Lady Penbrook's right-hand woman was probably his sister. Which, of course, would also mean admitting that he'd been sitting on that secret for months, meaning more grumpy faces.

Tips stared into his eyes. "You *will* wish to be telling her what you were about, Mr. Gunn." She switched to her Cockney accent. "'Cos I'll be telling her tomorrow or the next day, and you won't want her to hear it from me first. Understood?" Tips asked, still locking her gaze on his.

"Understood," Mick said grudgingly.

Her smile blended understanding and bullying. In her fancy accent, she cheerfully said, "Excellent, young sir, excellent."

The bells of a nearby church struck half three, and Tips dropped a sardonic curtsey. "Must dash, I'm afraid. Pressing engagements, you understand." With that, she stepped back onto the pavement and walked briskly away.

Mick stayed where he was, assessing his situation. First, he was definitely an idiot. Second, he was probably in trouble. The real question was how much trouble. He started walking back to the Institute, trying to figure out the best way to tell Alison and then, hopefully with her help, to tell the others.

. . .

Mick made it back to the Institute in time to exercise a bit. He thought about joining Leech's pick-up game of footie, but the players were mostly teenagers Leech's age or a couple years older. They were bigger, faster, and stronger, and some of them made a point of knocking around little kids who dared to play soccer with them. Mick could remember when the same kids had done that to Leech, but Leech had grown at least a couple inches since Mick had dropped into 1853, and he'd also filled out some in the shoulders. Mick had also gotten taller. According to Miss Weathers' measurements, he was now four foot nine and a quarter, meaning that he'd grown about two inches since dropping into 1853. By 2024 standards, he was probably a bit short for an eleven-and-a-half-year-old boy, but he was a little above average at the Institute and well above average for a real Victorian, especially a Victorian who came from a family that, like most Victorian families, couldn't afford to feed its kids properly. Regardless, the teenagers still towered over him.

Watching Leech execute a slick dummy to set a teammate up for an easy shot, Mick remembered watching soccer with his abuelo, first the Mexican league and then the Spanish league after his abuelo had sworn never to watch the Mexican league again after Mazatlán stole Morelia's team. His abuelo had always made a point about how really skilled players could hold their own against bigger, stronger players. Sadly, Mick wasn't really skilled. Plus, the Spanish league had referees to enforce the rules. The teenagers' pick-up game didn't have refs. Mick wasn't sure it had rules.

So Mick contented himself with waving at Leech and then at Stephen Burton, who was also playing in the game. After Gail's promotion to don, Stephen was now a greet team thane. Mick still secretly thought of him as Stephen the Snob, but, after a rocky start, they had gone from frenemies to something like actual friends, although Mick didn't see him very often anymore. And when he did, it was awkward because Stephen was a huge fan of Lady Penbrook. Mick couldn't be mad at Stephen for that since Stephen had no way of knowing about all the bad stuff she was involved with. But it meant that Mick had to be cautious about what he said around Stephen, especially since Stephen was a bit of a suck-up who had a history of over-sharing to try to impress Lady Penbrook.

Having ruled out footie, Mick decided to practice course. There was a course already set up and in use by a few dons, who were used to letting him join in as long as he didn't slow them down. The dons were even bigger and faster than the soccer-playing teenagers, but, after some extra tips from Miss Mitchell, Mick had gotten much better at navigating the obstacles and, even more importantly, had gotten very good at staying out of the dons' way.

He was disappointed but not surprised that Miss Mitchell wasn't one of the dons running course. Although Miss Mitchell no longer had to supervise the dons' night shift, she still didn't seem to be at the Institute much during the day. He only ran into her close to curfew or maybe doing condy first thing in the morning, and for a long time, Miss Mitchell hadn't been able to do condy at all because of the ribs Miss Jennings had broken to prevent Miss Mitchell from traveling back to 1767. Gail had told Mick that Miss Mitchell was taking Miss Jennings' sacrifice hard.

To distract himself from his messy situation with Tips and Alison, Mick went extra hard at the course and ended up hurting himself worse than the teenagers would have hurt him during footie. When he showered, both shins and one forearm were already red with irritation, and he knew they'd be black and purple by morning.

After that, he and Leech walked to the dining hall to meet Alison and Dolly for dinner. Distracted by trying to decide how to raise that afternoon's Catherine Collins episode with Alison, Mick didn't really taste his food and only half-heard his friends' conversation. He *really* didn't want to tell Alison. She was going to be disappointed in him, which he hated. But she'd be disappointed *and* angry if she heard it from Tips first. Besides, it might be important information.

Fortunately, not long after Dolly excused herself to "conduct research," Alison gave Mick an opportunity to get the ball rolling by asking him, "Are you quite all right, Gunner?"

"Yes, you're quiet as Miss Winchwood," Leech said, nodding to Samantha Winchwood, the tiny Sixer sitting a few seats from Mick. Miss Winchwood often sat near the Squad at meals but had only said a handful of words to them since Mick had come to the Institute, and most of those had been "I'm a most particular eater."

Mick forced himself to say, "I have something to discuss with you after dinner, if that suits you." He looked at Leech. "Just Alison. It would take too much time to explain the big words to you." He gave Leech a grin so that Leech would know he was joking.

Making offended noises, Leech stood up in a mock huff and carried his cutlery and dishes to the sideboard before heading to the exit.

"What is it, Gunner?" Alison asked.

Mick waved his hand vaguely toward the dining hall door, and Alison got the hint. They both cleared their cutlery and dishes before she led him to a bench beneath a field maple in the Institute's garden. They were alone, given the chill weather and light drizzle.

"So?" Alison asked.

Avoiding names and other obvious identifying information, Mick walked her through his efforts to keep tabs on Catherine Collins, including Tips' ultimatum and the ridiculous swan incident. He was relieved when she smiled about the swan because it meant she couldn't be too mad. At the last minute, he decided not to mention that Catherine Collins was probably his sister.

"Oh, Gunner," Alison said when he'd finished.

"I know," he said. "I'm sorry."

She waved her hand dismissively. "I don't think, technically, you've done anything in violation of Institute rules. Or the other rules, for that matter."

Mick assumed she meant the Palladians' rules.

"I guess not," he said. "But Miss North is going to give me that strangle-disappointment look. And probably Mr. Victor too," he said, shuddering. Mr. Victor had eyes like angry icicles, and nobody glared better than he did, not even Miss North.

Alison sighed and nodded in agreement. "We'd best start with Miss Emmet, then. She's likely in her office yet. No time like the present."

"If you ask me, this nonsense is the past," Mick said, gesturing at all of Victorian England with only somewhat exaggerated irritation.

With Alison sitting beside him in front of Miss Emmet's desk, Mick explained what had happened. Miss Emmet was amused and irritated in equal measure, except for the swan incident, which she found wholly amusing. Maybe a bit too amusing, Mick thought sourly, as she slapped her desk and wiped away tears of laughter. Miss Emmet agreed that Chris should be told that Catherine Collins had probably spotted Mick following her and said that she'd also let Miss North and Mr. Victor know. The good news was that she agreed that Mick hadn't really broken any rules or ignored any instructions.

"Still, Mr. Gunn," she said, "henceforth, if you are about to do a thing and you're not sure whether you ought, please refrain. At least until consulting Miss March or, better, an adult. As I understand it, today's pantomime involved not only your following Miss Collins but also two Eyes, one or two dons, and Miss March's friend." She raised her eyebrows until Mick nodded. She continued, "Miss Collins is neither dull-witted nor unobservant. She doubtless assumes that she will be spied upon anytime she goes forth openly in public, and she likely will detect most of those spying upon her. Still, we shouldn't make a mummer's farce of it all."

Mick blushed a little. He didn't know all the words Miss Emmet had just used, but he knew that the basic message was, *Maybe from now on, try not to be a total dumbass.*

Miss Emmet turned to Alison. "Miss March, perhaps you could tell me a little more as to what Miss Corcoran— 'Tips,' I believe?"

Alison nodded.

"Perhaps you could explain how Tips came to witness today's events? Did you also ask her to spy upon Miss Collins?"

Alison blushed and shook her head.

"Miss March, is that possibly, just possibly," Miss Emmet said, turning her eyes to Mick, one eyebrow raised, "because

you know that we Palladians are not a waddle of dodos incapable of taking obvious measures? And therefore you were able
to imagine that we might *already* have Miss Collins under observation?" She gave Mick a tiny smile to take some of the sting
out of her words.

Alison's lip twitched with a smile as well. "Yes, miss."

Miss Emmet turned her gaze back to Alison. "So how did
Tips come to be following Miss Collins, then?"

"To be precise, Tips was following Gunner."

"*Me?*" Mick asked.

Despite blushing faintly, Alison looked at him unwaveringly.
"Honestly, Gunner, you've been peculiar ever since, well, that
day on the bridge, and then—"

"So have Dolly and Leech," Mick said. "Dolly is always 'con-
ducting research,' and Leech is…" Leech sometimes seemed
like he wanted to set fire to all of Lady Penbrook's houses. But
Leech wasn't actually going to commit arson, so Mick didn't
want to get Leech in trouble just because he was annoyed with
Alison.

"Yes," Alison said, "and doubtless I've been peculiar as well.
But you're the only one who spent has such a great deal of time
in London by yourself, without telling any of us why."

"I'm a real greet now," Mick said. "I'm allowed—"

"Simply because one *may* do a thing doesn't make it wise,"
Alison said testily.

"Like spying on your friends?" Mick asked, also testily.

"Tempers, children," Miss Emmet said firmly.

Mick and Alison fell silent. Mick looked at Alison's
worried face and felt bad. He knew he'd been acting weird.
Deep down, he knew it had been dumb to try to spy on
Catherine Collins. And he knew it looked dumber to Alison

and Miss Emmet because they didn't know why he was
doing it.

He once again tried to gather the strength to tell them that
he was pretty sure Catherine Collins was his sister, and he
might have succeeded if there hadn't been a knock at the door.

At Miss Emmet's invitation, Clarissa Mitchell and Gail
Atkinson opened the door.

"Oh, good evening, Gunner," Gail said. "Miss March."

They all murmured greetings and nodded at one another.
Gail and Miss Mitchell were both wearing regular Victorian
dresses, so they took a moment to gather them up and settle
into chairs. Mick retrieved a slim volume of poetry that Gail's
skirts had swept to the floor. He offered it to Miss Emmet, who
smiled ruefully and said, "I really should accept the Vicar's offer
of a larger office."

"We've just come from Hidden Thorns," Miss Mitchell said,
using a nickname for the Ladies Society for Moral Advancement
and gesturing down at her frilly dress.

"Indeed?" Miss Emmet asked. "Are your elocution lessons
proceeding apace?"

"Oh, I'm learnin' to talk real purty," Gail said in an exaggerated American southern accent. "Though when Mrs. Milner and
her friends get to talkin', I do still use me some curse words."

The joke got a laugh from everybody, including Mick. But
Mick remembered that Gail had once used a similar accent with
him when she hadn't been kidding. He suspected that her original accent wasn't too different from the one she'd just used. He
wondered if 1854 American Southern accents sounded the same
as the ones he or Gail had grown up with. Then he wondered
when the American Civil War was going to start. He wished he
could remember the date. But it might be soon. Every once in a

while he'd see something in a broadsheet suggesting that things were getting pretty tense in America over slavery.

Thinking of slavery made him think about Miss Jennings' sacrifice for Miss Mitchell. He snuck a look at Miss Mitchell, who seemed calm on the outside and no longer in pain from the ribs Miss Jennings had broken. Mick had been trying to keep an eye on Miss Mitchell. She'd always gone out of her way to be kind to him. Plus, he'd stolen her fake last name to use as his fake first name, which made him feel connected to her.

"Other than cursing Beatrix Milner, as all right-thinking women must," Miss Emmet said, "have you anything to report from the Ladies Society?"

"Not from the Ladies Society itself," Miss Mitchell said.

"Goody-goody biddies," Gail said with a sniff.

Miss Mitchell smiled in agreement. "But while there, we did chance to speak with Eliza Richardson, the mechanical, who mentioned having spoken with some dons from Gee Street."

Mick fondly remembered Miss Richardson. She was one of the engineers who worked in the mysterious workshops in a hidden corner of Demeter Farm that made devices related to alley phenomena and, Mick suspected, devices that should not yet have been invented. She was a short blonde woman who swore like a sailor and did really good impressions of people like the stuffy Demeter Manor butler Mr. Anderson and even Lady Penbrook herself. Miss Richardson had helped Elmer Maxwell with the steam engine on the narrowboat that Mick and some of the dons had taken to the Hungerford Bridge to stop the Realignment.

Miss Mitchell continued, "The dons told Miss Richardson that they have been noticing odd alley phenomena for the past week or so. They have consulted with dons at the other outposts, and it would seem some of them may also have seen oddities."

"Oddities?" Miss Emmet asked. "How so?"

Miss Mitchell frowned. "Well, they seemed rather stuck for words. But it sounded like something to do with hues and brightness. Am I mistaken, Miss Atkinson?"

"No, that's quite right," Gail said. "There don't seem to be any changes in the size or the timing of the apertures or in their health. No inappropriate fawkeses. No time lightning. But the colors are apparently ... surprising, and sometimes the lights are darker or brighter than one might expect."

"It may, of course, be nothing," Miss Mitchell said.

"It usually is," Miss Emmet said. "Until it isn't. Have you informed Miss North?"

Miss Mitchell nodded. "She was with us at Hidden Thorns when we spoke with Miss Richardson. She said that she would inform the others in due course."

Mick hesitated to speak up, especially given the reason he was in Miss Emmet's office in the first place, but he felt like he needed to say something. "You said it started a week ago, right? That's when Catherine Collins got back."

"We were all striving our utmost to forget that fact, Mr. Gunn," Miss Emmet said with a wry grin.

"Quite rude, Gunner," Gail said, winking at him.

He always liked it when Gail winked at him, and the fluttering sensation it caused this time distracted him for a couple seconds from Catherine Collins. "It's probably her, isn't it?" he asked. "Catherine Collins?"

The others all looked at one another intently. After a long silence, Miss Emmet said, "Certainly, it would be foolish to conclude that it could *not* be she."

"Is there anything we ought to do?" Gail asked.

Miss Emmet pursed her lips and looked at Miss Mitchell, who shrugged. "We should let our investigation of this new phenomenon proceed just as any such investigation would normally proceed," Miss Emmet said. "Though, naturally, we must ensure that some of our people are among the investigators. And we shall need to ensure that Mrs. Cutter is furnished with any data that might fire the furnaces of her fearsome mathematics. Yes?"

Miss Mitchell and Gail looked at one another, each nodding her head slightly before looking at Alison and Mick, who both also nodded.

"If that's all," Gail said, "I would be grateful to change into something less voluminous."

Gail and Miss Mitchell took their leave, being careful not to jostle any more of Miss Emmet's books.

Shortly after, Alison also began to leave but stopped in the doorway when she saw that Mick was still sitting. "Gunner?" she asked.

Mick sighed. "Could you close the door?" he asked. "Please."

Alison did. After a moment's hesitation, she returned to sit next to Mick.

"Mr. Gunn?" Miss Emmet asked gently.

Mick thought it through. If this new thing turned out to be dangerous and if, as he believed in his bones, it was Catherine Collins' work, people were going to have to know she was his sister.

Mick said, "So the first thing is, I think Dolly is right that only certain materials can survive in a time alley. Like, for example, if you make a teddy be— poppet out of all-natural fabrics, it'll come through fine. I know this because I found my baby sister's poppet on Catherine Collins' bed when Chris and I searched her lodgings after Hungerford Bridge. And Catherine Collins looks almost exactly like my mother did, back when she was about as old as Catherine Collins is now. So I think, well, I think she's my baby sister. Only, she's pretty big for a baby, I guess."

He chuckled, not so much at his stupid joke as at the absurdity of it all. Also, the stunned, open-mouthed expressions on Miss Emmet's and Alison's faces were pretty hilarious.

There was a long silence.

"You're in earnest?" Miss Emmet asked him.

Mick nodded.

"And you're certain that the poppet is indeed your sister's? Not just a similar one?"

Mick nodded. "I could explain, but I'd need to say stuff about the future."

Alison was staring at him hard, her expression impossible to read.

"Well," Miss Emmet said, her face a mix of amusement and shock. "Well, well." She paused for a while. "We must inform the others." She paused again. "As soon as possible."

Alison was still staring inscrutably at Mick. He realized that what he'd just said was probably bringing up terrible memories of how she had gotten separated from her brother before he'd died.

After checking her wristwatch, Miss Emmet muttered inaudibly to herself before asking, "Miss March, are you familiar with the Longshanks coffee house?"

Alison blinked. "Opposite the Raymond Buildings?"

"The very one," Miss Emmet said, digging through the piles on her desk until finding a blank scrap of paper. She wrote a sentence or two, blotted the ink, and waved the paper in the air before handing it to Alison. "A permission," she said. "It says you are to take a cab to Orphans and that the warden should provide you with return fare. If anyone, whether the warden or your friends or the local beadle, asks your destination, you will tell them Orphans. If they ask the purpose of your visit, you are to say that a professor instructed you to collect certain sheet music that he urgently needs by morning, he having kindly remembered that Miss March has friends there she might wish to visit and thinking it wise to send Mr. Gunn along to become more familiar with Orphans. If obliged to name the professor who sent you, give Mr. Phillips' name. I have taken the liberty of signing the permission in his name."

She held up her finger. "However, you are actually to go to Longshanks. Do not go directly. Change cabs along the way, more than once. Walk a mazy path for five or ten minutes at each stage, though do of course avoid perilous quarters. At quarter past eight, knock up Alberts & Samuels on Bedford Row. They're solicitors. You will be met there and shown to Longshanks."

She made each of them repeat the instructions before nodding her approval.

Mick could see Alison choke back a question before nodding slightly, folding the paper, and carefully placing it in her satchel.

With Mick close behind her, Alison had just placed her hand on the doorknob when Miss Emmet said, "Quarter past eight, children. Until then, be cautious and, above all, speak of this to no one, not even one another."

. . .

By adding "not even one another," Miss Emmet spared Mick a million questions from Alison but earned him a million quizzical glances. On the whole, he would have preferred questions because the glances came with the silent treatment, which lasted until they made it to the Tory Six common room. There, Alison said only, "At the warden's door at seven o'clock." She looked across the common room, spotting Leech beside the fire with a couple of grinds, laughing uproariously at something.

"I shall go directly to my room to avoid Leech," she said. "Dolly is doubtless still at her researches in the library."

Mick nodded, knowing that Alison meant that Dolly wouldn't be in the room the two of them shared to ask any awkward questions. He thought about apologizing to Alison for not telling her earlier about his sister. But then he decided that if a kid travels almost two hundred years into the past, fumbles around for a few months, almost getting killed a couple times along the way, and then finds out that his baby sister is now twenty-one years old because she traveled even further back in time and, by the way, might be a villain... Well, maybe that kid gets to take a little bit of time to process.

As Alison was walking briskly toward the girls' rooms, Mick thought about going to his room until it was time to meet back up with her downstairs. But Leech might decide to come chat, and Mick didn't want to answer Leech's questions any more than Alison did. Also, Mick was already wound up and didn't want to sit there for a half hour or so just fidgeting. So he left the common room. He wasn't sure where he was headed until he found himself stepping through the half-open door to the nursery, which doubled as Ellen Weathers' office and bedroom. Across the room, the Institute's eight or ten toddler alley rats were clustered on the carpet near the windows as a boy a few years older than Mick read to them, making dramatic gestures. Though he wasn't sure, Mick thought he recognized the boy as a greet from Tory One.

As usual, Miss Weathers was seated in the glow of an oil lamp with her long, dark hair pulled back as she read a hefty medical tome. She was about seventeen years old but had the calm self-possession of somebody much older. Mick always felt comforted by the sight of her, partly because she reminded him of his no-nonsense Tía Verónica and partly because she had once saved his life with one of her textbooks. Of course, she'd used it as a club rather than as a medical reference, but Mick definitely still counted the save.

When he was a few yards away, without looking up from her book, she said, "Ah, Gunner, do sit." She held up a finger as he sat, and he stayed quiet for a couple minutes until she closed the book and looked up at him.

"A pleasure to see you," she said. "You're well? Staying out of trouble?"

Mick made a wry face.

Miss Weathers laughed. "Well, trouble does seem to pay you frequent calls. Perhaps you oughtn't serve it tea and biscuits quite so generously."

Mick smiled faintly, wondering if maybe he did invite trouble.

"Is there anything you wish to discuss?" she asked him in a friendly but serious tone.

Mick wanted to discuss his sister so badly it hurt, but he wasn't permitted. "Not really." He looked over at the older boy reading to the toddlers. "Not your job anymore?" he asked.

"Only on Sundays, Mondays, and evenings, thanks to Mr. Reeve there," she said. "The younglings are quite enchanted with him, and I'm quite enchanted with being able to revise without constant interruptions to read fairy tales or to convene courts of equity to ensure the just allocation of boiled sweets."

"When did you get an assistant?" Mick asked.

"With the new term, though I have been owed one since passing my sorting exams last summer."

"Are you officially a don now?"

"Not precisely," she said. "In essence, I'm Dr. Quinn's apprentice. In seventeen months, she will determine whether I am fit to continue the study of medicine."

"And then what happens? If you are fit?"

"I shall be smuggled in the back door to the Learned Society of the Great Globe, where I shall officially be deemed a student of medicine by one of our esteemed London medical colleges. Of course, at the very same time, I shall absolutely be deemed no such thing because it would be unnatural to permit a mere woman to pursue demanding studies likely to induce hysteria and to plunge her fragile feminine mind into madness. Eventually, if all proceeds to plan, I shall be a fully trained medical doctor, like Dr. Quinn, with impeccable credentials, even if those credentials remain rather shrouded in secrecy and misapprehension."

"That sounds … messy," Mick said.

"Exceedingly so," Miss Weathers said with a wan smile. "But vastly better than going into service. Or training to be the wife of some gentleman who might prove useful to the Project."

Mick again thought how odd it was that Lady Penbrook seemed to be doing so many awful things but also seemed genuinely committed to giving people like Miss Weathers opportunities that Victorians wouldn't normally allow. It was weird to be fighting against someone who was trying to help women become doctors so they could save lives. On the other hand, it was weird to try to help people become life-saving doctors by getting a bunch of kids killed. Mick let the thought go because he still didn't know what to do with it.

Then he wondered, again, what *he* would do for a living if he stayed in the past. As usual, he reminded himself he should be trying to return to the future, not staying in the past. But probably not a doctor, though. Miss Weathers' medical books weighed more than he did.

After a silence, Miss Weathers asked, "And you're certain that there's nothing you wish to discuss?"

Mick shook his head and pulled out his pocket watch. He still had almost twenty minutes before he had to meet Alison. "If it's not a bother, I'd just like to sit here for a quarter hour or so. I'll be quiet."

"See that you are," she said, "or I'll send you to Mr. Reeve for discipline and you won't have any pudding on Sunday."

Mick smiled at her. That was the kind of joke Tía Verónica would make. Or his mom had made, for that matter. A wave of loss assailed him suddenly, reminding him of losing his mother and then, less than a year later, losing the rest of his world. He closed his eyes, breathed slowly, and tried to let it pass. Such waves of loss still washed over him sometimes, pulling him into their curl and carrying him through cold waters. He'd gotten better at riding them out without screaming or crying. *Keeping a stiff upper lip*, he thought. Maybe he was becoming a Victorian despite his best efforts.

4

LONGSHANKS

After twice switching cabs as Miss Emmet had instructed, Mick and Alison still had a little extra time, so Alison instructed the driver to drop them at Barnard's Inn. From there, they made a short walk long by taking a lot of extra turns.

"I don't see anyone following us," Mick said. "You?"

"I should have mentioned if I did," Alison said crisply, still sounding irritated with him.

"I wondered about the man in the green frock coat," he said, carefully keeping his tone neutral.

"I did too," she admitted. "But I believe he was merely full of gin."

After sheltering from the cold drizzle in a nearby entryway until the appointed hour, Mick and Alison presented themselves at the unassuming door of Alberts & Samuels, its tarnished brass plate barely legible in the fog-shrouded light from a gas lamp across the street. Alison had scarcely begun to lower her hand after knocking when the door opened partway.

A woman's voice from behind the door told them to enter.

With only slight hesitation, Alison and then Mick stepped inside.

A young woman in a drab domestic's dress and bonnet led the way, her candle lamp gently illuminating an office door and then a narrow hallway that dead-ended into a narrower stairway. Moving single file, they ascended the steep stairs, which eventually began to curve into a darkness only slightly dented by the lamp. Then there was another narrow hallway, with a door at the end that the young woman unlocked with a heavy key. That led them through what felt like a funhouse maze before the young woman knocked a quick, precise rhythm at a heavy door. The door opened after a slight delay.

Alison and Mick followed the young woman through the door, which she closed and locked behind them. Once the other two took a few steps forward, Mick could see that they were in a small, quiet, windowless room cheerfully lit at one end by oil lamps and a well-fed coal fire. There were several chairs arrayed in a horseshoe around the fireplace, two of them occupied by Miss Emmet and Miss North. When the man who had opened the door for them settled into a seat, Mick realized it was Mr. Victor, and when the young woman who had led them to the room removed her bonnet, Mick saw it was Chris.

Chris also took a seat, which left the two chairs nearest the door. Mick and Alison looked at one another and settled in. Mick's chair wobbled slightly on the uneven floor. He tried to move the chair around to get it level but gave up when he realized everybody was watching him fidget.

"Level floors are not among Longshanks' virtues, I'm afraid," Miss Emmet said.

"We're above the coffee house, are we?" Alison asked quietly.

"Indeed we are," Mr. Victor said.

Alison nodded, looking troubled.

"Is something giving you pause, Miss March?" Mr. Victor asked.

Alison frowned. "Longshanks has a reputation for being home to rather a lot of intrigue. And I'd imagine that our, ah, likely subject of discussion is, well…"

"Delicate?" Mr. Victor said. "Quite so. However, the proprietor maintains this room precisely in order to afford certain individuals the privacy necessary to discuss delicate topics."

"And he is…?" Alison trailed off.

"Trustworthy?" Miss North asked. "Not, perhaps, in all instances. But he is a friend of the Vicar's."

"And the Vicar," Mr. Victor said, "has an understanding with the proprietor that, when discussed in this room, our secrets"— he pointed to the other adults in the room—"are the Vicar's secrets. Here, you may speak freely, although it is perhaps wise to err on the side of also speaking softly."

"Speaking softly is often advisable," Chris said, "but the room is lined with rather a lot of cork, among other things. That muffles sound and makes eavesdropping difficult. And I had a rather thorough reconnoiter earlier to confirm that our sanctum appears to be intact."

"On that theme," Miss North said, "unless expressly instructed contrarily, do avoid repeating conversations such as this. To anyone." She paused and added half-apologetically, "As you already know."

The adults exchanged glances amongst themselves for a

while. Alison and Mick did the same until Alison remembered that she was mad at Mick and turned her gaze to the fire.

"Miss Emmet?" Miss North asked gently.

"I am the one who convoked this assembly," Miss Emmet said, "but it's Mr. Gunn who must speak, I think."

Mick swallowed deeply. He'd been hoping that Miss Emmet would explain the main point, ideally after emphasizing that he'd done nothing wrong. He hesitated for a moment, hoping that she still might.

"Mr. Gunn?" Miss North prodded.

Oh well. Mick nodded and tried to think of a graceful way to ease into the fact that Catherine Collins was his sister. What he came up with was: "Catherine Collins is my sister."

The dumbfounded looks from Chris, Mr. Victor, and Miss North indicated it hadn't been very graceful.

"Come again?" Chris managed.

Mick swallowed. "You remember when we were in her rooms?" he asked Chris. "I was in her bedroom, and you saw me holding a poppet?"

Chris nodded. "You were looking at it as if it had come to life and given you a message from on high."

"A message from the future, I guess," Mick said. "The poppet was my sister Em— my sister's."

"How can you be certain?" Mr. Victor asked.

Mick paused. "I think I maybe need to talk about the future, so..."

"I have done some thinking on this point since Mr. Gunn dropped this mortar in my office this afternoon," Miss Emmet said. "This, I would submit, is one of the rare circumstances in which it might do well for Mr. Gunn to provide us with full information, even at the risk of inadvertently sharing scraps about the future."

Miss North and Mr. Victor looked at one another for a while before nodding. "Very well," Miss North said. "But, Mr. Gunn, please do not unnecessarily reveal any details about the future."

"We shall ask questions as necessary," Mr. Victor said. "And we may interrupt you to prevent you from discussing topics that ought not be discussed. Understood?"

Mick nodded. First, he explained that he'd recognized Swaggy Bear just by looking at it.

"But surely many poppets resemble one another," Miss North said.

"Well," Mick said, "the, uh, person who made it isn't really great at sewing, so there were some lumps and things like that that I recognized. Also, the person who made it sewed a couple letters into my sister's bear, and those letters were in the same place on Miss Collins' bear."

"And that's all?" Mr. Victor asked. "Similar poppets with similar monograms?"

"Also, there was a picture of my mother," Mick said. "A photograph. In the future. I kept it in my room in the future and looked at it a l— often. Very often, after my mom—" he stopped himself, realizing he probably didn't need to explain that after his mom's death he'd spent a lot of time every day looking at the photo of his mom and dad. "Anyway, the picture showed my mom when she was about the same age as Catherine Collins. From the first time I saw Catherine Collins, she reminded me of someone, but I couldn't figure out who. Then I figured out Catherine Collins looks almost exactly like my mom."

"Is there anything else?" Miss North asked.

"Well, the math works. The mathematics," he corrected

himself. "My sister was about a year old when I got pulled into my time alley, and Catherine Collins was about a year old when she dropped in 1833. Also, the log for the day Catherine Collins was found said she had an animal poppet with her."

Miss North frowned. "Unless I am mistaken, when you dropped, Mr. Gunn, you made no mention of a sister traveling the alley with you."

"She didn't travel with me," Mick said. "We were together in the future, and I was trying to pick her up when the alley pulled me in. But just me. I didn't know she came back in time too. Not until I saw Sw— the poppet."

"If she did in fact travel back in time," Mr. Victor said. "Perhaps, however, your sister and Miss Collins are simply different people."

"Too many coincidences for that, wouldn't you think?" Chris asked.

The other adults nodded thoughtfully.

Miss Emmet said, "I think we must accept that it is possible, even probable, that Miss Collins is indeed Mr. Gunn's sister. For the moment, let us say that she is. Is that of consequence?" Her eyes met Mick's. "To the Palladians, I mean to say. Clearly, it is of the utmost consequence to Mr. Gunn himself."

"Might knowing more about Miss Collins help us to better understand how she manipulates alleys with such facility?" Mr. Victor asked. "Admittedly, she was an apt pupil at the Institute and then at Lady Grenville's, but—"

"I am now convinced," Miss North interrupted, "that she was even more intelligent than she let on. And clearly, she concealed from us a prodigious alley sight."

"But is that alley sight enough to explain her mastery over

alleys?" Mr. Victor asked. "Mr. Gunn likely has a similar alley sight, but he has shown no signs of mastery over the alleys."

Miss North leaned forward. "Mr. Gunn, *do* you have any such mastery?"

Mick shrugged. "I've never really tried, but I don't think so."

"And are you able to tell whether Miss Collins' alley sight is better than your own?"

Mick shrugged again. "The only way I know about people's alley sight is if their eyes have the alley glow. I think the brighter your eyes are, the better you see alleys. My sis— Catherine Collins' eyes are really bright. Probably brighter than mine. Maybe even brighter than Cassandra Halliwell's."

"Which raises an interesting point," Mr. Victor noted. "Cassie Halliwell never displayed any great alley sight when she was at the Institute. Quite the opposite, in fact."

"Perhaps she hid her light under a bushel, just as Miss Collins did," Miss Emmet said.

"Perhaps," Mr. Victor acknowledged. "But C— Miss Halliwell's alley sight was always rather poor—or at least always appeared to be rather poor—even when she was a very small child, which was long before she could have had any reason to deceive us. In contrast, Miss Collins seems to have pretended to lose her alley sight only when she was nearly ready to stand her sorting exams."

"If we ever manage to unravel what Lady Penbrook is attempting to accomplish," Chris said, "I suspect we shall find that Miss Collins began pretending to lose her alley sight only after Lady Penbrook recruited her."

"Did Cassandra Halliwell also serve Lady Penbrook?" Alison asked.

Mick hadn't thought of that.

Miss North shrugged. "Quite possibly. Or perhaps she served Lord Harrowgrave. Or both."

"But," Mick said, "didn't Cassandra Halliwell just want to go back far enough in time that she wouldn't get…" He trailed off, not wanting to say "that she wouldn't get burned to death by birth flame, which is caused by the cruel and mysterious barrier that makes it impossible for alley rats to travel forward in time beyond the days they were born."

"Such was her goal," Chris said. "But whoever gave her the future journals that she used likely had some other aim. And also, of course, that person had access to future journals that should have been locked deep in the Vault."

Mick had almost forgotten the future journals that had given Cassandra Halliwell the information she needed to waylay at least one lift alley.

"My initial point," Mr. Victor said, "was that it may be that Miss Halliwell acquired her apparently excellent alley sight only *after* she began waylaying alleys. Many scholars of alley sight believe that one's alley sight improves as the result of being within an alley. The longer one is within the alley, the better one's alley sight becomes." He paused. "Mr. Gunn, please answer yes or no only. Do you come from further in the future than the average rat?"

"Notably so," Miss North said before Mick could answer.

"I rather suspected," Mr. Victor said with a nod. "Then if Miss Collins is indeed Mr. Gunn's sister, her alley took her twenty years further back in time than Mr. Gunn's already unusually long alley, which might account for her excellent alley sight."

"But," said Miss Emmet, "when waylaying alleys, Cassandra Halliwell only managed to travel backward a few additional years in time altogether. And before that, in her initial alley, she traveled fewer than perhaps forty years backward. And yet Mr. Gunn reports that her eyes were as bright as Miss Collins'."

Miss North and Mr. Victor nodded at the same time. "Just so," Mr. Victor said. "It seems that time, as measured by the conventional calendar, is only part of the time spent in the alley. In the world of the alleys, time moves differently, by all accounts."

"If I might…" Alison said, starting to ask a question before stopping and looking nervous.

"Pray continue, Miss March," Miss North said.

"If I might ask Mr. Gunn a few questions?" Alison said.

"Proceed," Miss North replied. "However, Mr. Gunn, do not *answer* any question until given permission."

Mick nodded.

"Gunner," Alison said, "did you perhaps, in your time alley, stop at a way-world? Or perhaps even more than one?"

Way-worlds were moments in the ordinary world, or at least what felt like the ordinary world, that some rats popped in and out of while their alleys dragged them back in time. Mick looked at Miss North, who nodded to indicate that he should answer. "More than one," he said.

"Many more than one?" Alison asked.

With permission from Miss North, Mick said yes.

"How many more?" Alison asked.

"Hold a moment, Mr. Gunn," Mr. Victor said. "Miss March, is it your idea that the more way-worlds one passes through, the greater one's exposure to the alley? Or, one might say, the longer one spends in the alley as measured in alley time, rather than the time of our world?"

"I've seen the notion proposed in more than one text,"

Alison said. "Rhys-Edward's *Apertural Oddities,* and also, I believe, something by Philomena Blake. *Chronal Esoterica,* perhaps. And possibly also Braithwaite's *Principia Aperturarum.*"

"I do seem to recall such a passage in the *Esoterica,*" Miss Emmet said.

"And I in Rhys-Edwards," Mr. Victor said. "Very clever, Miss March. Very clever."

That was high praise indeed. Mick tried to remember the last time he'd heard Mr. Victor praise anyone. It had probably been Miss Jennings. He felt a pang of loss.

"Do answer, Mr. Gunn," Mr. Victor prodded. "How many way-worlds did you pass through?"

"A l— A great many," Mick said. "I'm not sure exactly how many."

"Hazard a guess," Miss North instructed.

Mick paused. "They, well, the thing is, they sped up at the end. They went by so fast I couldn't tell them apart. But before that ... dozens? Maybe a hundred?"

Well, Mick thought, whatever else they might think about him, they couldn't say he bored them. They all looked at him with stunned expressions on their faces.

"Are you absolutely certain, Mr. Gunn?" Miss North asked. "It would be an easy thing for even the calmest adult to exaggerate."

Mick shrugged. "There were too many to count. But at least several dozen."

"Some say," Miss Emmet noted, "that alley rats who pass successfully through way-worlds are likely to be calmer or cleverer than those who did not. It is easy to panic in a way-world and do oneself harm."

Mick happened to notice that there were tears in Alison's eyes.

"You and your brother went through way-worlds?" Miss Emmet asked her.

Alison nodded.

Mick reached out and squeezed her hand. She smiled at him faintly. Eventually, she lifted his hand off hers, and he pulled his hand back to his lap.

Miss North looked at Alison and then back at Mick. "It is said that the drop aperture and subsequent lift aperture in each world can sometimes be in different places. Did that happen to either of you?"

Alison and Mick both nodded.

"From the very beginning?" Miss North asked.

Mick nodded again, but Alison shook her head. "Only after I lost my brother."

"But," Miss North said, "it happened to you from the very beginning, Mr. Gunn?"

Mick nodded slowly, running through his memories as best he could. "I think so. Sometimes they weren't as far away as other times, and by the end I think they were all in the same place. I didn't have time to move from one place to another."

"Why *did* you move to the next aperture?" Chris asked curiously. "I didn't pass through any way-worlds, but my journey through the alley was quite miserable enough as it was. I doubt I would have been eager to step into a second aperture."

"I hoped the new aperture might take us back home," Alison said. "And I was somehow drawn to each new aperture and even filled with ... something like a certainty or a fear or a ... a *faith* that something dreadful would happen if we didn't enter the new aperture."

The others nodded.

"Mostly," Mick said, "I followed the alley song."

"I had nearly forgotten," Miss North said, almost to herself. "So few possess that ability."

"Mr. Larson could hear it too," Mick said. "The Collapser. He talked about it on the Hungerford Bridge before— before everything happened. Chris told him to stop making so much noise."

Chris' lip twitched with a grin. "I did, didn't I? Well, we were meant to be sneaking at the time."

"One wonders," Mr. Victor said, "how Miss Collins managed to navigate so many way-worlds as an infant, if indeed she is Mr. Gunn's sister."

Mick hadn't thought of that. He remembered how confused, battered, and tired he'd been by the time he dropped in 1853. There was no way a baby could have done it.

"Quite possibly one person's experience of an alley is different from another's," Miss North said. "Certainly, a passenger's experience differs from an alley rat's. So few rats have ever shared an alley that we really haven't any way of knowing how their experiences might differ."

Everyone fell silent for a while.

"I shall shortly need to take my leave," Chris said, "Have we learned all that we can for the moment?"

The other professors all nodded.

"For now, I think no one else needs to know of this," Mr. Victor said. "Agreed?"

Everyone nodded.

As instructed, Alison and Mick took a couple cabs back to the Institute. Since it was after hours, Alison tugged the bellpull at the Boys' School gate, and they waited to be let in.

"I apologize for being cross with you, Gunner," Alison said. "If your secret had been my secret, I likely would have guarded it just as you did."

"I'm sorry," Mick said. "I didn't know the right thing to do."

"I seldom do. Even when I think I do," Alison said with a sigh.

A muffled thudding and clunking warned that the door would soon open.

"I do hope," Alison said, "that the fates will be gentle when they teach us yet again that we do not know what we think we know."

5

THE RUMNESS BEGINS

"Fairy Six, estimated dimensions steady, approximately seven foot by four," Mick said, settling into the crisp, neutral tone and cadence of a spotter cataloging a live aperture. In a detached way, he noticed again that for some reason it was easier for him to maintain a halfway decent posh London accent when he was reporting on alley phenomena than almost any other time. "Primary monochromatic, polished steel. Calm pulse. Frame inchoate, luminescent, primary cerulean with dotted obscurities tending to black."

Having noted all of that in her little notebook, Alison asked, "Amendments?"

Leech and Dolly shook their heads.

"Alley song?" Alison asked.

"Quiet, but I can hear it," Mick said, still eying the aperture. It was a cold, damp afternoon, and the occasional wagon or carriage passed quietly on the softened roads. Mick could just make out repeated cracks from batting practice at Lord's New Cricket Ground.

Mick stared a little while longer at the aperture, then let his eyes wander beyond it to Punker's Barn in the background. There was enough fog that the world grew hazy by the far end of the barn, and the fog conspired with the low, heavy clouds to form a slate gray ceiling above them.

"Time till opening?" Alison asked.

All of them, including Alison, squinted at the alley for a bit, trying to select the right formula and do the math in their heads. Mick was getting better at picking the formula, but he almost never knew enough math to do the calculations.

"A quarter of an hour, I'd venture," Leech said.

"Closer to twenty minutes, perhaps?" Dolly said. "But I shouldn't be surprised by a quarter hour."

Alison nodded in agreement.

Something was off with the alley, though Mick couldn't figure out what it was. He squinted and turned his head side to side. He looked with one eye closed, then switched eyes. He listened with a finger in one ear, then switched ears, even though the alley song wasn't really a sound, at least not entirely. He even turned briefly to look at the muddy canal waters behind them to make sure their colors seemed normal.

"The aperture still feels wrong," he said. "Doesn't it?"

"It does," Leech said, "though I couldn't say how."

Alison and Dolly shrugged and nodded.

After a moment, they all turned to face the canal. Dolly and Leech took turns listlessly trying to skip stones across its widest part. Nobody was close enough to see their faces, but they had been patrolling so long that it was second nature to disguise what they were actually looking at. Besides, they were only a couple hundred yards from the Cricketers lookout, and you never knew who the Eyes reported to these days. Although Mick was pretty sure the building opposite the barn blocked the lookout's line of sight.

After a moment's silence, Alison said, "I believe..." She paused to consider. "I believe it's the hues. They should be reversed, shouldn't they? Cerulean framed in steel would surely be more natural."

Retying her bonnet strings, Dolly snorted at the word "natural."

"As natural as a time alley could be," Alison acknowledged. "But I do rather think the hues are reversed."

Mick tried to remember alleys he'd seen, either in person or in reference books. Aside from a few overconfident books grown dusty with disuse, he'd never heard of anybody claiming that there were clear, predictable rules about the colors and brightness of time alleys. *Broome's Taxonomy* was full of footnotes that, translated from ye olde professor, basically said, "Or whatever. It's not like there are actually any rules for this stuff."

Still, there did seem to be patterns, and even if you couldn't always put it into words, you learned to recognize when something seemed off. And Alison was right. If the aperture had been sky-blue with a steel-colored frame, Mick wouldn't have thought twice about it. But steel-colored with a sky-blue frame was weird.

After a few minutes, a subtle tone of surprise just detectable in her voice, Alison said, "Even the fairy path agrees with us, it would seem."

Like the others, Mick turned slowly to face the fairy path again. The colors had reversed themselves. It did indeed look a lot more correct that way, except that Mick had never heard of an aperture reversing colors.

"Gunner," Leech asked, "I don't suppose the alley has grown ears, by any chance?"

Mick chuckled and then listened for a moment. "I think the alley song sounds more normal now. Maybe."

"Are there any other changes?" Alison asked him.

Mick mentally ran through the catalog again. Same size, same basic brightnesses during both the dull and bright phases of the slow, almost imperceptible pulsing. "Not really, but it's probably going to fully frame up soon." Before Alison could ask, he added, "No more than three minutes."

"Time of opening apparently unchanged," Alison said, discreetly checking her pocket watch.

Dolly, and then Leech, nodded in agreement.

Almost exactly eleven minutes later, the aperture opened. Mick closed his eyes to keep from getting blinded by the light show.

"Dropper," Leech said.

"Droppers," Dolly corrected.

Mick waited until the aperture's closing flare faded from his eyelids before opening his eyes. He looked across the canalside path and patch of grass to the muddy ground about thirty yards to where the aperture had been and saw two droppers, one kneeling, the other lying on the ground.

Pretending not to hurry, the Squad walked briskly toward the droppers. As they drew closer, Mick could see that the kneeling one was a girl about his age and the other was a little kid no older than four or five. The little kid seemed to be unconscious, and the girl was wide-eyed and a bit panicky.

"Where...?" the girl asked when they drew near. "What...?"

"It is important that you do *not* tell us your names," Alison told the girl. "Not yet. Is the child in distress?" she asked, nodding to the unconscious kid.

"I..." The girl's expression became even more panicked.

Alison knelt and checked the unconscious kid's wrist for a pulse. "Alley sleep, I'd wager. Not," she said as she stood back up, "of the utmost urgency, I'm pleased to say. Still, we should alert Dr. Quinn and Miss Weathers."

Leech asked, "Blandford Square?"

Mick realized Leech was confirming the nearest telegraph relay. Mick wondered whether they could trust whatever Eye was running that relay. But that shouldn't matter for routine alley business like this.

"Indeed," Alison told Leech, keeping her gaze on the droppers.

Leech took off at a brisk trot.

"My cousin," the girl said, "is she all right?"

Mick's best guess was that the girl's accent was Welsh or Scottish. Probably Welsh. Maybe. He sighed mentally. He was supposed to be able to tell them apart, and he'd already offended a couple kids from Tory Four more than once by getting the two accents mixed up.

"She will be tended to," Alison said. "You both will. Again, please, strange though it may seem, do not tell us your names or where you are from."

"Yes, but—"

"Truly," Alison said. "All will become clear. Or, much will become clear, at any rate. I shall ask you a few questions. Kindly answer them, and you'll soon be in clean clothes before a warm fire."

Mick noticed that the droppers' clothes were filthy but mostly intact. They also seemed fairly dry, unlike the soaking wet scraps Mick had been wearing when he'd dropped almost a year before. He flashed back to his own drop alley, when Alison had run through the same routine with him. Mick had later learned that he'd been her first dropper. She, Dolly, and Leech hadn't been greets back then, so it hadn't been their job to run the steps for new droppers. They'd only done it for Mick because his alley had opened up by surprise and there hadn't been a greet team nearby. Since becoming a greet team, the Squad had run through the steps a few times, and Alison was already much smoother at it. She made sure to explain things and to wait for answers, which she hadn't really done with Mick.

The extra explanation and patience eventually helped calm the girl down, despite the fact her cousin wasn't waking up. Fortunately, the little cousin seemed healthy enough. Just thoroughly unconscious. By the time Leech returned to say the carriage was on its way, Alison had extracted most of the required information. Since there were two droppers, the usual tactic of temporarily calling the new dropper "Miss Stone" wasn't enough to identify them, so Alison coaxed the elder dropper into picking temporary first names for herself and her cousin—"Sally" and "Mally." Thanks to Alison's skilled touch, Sally made it through the interview without too much distress. Still, the arrival of the Institute's sleek black carriage seemed to strip away Sally's denial, and she looked pretty miserable to discover that it really was 1854.

Miss Weathers, who had arrived with the carriage, lifted Mally to her hip and put a consoling hand on Sally's shoulder as she escorted the girl to the carriage. Once Sally and Mally were in the carriage, Miss Weathers clambered up and closed the doors behind herself.

The Squad waited for a while, presumably while Miss Weathers conducted initial health checks in the privacy of the carriage. Several minutes later, she returned to huddle with the Squad a few yards from the carriage. In quiet tones, she asked, "Any signs of the Rumness?"

"The what?" Mick asked.

"The latest disturbance in the alleys," Miss Weathers said. "The odd hues and brightness."

"They're calling it the 'Rumness'?" Alison asked.

"I've also heard it called the 'Obliquity'," Miss Weathers said with a small smile. "But I think 'Rumness' will carry the day." She looked at Mick. "Nothing to do with liquor, by the by. 'Rumness' just means 'strangeness.'"

Mick wanted to be offended that Miss Weathers thought he'd need the explanation. But then, he *had* needed it.

"There were disturbances with the hues of their alley," Alison said. "Is that of interest? Medically?"

Miss Weathers pursed her lips thoughtfully. "The alleys forever contrive to surprise us. Dr. Quinn will of course need to examine both droppers. Still, the Rumness doesn't appear to have done them any harm. The little one seems to have a case of alley sleep, but she should be none the worse for it when she awakes. The elder girl seems quite well."

"The little one is the passenger, then?" Leech asked.

"I should think so," Miss Weathers said. "I've only ever heard of passengers suffering from alley sleep."

"They both should be tended to promptly at the Institute," Dolly said firmly, inclining her head toward the carriage.

"Agreed," Miss Weathers said. "The warden asked me to tell

you that Miss North wishes you to present yourself at the solarium at half-two."

Mick checked his pocket watch. They had just over three hours. Plenty of time to finish patrol and, hopefully, to get lunch before the food ran out.

Miss Weathers gathered her dress and began to turn toward the carriage but paused and pulled a note from the pocket pinned to her dress. "From Miss Emmet," she said, handing Alison a note.

Alison murmured her thanks as she turned the note over in her hands to inspect it. Mick noticed it was sealed with wax, which was almost unheard of for notes addressed to students.

"Can you decipher it?" Mick asked, assuming it had to be written in some sort of code, maybe a double-cipher like the dons used—one layer of code, one layer of inside jokes.

Alison frowned.

"If you need my help with the finer points of cryptography, don't hesitate to speak up," Leech said with a grin.

"You've scarcely mastered the rudiments of orthography," Dolly told him.

Leech laughed harder than Dolly's joke deserved. Mick figured Leech was just glad to hear a joke from Dolly for a change.

"Is it ciphered, Alison?" Dolly asked.

Alison frowned again. "Only in the sense of being all sixes and sevens," she said.

She handed the note to Dolly, who read it several times.

"This is nonsense," Dolly eventually said. "Or possibly monstrous."

With an exasperated *tsk*, Leech snatched the note from Dolly's hand and read it several times, even holding it up to the dim sunlight as if looking for invisible ink. "It must be a cipher, mustn't it?" he asked. "This can't be the actual message."

"Seriously?" Mick asked, annoyed.

"Apologies," Leech said, handing Mick the note.

As soon as Mick read it, his annoyance gave way to the same mystification the rest of the Squad was showing. He looked up, ready to ask Miss Weathers whether it was a joke, but the carriage was already a hundred yards away.

It was a very short note: "Miss Paisley will return to the Institute tomorrow, with my approval."

The Squad all looked at one another in bafflement. Angela Paisley was returning to the Institute. Angela Paisley was a surly girl with a hairdo full of ribbons and a head full of creepy notions—including the notion that it would be okay to try to help Cassandra Halliwell waylay time alleys and kill the kids inside them. And she was being allowed to come back to the Institute, a place full of kids no different from the ones who had died in the alleys. Angela Paisley, who might still be loyal to their enemies, was returning to the Institute, and Miss Emmet approved.

Mick resisted the urge to hold the note up to the sunlight like Leech had. "Well," he said, not quite sure what to say past that.

"Some people should be allowed to come home," Dolly said indignantly. "And some should not. The very idea of Angela Paisley's returning when the Collapsers are forever..."

Ah, Mick thought. *Right*. No wonder Dolly was upset. To help alley rats—and everybody else—the Collapsers had put themselves at great risk. At best, they had stranded themselves in 1767. At worst, they had been killed. Despite all her research, Dolly hadn't been able to figure out which. Either way, they were never coming back to the Institute. But Miss Paisley was.

For a sickening moment, Mick wondered whether Miss Emmet was actually working for Lady Penbrook. Why else would she let Miss Paisley come back?

"I highly doubt Miss Emmet is colluding with our adversaries," Alison said, apparently reading his mind, or at least his expression. "Come, we've patrol to finish." She led them along the canal's south bank toward Regent's Park.

"Still, Miss Paisley oughtn't be allowed to return," Dolly said, as they passed the cottages and other small buildings along the bank. "She betrayed the Institute."

"Perhaps she has repented and made amends," Alison said blandly.

"Perhaps she was chained in the Tower, tortured every day by fiendish devices," Leech suggested, but Dolly didn't bite.

They continued patrolling and grumping all the way to the last stop on the greet sheet. After that, they circled back to York Terrace to buy spice cakes from Mayor Cakes. The spice cakes improved Dolly's mood, but she was still slightly surly when they returned to the Institute and managed to scrape together most of a lunch from the remaining food at the Sixers' table. After that, they trudged upstairs to the solarium, arriving with five minutes to spare.

Slightly to Mick's surprise, it was Miss Weathers rather than Miss North who opened the door and escorted them across to the sitting area near the fire.

"Do sit," the Vicar said, sweeping a hand to indicate the sofa and various chairs. "Our newest alley rat is in the antechamber." He smiled broadly. "And young Mr. Asquith should be bringing tea and biscuits momentarily."

The Vicar seemed to be tormented by the possibility that, somewhere, an Institute student or professor might be suffering from a deadly tea deficiency. It was endearing. It was also a little funny once you knew to look for the flicker of disappointment that played across Miss North's face whenever the Vicar offered tea. Gail had pointed out to Mick that Miss North was a coffee addict who didn't get to drink nearly as much as she'd like because coffee wasn't a ladylike beverage. Apparently, she stashed a fireplace coffee pot in the kneehole of her desk just so she could make it through the day.

"Miss Weathers," Miss North said, "while we await Mr. Asquith, perhaps you could inform us regarding the health of our most recent droppers? What are we calling them, by the by?"

"Sally and Mally Stone," Alison said. "I've spelled them the English way for now."

Miss Weathers said, "Sally, the elder girl, is in good health, allowing for her ordeal. The little one, Mally, is indeed in a state of alley sleep, but her color is good, and her breath and pulse are untroubled. Dr. Quinn and I wouldn't be surprised to find her awake tomorrow."

A bell rang. "Thank you, Miss Weathers," the Vicar said. "The bell should signal Mr. Asquith's arrival with the tea. Mr. Gunn, would you be so kind as to admit him? And do ask the elder Miss Stone to join us as well."

Mick circled around the chairs to the antechamber door, opening it wide to allow admittance to the large silver tray bearing tea service and biscuits being held by Mr. Asquith, who turned out to be a don with astonishingly thick, dark hair and a stoic expression beneath a heavy brow. After Mr. Asquith passed by, Mick took a few steps into the small antechamber.

The new dropper, Sally Stone, was standing awkwardly beside a delicately ornate chair. Somebody had given her an instisuit and helped her brush her hair and wash her face. She was cleaner but still looked quietly panicked.

"The Vicar and Miss North wish to see you now," Mick told her, inclining his head toward the solarium. He realized he'd reflexively used his fancy London accent. In his own accent, he said, "It'll be all right. They're actually really nice. For English people, anyway." He smiled. Switching back to his London accent, he said, "And there are biscuits."

She managed a faint smile. "It's— is it... Is it *really* 1854?"

"I think so." He smiled. "Though, I suppose it could be the world's best practical joke. I'm called Mitchell Gunn. We're calling you Miss Stone, I think?" he asked, stepping aside to let her through the door.

She blushed slightly and nodded before walking past him. Before he could close the door, Miss Weathers breezed by in the other direction, patting him on the shoulder as she did. "Must dash, Gunner," she said over her shoulder.

"Bye, Miss Weathers," Mick said. He waited a moment longer for Mr. Asquith, now empty-handed, to follow Miss Weathers out of the solarium. Then Mick stepped back into the solarium and shut the door. In the sitting area near the fire-place, the Vicar and Miss North were sitting on the sofa with Dolly, and Miss Stone, Leech, and Alison were in the three stuffed chairs facing the sofa across the coffee table. That left Mick the small chair at the end of the coffee table farthest from the fire.

The room was awkwardly silent except for the Vicar asking everyone how they took their tea. It was surreal to watch things play out so much as they had when Mick had been the new dropper. Obviously in need of comfort food, Miss Stone was working her way through a stack of biscuits that the Vicar had placed on a small blue china plate for her, much as Mick had done when he'd first arrived. Also much as when Mick had arrived, Alison was nibbling absently at a ginger nut biscuit while reviewing her notes from that morning's time alley, and Leech kept trying to sneak extra biscuits off the plate on the coffee table until Miss North grabbed his hand. Although Dolly now seemed more relaxed as she dipped an Albert biscuit in her tea.

Eventually, they debriefed. Alison went through the various phenomena leading up to the alley, with the Vicar and Miss North frequently interrupting with questions. Alison mostly handled the questions, though Mick had to answer the ones about the alley song and a few about the more subtle details of the alley's appearance.

They spent several minutes discussing nitpicky points about the alley's reversal of colors between the frame and the primary, and Mick happened to catch an expression of total confusion on Miss Stone's face. At first, Mick thought she was struggling with all the technical jargon. Then he remembered that during the debriefing for his own alley, he'd been baffled that everybody was obsessing over tiny details about the time alley instead of focusing on the fact that he'd *traveled backward in time*. It was startling to realize that, in less than a year, he had started to take time travel for granted.

During a lull in the conversation when the debriefing seemed mostly wrapped up, Mick looked at Miss Stone and said, "Time travel is real. You get used to it." He paused and tried to think of something more helpful to say, but all he could come up with was pointing to the biscuit plate and saying, "If you like almonds, the ratafias are really good."

The Vicar chortled. After confirming with Miss North that the Squad was free to go, the Vicar turned his gaze on Leech. "Mr. Charles, as it is a Sunday afternoon, the kitchen fires are cold, which means that Mrs. Robbin and the others were unavailable to make biscuits."

"Yes, Vicar?" Leech asked politely.

"The biscuits on the tray, therefore," the Vicar said, "are from my personal and precious hoard of Huntley and Palmers, and I should therefore very much like to restore to the tin those biscuits still on the tray."

"Most understandable, Vicar," Leech said cheerfully. "So should I, in your position."

"See that you allow the Vicar to do so in *your* position as well, Mr. Charles," Miss North said.

Mick grinned. Leech liked to play Robin Hood with the Vicar's biscuits, but now he would have to leave with his pockets empty.

The Squad rose to leave, and Miss North escorted them across the solarium to the room's main door. At the door, she stood with a hand on the handle and said quietly, "One other thing, if you please. I believe you've had a note from Miss Emmet about a returning student." Possibly seeing the indignant look on Dolly's face, Miss North held up her palm. "Please direct your inquiries on the subject to Miss Emmet. She also asked me to deliver an additional message, which is, and I quote, 'Consider the possibility that I am not an utter fool.'"

With that, she opened the door, shooed the Squad out, and latched the door shut behind them.

"I'll consider the possibility," Dolly told the closed door. "But I may decide against it."

"I look forward to watching you tell Miss Emmet that," Leech said as they started walking toward the stairway that switchbacked down the Great Hall.

At the top of the stairway, Leech pulled biscuits out of his pocket and handed one to each of them before popping a ginger nut biscuit into his own mouth.

"Oh, Leech," Alison said, eyeing the biscuit in her hand. "You promised the poor Vicar."

"The Vicar restricted his request to those biscuits still on the tray, if you'll recall," Leech said.

Dolly thought about that for a second. "So he did," she said, breaking the biscuit in half and quickly devouring both halves.

Mick did the same with his, gratefully noticing that Leech had given him a ratafia.

Alison held out only half a flight of stairs before eating hers. "The Albert biscuits *are* rather good, aren't they?" she asked, giggling slightly.

6

THE NEED FOR PUPPETRY

That Monday, the start of Epiphany Term, there was Angela Paisley breakfasting at a dining hall table shared by the Twos and the Fivers. She was sitting alone at one end of the table, empty stools separating her from the other kids. Apparently, Mick and his friends weren't the only people who hadn't forgiven her.

Mick wasn't sure he would have recognized Miss Paisley just by looking at her. Her face probably didn't look too different— pale, rectangular, unremarkable, and set in a bland mask. But she'd always been instantly identifiable by her thick mane of light brown hair decorated with countless ribbons. The hair was still there, but the ribbons were gone, except for one tied neatly around her ponytail.

Miss Paisley didn't look at any of them as they walked by, but she had always avoided eye contact with Mick, even when he'd sat directly across the table from her.

The Squad settled into its accustomed spot at the Sixers'

table. There was little Miss Winchwood, eyes focused on her plate as befitted a most particular eater. Before sitting down, Mick scanned the table until he realized he was looking for Owl. He still did that sometimes. He settled onto his stool, feeling silly and sad.

Most of the week went by, but they were all too busy with patrol and tutorials to corner Miss Emmet and ask her about Miss Paisley. Mick met daily with Mrs. Cutter in her ruthlessly tidy office, a spacious, well-lit room down the hall from the solarium. Mrs. Cutter was a gray-haired woman about Mick's height. She looked like a Keebler elf but had a mind like a samurai sword, and she was trying to teach him the formulas that every greet needed to know to predict the timing of alleys. Sometimes, there were other, older students in the tutorial, including Alison, but that Friday, it was just Mick. So, after taking a swing and a miss at a linear approximation for an unframed glow-orb Seven, Mick risked asking, "Isn't this a bit basic for you? I thought you only taught dons and mechanicals and, like, other professors."

Mrs. Cutter smiled. "This material is more introductory than I typically teach, yes. But Mr. Neill has been seconded to Orphans for the term, so one does what one must. Besides, it affords me an opportunity to speak freely with you, which I suspect we shall need if this Rumness turns out to be a genuine illness of the alleys." She grinned crookedly at him. "Besides, I quite enjoy your accent."

"Oh," Mick said. "I thought it was getting better."

"Not your spoken accent, which is indeed becoming more correct. Your mathematical accent. People who learn mathematics in different places and times often have different ways of approaching the same problem. Yours is new to me."

"I hadn't thought of that," Mick said.

Sometimes, he was amazed that the Institute—and the entire the Project, really—managed to fly under the radar so successfully. If people paid close attention to you, as an alley rat, you were always giving yourself away. The words you used, your tone of voice, your accent, how you dressed, how you gestured, and apparently even how you did math. But he guessed the key was that nobody looked for time travelers. When he'd been back in his real life, if somebody had put him in a room of a hundred kids his age, it probably wouldn't have taken him too long to figure out whether any them were only pretending to have grown up in the U.S. But he would never have caught on that one of them had been born in 2195. Even if some kid had straight-up *told* him about being from the future, Mick wouldn't have believed it.

Mick snapped out of it to find Mrs. Cutter's bright alley rat eyes regarding him with amusement. "Welcome back, Mr. Gunn."

Mick blushed. Surprising himself, he asked, "Did Lord Harrowgrave or Lady Penbrook have different mathematical accents? Or Catherine Collins?" He paused. "No, wait, Catherine Collins wouldn't, would she?"

"I never taught any of them, I'm afraid. I became a professor here only a decade ago."

Mick hadn't known that. "What did you do before?"

"I made people who were taller and more male than I look nearly as clever as I was."

Seeing Mick's confused look, she explained, "I was a mathematician for the Project, assigned to the Seat. I devised solutions to various thorny questions that had thwarted the men working on them, and then they or someone else would find ways to ensure that my involvement was not generally known."

The Seat (Society for the Enlightened Advancement of Trade) was what the Project's headquarters called itself, especially to the outside world. The Seat, or at least parts of it, had the reputation for being the chosen workplace of the snobbiest alley rats—mostly the snobbiest male alley rats. It sounded like a great place if you were into sucking up, insider trading, and helping yourself to stuff that belonged to people from other countries.

Victorians didn't say, "That sucks," so Mick didn't say it either. "That sounds ... frustrating," he said.

Mrs. Cutter smiled faintly. "Often immensely so. But it granted me a handsome stipend and afforded me the opportunity to solve a great many challenging problems without too often being cursed as a confounded unnatural female. And a few worthy souls did recognize and respect my capacities, which really is all any of us can hope for. Especially since one of those souls was my late husband, may angels guard his rest. He was no more handsome than I, and far less handsome than my stipend, but he was an intelligent, honest man, and, rarest of all things, possessed of the ability to see accurately what was in front of him, not what he expected to find there." She paused. "I made his acquaintance at the Society for Chronal Fancy, if you can imagine."

Mick seemed to remember Miss Jennings saying something about that once. He felt a pang at the thought of Miss Jennings.

"Yes, 'tis a foolish place," Mrs. Cutter said. "Yet I am forever grateful to it for introducing me to my dear Mr. Cutter. And, of course, one of its founders was Sir Oswyn Yates, a forward-thinking man of means who endowed the stipend I received from the Seat." Her gaze turned to some faraway memory. "That night at the Society for Chronal Fancy was not so very long before the Institute relocated here, as it happens. I was escorted by a handsome and very clever arrow, a Mr. Amos. Or was it Mr. Abrahms? But he fell into disputation with another gentleman and stormed off, quite forgetting me. Mr. Cutter, recognizing me from our time together as students at Young Scholars, took up my cause, as it were. We were wed not six months later."

Mick nodded encouragingly. Grown-ups liked to talk about their pasts. And listening to Mrs. Cutter's story was better than getting formulas wrong.

Mrs. Cutter continued, "It was when Mr. Cutter escaped this vale of woe that the Vicar prevailed upon me to serve as a professor here. The salary is rather disappointing, but I am spared the need for dreary Punch and Judy puppetry whenever I wish to engage in interesting mathematics."

"And, Mr. Gunn," she said, pressing on the arms of her chair to get to her feet and taking a few careful steps to stand in front of the small blackboard, "most mathematics are interesting if one approaches them with the proper attitude of mind," she said.

"And if one understands them," Mick said with a small sigh.

"Quite so. Now, let us try again, shall we? Only this time, do try to bear in mind the rudiments of addition and subtraction."

Mick sighed again.

On a late February Sunday morning a few weeks later, after bruising himself by going hard at course, Mick realized that the Squad didn't have patrol. He had the whole day in front of him and decided to spend a chunk of it walking all the way around Regent's Park.

He went by himself because Alison was visiting Tips and the others at Orphans, Leech was at Mass, and Dolly had begged off so she could continue researching the Collapsers.

Mick worried sometimes that Dolly was becoming obsessed with the Collapsers, but Alison and Leech were less concerned, and they had known her way longer than Mick had. Then again, they also had been learning to sleep under the Victorian blanket of silence way longer than Mick. Maybe they figured that Dolly had to be okay if she wasn't crying or screaming.

In any case, Dolly told him twice, politely but firmly, that she didn't want to go for a stroll. And, honestly, sometimes it was nice to go out by himself. He remembered that when he'd first arrived at the Institute, he'd worked very hard to figure out a way to escape, just in case he needed it. During all the danger and drama with Miss Paisley and Cassandra Halliwell, the professors had blocked up the basement escape route that Miss Emmet had told him about, but now that he was taller and stronger, he was pretty sure that he could climb the garden gate if he had to. He already knew that he could shimmy down the drainpipe leading to the Little Castle alley, but he'd promised himself and others that he wouldn't do that again because it had been massively stupid. Also, since then he might have gained enough weight to pull it off the wall.

These days, rather than devising a complicated escape plan, he could just PV himself out with the warden ("PV" stood for "*propriae voluntatis*," which was Latin for something like "doing my own thing").

Not that he wanted to escape anymore. When he'd first arrived, the urge to escape had been strong but irrational. Back then, he'd felt like escaping from the Institute would somehow let him escape from Victorian England. But that wasn't how it worked. Even if he left the Institute and somehow figured out a way to get some trains to Liverpool and then a ship to America and then some more trains or covered wagons or whatever to Chicago, he'd still get there seventeen decades before he'd stepped into his time alley. None of his family or friends had been born yet. And his ancestors were probably still in Michoacán and Cork. Well, maybe the ones from Cork were already in America. His dad had said something about them running out of potatoes before the American Civil War and going to London and then New York or Boston or somewhere like that before eventually ending up in L.A. Anyway, the point was that his real life wasn't anywhere in 1854. Leaving the Institute would get him nothing except loneliness and hunger.

In fact, if he was ever going to get back to his real life in the future, he needed to be in London. Time travel required time alleys, and the only ones he knew about were in London. Most alley rats figured there had to be time alleys elsewhere, probably in other big, important cities—maybe Peking, Rome, Paris, Cairo, Constantinople, Moscow, and a few others. But nobody seemed to know for sure.

Besides, everybody thought that traveling into the future, at least more than a few days, was impossible. And everybody agreed that it was totally impossible to travel into the future later than your birthdate because the universe would literally burn you alive as soon as you got to the instant of your birth. And that wasn't just a myth—Mick knew at least one person it had happened to. He definitely needed to solve that problem before trying to time-travel more than a decade after his birthdate.

So to get back to his real life, Mick needed to be around time alleys and people who understood them. Which, he grudgingly reminded himself as he passed the Marquis of Hertford's enormous villa, meant that he needed to be at the Institute. Of course, everybody there thought what he wanted to do was impossible. Maybe they were right. If they were, he had no place else to go. And if they were wrong, he still needed their help.

As that sank in deeper than ever, he walked without noticing his surroundings until a thought occurred to him that forced him to step to the side of the path and stand still. If he really wanted to talk to somebody about getting the most out of time alleys, he needed to talk to Catherine Collins. She obviously knew how to do things with alleys that nobody else did.

Of course, she worked for villains, so maybe he couldn't trust her.

"Maybe," a snide voice in his head said mockingly. Okay, *probably* he couldn't trust her. Almost surely. But she might be the only one who knew what he needed to know. Maybe learning was more important than trusting.

He started walking again, different parts of his brain arguing with each other about whether and how to try to ask his sister how he could go home. How *they* could go home?

He was so distracted that the Eye in Park Square got within ten or fifteen yards before Mick noticed that she was an Eye. In his defense, she didn't have alley rat eyes, and she had done a very good job of looking like a wayward street urchin of perhaps fifteen or sixteen. Still, beneath her tattered clothes and a careful layer of grime, she had the glow of youthful good health, at least grading on the Victorian health curve.

As the Eye closed the gap between them, Mick quickly

scanned the area for red flags. He didn't see anything obvious, which was all he had time to look for before the Eye started loudly wheedling him to buy a hairbrush. Mick did his best spoiled London rich kid impression by simply ignoring the Eye. When the Eye was close enough to thrust a brush in Mick's face, she said quietly in a cockney accent, "There's a young gentleman waiting for you at Manchester Square. 'E says you'll know him from the crow." Raising her voice and the hairbrush, she added, "Joey and ha'penny for the hairbrush, young master, and you'll not regret it, I'm sure."

Mick had a shilling in the purse in his satchel, plus tuppence and a few farthings in his pocket. That money had to get him through the week, and he wasn't going to spend a third of it on a dirty hairbrush. But he figured he probably owed the Eye something for delivering the message, so he gave her a farthing. When she gave him a wounded look in return, he added another farthing and a loud insult about paying her to leave him in peace. She thanked him in a loud street seller whine that was more curse than thanks. Returning the hairbrush to her basket, she winked at him and wandered off.

Finding a tree to lean against, Mick surveyed the square again, scanning for threats and trying to figure out what the Eye's message could have meant. He didn't know anybody who lived or worked at Manchester Square, and he had no idea what "You'll know him from the crow" might mean. He knew from Alison that thieves and burglars sometimes called their lookouts "crows," but it wasn't like he was out doing burglary as a side hustle.

He wondered whether he should return to the Institute to see if somebody there had any ideas about what to do next. But by then the "young gentleman" waiting for him might have disappeared. And using the nearest Institute telegraph relay wouldn't be any faster. Besides, you never knew who was reading those telegraphs. If the young gentleman wanted to talk to him in secret, sending a telegraph might be exactly the wrong move.

Maybe the young gentleman was actually a young lady—was Catherine Collins keeping watch on him? He decided that was a stretch. Just because he'd been thinking about her didn't mean she'd been thinking about him. And, as far as he knew, they had no shared connection to crows. Murderous swans, maybe, but not crows.

In the end, Mick took a winding route to Manchester Square, arriving twenty minutes later. By then, he'd started to think the young gentleman had to be Chris, in part because she'd shown him the Crow's Nest at Demeter Farm. Also, who else would send Eyes to deliver messages to him?

It had to be Chris, he thought as he stood at the edge of the square, looking around.

"Greetings, Mr. Gunn," said a quiet voice a few paces behind him.

Or not Chris, he thought as he turned to see the earnest face of Ward Carlton, a boy he'd befriended the past summer at Demeter Farm. Ward was wearing his Sunday best and a nervous grin.

"Greetings, Ward," Mick said after his brain caught up to reality.

"You seem startled, Mr. Gunn," Ward said.

"Please call me Gunner," Mick said. "And I'll call you Ward, as before."

Ward nodded hesitantly. "Thankee. I apologize that haven't

the knack for privy messages. I'm afeared to be too bold in saying just what I mean, so they end up too bashful by half."

To be polite, Mick said he blamed himself for not understanding the message. And, in fairness, he and Ward had spent a fair amount of time together in Demeter's Crow's Nest, so it hadn't been the worst clue in the world. To cheer Ward up, Mick asked about people he knew from the farm, especially the Maxwells. The Maxwells operated the farm's canal boat. Ward had a huge crush on Rosie Maxwell, a girl about their age, and he admired Rosie's older brother Elmer.

Talking about the Maxwells perked Ward up enough that Mick eventually decided it was safe to ask why Ward had sent the message in the first place.

"I'm to take you to meet someone," Ward said. "I don't know who."

The lack of specifics was a little alarming, but Mick couldn't see Ward leading him into a trap, at least not on purpose. Mick wanted to ask more questions, but asking people questions often ended up giving them information. And he had to be careful not to give Ward too much information. Ward was a good guy, but he wasn't an alley rat, much less a Palladian.

"We're only going to Portman Square," Ward whispered as they set off, "but we're to take a twisting path." As they walked, Ward quietly explained that he had been working some days as an Eye in training, although Ward didn't actually use the term "Eye." Chris had told Ward, more or less accurately, that Lady Penbrook and other wealthy people such as herself liked to keep an eye on developments in London to protect their interests, including trying to prevent attacks like the one that had badly wounded Elmer Maxwell the summer before. Chris obviously hadn't told Ward, who lived in awe of Lady Penbrook, that Lady Penbrook had almost certainly ordered that particular attack.

"But all is gas and gaiters with the Maxwells now, Elmer included," Ward promised Mick earnestly.

"Gas and gaiters," Mick thought in frustration. He was never going to learn to speak Victorian.

"I'm pleased to help her ladyship, so I am," Ward said. "But what I like most is helping kids as have nowheres to go. You know how it was with me, after I left the workhouse." He spat on the pavement to express his opinion of the place where he'd been starved and beaten. "Chris has set me to search out kids as are sleeping rough but might have it in them to earn an honest penny, and I commends them to Chris or one of the others, and then maybe the kids get some food and even a roof over their heads." He paused and added with a shy smile, "I enjoy telling 'em they'll be helped, and they look at me with phizzes saying 'walker,' but I know it's God's truth. And I know they'll know it too."

Nope, never gonna learn to speak Victorian. "So you're not still working at the farm?" Mick asked.

"Mostly, I am. It's my home, y'see. But some days, as needful, I cross the river into the kingdom of the swells here, like a brave explorer, and all."

Ward came to a stop, and Mick realized they had reached Portman Square.

"You're to wait here, but not long, I don't think," Ward said. "And I'm to return home." He looked both ways and leaned in, bringing his face a few inches from Mick's. "Chris gave me enough money to take a cab from the river, but if I walk home, I can keep the coins."

"It's a long walk," Mick pointed out.

"'Tis, and no doubt," Ward agreed. "But it's a fair few ha'pennies as well, and if I leave now, I'll be home while the sun is still above the trees."

They said their goodbyes. Mick stood with his back to a broad tree trunk, scanning the square closely while pretending to be idly reading *Wilson's London Guide*. After five minutes, he was feeling fidgety and realized he should have pressed Ward harder for details about who would be coming when.

Then he spotted the young Mr. Davies, whose waggoner uncle sometimes provided Chris with transportation—and cover —on her London excursions. The uncle was a quiet man with a sneaky sense of humor. This young Mr. Davies seemed like the kind of guy who would charm you so he could steal your purse and then charm you into forgetting he'd stolen your purse. But Chris seemed to trust him, or at least find him useful.

Mr. Davies puttered about the square for a moment, looking at trees and doffing his new hat to a few elegant young ladies. Eventually, without once looking in Mick's direction, Mr. Davies walked past Mick when nobody else was within a few yards. Without slowing, he said just loudly enough for Mick to hear, "Follow me at fifty paces."

Mick followed Mr. Davies until Mr. Davies pretended to stop Mick at random to ask him the time. He then gave Mick quiet, terse directions for how to duck down an alley and cut through a back garden to get to the top floor of a particular house. If anybody stopped him, Mick was supposed to ask for "Mr. Samuel."

After tiptoeing past dustbins and actual, four-legged alley rats, Mick found himself at the rear entry to one of the fine houses facing Grosvenor Square. Making sure to look like he knew precisely where he was going, Mick strolled through the plaster dust in the garden, took the servants' stairs at the rear, and ascended to the top floor. Fortunately, since it was Sunday, there were no workmen around. Well, he realized, not *fortunately*. Whoever had summoned him had known there wouldn't be workmen on the building site on the Sabbath.

He'd been ninety-five percent sure that Chris would be waiting for him, and he was glad to be right. She was sitting in a padded chair in front of a corner window, peering through a surveyor's transit aimed at a gap in the curtains. That day, she was dressed much like Mr. Yardley had dressed, in the sort of suit worn by an engineer who spent most of his days in the office but who might occasionally need to go whack greasy machinery with a hammer.

"Greetings, Gunner," she said as he settled into a wooden chair beside her.

"Mr. Samuel?" he asked.

"I am so known on my visits here. In honor of Samuel Pepys," she explained. Looking up from the transit and seeing that he didn't get it, she added, "Because my hours here are spent peeping through curtains."

"Oh," Mick said. "Peeping at what?"

Chris slid out of her chair and gestured an invitation to look into the transit. "Do try not to jostle the focus," she said.

Mick sat where Chris had been sitting and peered through the transit, which turned out to be a cleverly disguised telescope focused on an elegant home.

Oh, right, Mick realized. *Lady Penbrook's townhouse.* The telescope didn't show all of the townhouse, but he could see most of the front stairway, some of the front entrance, and some other points of interest.

"Don't the owners mind?" Mick asked. "You being in their—What is this room?"

"Sitting room."

"They don't mind you being here with your telescope?"

"The Marquess hasn't any idea I'm here. And he hasn't any tenant at the moment, given the Cundifying afoot."

"The what?"

"The renovations," Chris explained. "For several more months, at the least, this house will be free of tenants while the Cundys make it look like the suburbs. During that time, the laborers here will know me as a member of one of the architectural firms assisting in the project. It's a lovely site for a spot of spying, I must say. I particularly appreciate my comfortable chair," she said pointedly.

Mick got out of Chris' chair. She sat back down and resumed peering through the telescope. Mick stood there awkwardly for a moment, expecting Chris to explain why she'd summoned him.

After the silence dragged on a couple moments, Mick said, "Well, nice to see you, then," and started to leave.

"Oh, do sit, Gunner," Chris said impatiently. "I'm in the midst of potentially important peeping."

Mick settled into his chair.

Getting increasingly fidgety, he waited a few more minutes until Chris said, "Well, I had hoped for a moment that might be Catherine Collins, but it was some fashion plate fizgig on the arm of a young gentleman who would have been excelled at the lists—shoulders like a blacksmith, head like a helmet." Casually, she asked, "May I assume you've also not seen Miss Collins recently?"

"I've been a good boy," Mick said.

"Well done," she said. She pulled back from the telescope and looked at him carefully. "I can only imagine how difficult it is not to seek her out. I still long to see my brother, and it's been twenty years since I dropped, and he's a century distant."

Mick nodded. He hadn't known that Chris had a brother.

Chris resumed watching Lady Penbrook's townhouse, but through the window rather than the telescope. "That, however, was not my main motive for wishing to speak with you. I believe that Lady Penbrook will soon summon you for an interview."

Yikes. "Why?"

"I'm unsure what reason she'll offer," Chris said. "No doubt it will be plausible. Possibly it will be genuine. You have now seen the Rumness, so possibly she will ask you to describe it. But I suspect the true purpose will be to determine whether you can be of use to her in some capacity."

"Like what?" Mick asked. "I mean, she doesn't know about my alley sight. Does she?"

Chris shot Mick a glance. "Almost certainly she does, at least to some degree. We have worked to understate your abilities in our official reports, but there are of course unofficial reports from so many sources. Each day, I work to determine which Eyes I can trust for which purposes, and each day I am less certain that I know." She sighed. "And deception is unnecessary where lack of discretion or innocent mistake will suffice."

Mick nodded.

"Besides," Chris added, "she needn't think you exceptional to find you useful. It may have been Lady Penbrook who selected Miss Paisley as a cat's paw for Cassandra Halliwell. If so, it was not because Miss Paisley had outshone others in some worthy field but instead because she was full of grievance and self-importance, which made her useful to Miss Halliwell."

"So I'm full of grievance and self-importance?" Mick asked, mostly jokingly.

"No more than most," she said with a small grin. "I simply mean to say that Lady Penbrook is adroit both at identifying those who will serve her purposes and at disguising those purposes. Perhaps she is interested in your alley sight. Perhaps it is the fact that certain professors trust you. Perhaps she sees in you an ambition to excel that she can twist to her ends, as she did with me."

Chris said the last part bitterly. Chris was usually so cheerful and droll that it was easy to forget that she felt deeply betrayed by Lady Penbrook. And deeply ashamed that she had let Lady Penbrook con her.

"If she knew that you believe Miss Collins to be your sister, she would assuredly find a way to twist that to her ends," Chris said. "Another reason to avoid contacting Miss Collins, I fear."

Although Mick hated to admit it, that made sense.

"If you are obliged to speak with Lady Penbrook," Chris said, locking her gaze with his, "say as little as possible, and even then to say only the blandest of things. Practice saying, 'I couldn't say, my lady' and 'It's not my place to say, my lady.'"

Mick nodded.

"Truly," Chris said. "Actually practice it. Those are useful phrases when dealing with powerful people."

"I will," Mick promised. "Will I have to go there?" he asked, pointing at Lady Penbrook's townhouse.

Chris shook her head. "Doubtful. Of late, her ladyship seems determined to limit her social engagements here in

Mayfair to the élite of London society. Demeter now generally serves for her more common connections."

Chris sat up attentively before leaning forward to press her eye to the telescope. "The lady herself."

"Lady Penbrook?" Mick asked.

"On the arm of that sleek toad Vossington."

"Who's he?" Mick asked.

"They've got into her clarence," Chris said, leaning back in her chair. "Vossington is one of the pretenders to the earldom of Harrowgrave."

"That's still going on?" Mick asked. "Figuring out who's going to be the earl?"

"Indeed," Chris said. "The late Lord Harrowgrave had no heirs, and his wife is not in the line of succession. Remember too that the late Lord Harrowgrave was an invention. Before the Project saw fit to smuggle him into the lordship, St. John Andrews was simply another alley rat, albeit one with glorious cheekbones."

"How did they do that?" Mick asked. He'd been wondering that for a while.

"Well, it's not the sort of thing that the plotters bruit about in the public square," Chris said. "But I suppose that they found a way to convince the then-Lord Harrowgrave, who was childless, that young St. John was his bastard son from, ah, a youthful dalliance."

"Does that mean 'sex'?" Mick asked.

Chris laughed. "That it does, my scandalous and improprietous youth. In any case, the old Lord Harrowgrave did indeed recognize young St. John as his heir. Likely there had been a youthful dalliance, and the plotters falsified sufficiently convincing proofs that St. John was its result. And doubtless those same plotters also retained very convincing evidence that those proofs were falsified."

"Why?"

"For a counterfeit earl to be useful to the Project, he must convince the world of arrows that he is a genuine earl. But a genuine earl is a very powerful man, and such men often would rather use their power for themselves than for the Project. So the Project ensures that it has ways of controlling them."

"Does that mean somebody has proof that Lady Penbrook isn't really Lady Penbrook?"

Chris frowned. "I have thought upon that extensively of late, and the answer is far more clouded. Lady Penbrook's claim to the viscountship derives not from her supposed blood but rather from her marriage to her husband, the legitimate Viscount of Penbrook. As I understand it, because such titles almost always pass to men, not women, she was allowed to inherit the title only after rather a lot of bribery, blackmail, and legerdemain in the court of chancery and the House of Lords. So, it seems quite likely that there are proofs of those irregularities somewhere, likely in the hands of the Undertaking. Whether those proofs would ever see the light of day, I cannot say, though I have my doubts."

Chris pressed her fingers to her eyebrows and rubbed her brow for a little while before looking at Mick. "For what it may be worth, my belief is that we must plan to stop Lady Penbrook in the time alleys, for she is likely to outmatch us in the chambers of the mighty."

"But we don't know what she's doing in the time alleys," Mick said.

"No, indeed we do not," Chris said. "Sometimes one's best hope is still a bad hope." She chuckled and grinned at him. "Now, away with you. I can't spend all day raising your spirits."

7

NONSENSICAL EYEBALLS

Trudging under a spiteful mid-March sky after a cold, wet patrol, the Squad was quarreling and quibbling to keep warm as they made their way to meet Gail and Miss Mitchell at the Ladies Society. Mick was trying to tune out the ill-tempered sniping between Dolly and Alison. He had long ago gotten used to Dolly and Leech squabbling with each other. But lately Dolly had been squabbling with everybody, even Alison, whom Dolly usually treated like a rock star.

As they passed the Learned Society of the Great Globe, Mick noticed a thin young man struggling to lower a wheelchair down the Learned Society's steep stairway (Victorians had never heard of wheelchair accessibility). The occupant of the wheelchair was spewing a torrent of insults far more lethal, and creative, than anything Dolly or Alison had come up with all afternoon. The wheelchair had a protective canopy, so Mick couldn't see its occupant, but he sounded like an old man. Mick could see the heavy silver head of a cane waving from side to side, emphasizing each insult. At last, the young man finished backing the wheelchair down the stairs, straightened his hat atop his thick blond hair, and pushed the chair away.

"Keep practicing your insults another threescore years," Leech told Dolly and Alison, "and you may rival even him."

"Shut up, Leech," Alison and Dolly snapped in unison, the first thing they'd agreed on all day.

Everybody shut up for the remaining brief walk to the Ladies Society, where they found Gail and Miss Mitchell waiting for them in the lobby. "How delightful you could join us," Miss Mitchell said in an excellent imitation of a cheery, airheaded socialite. "We know how demanding your studies must be."

That was a reminder that they needed to remember to act like respectable arrow children. Although the Ladies Society was a hotbed of alley rat intrigue, it had many arrow members and thus wasn't a safe place to discuss time alleys.

"It's such a shame you missed the lecture," Miss Mitchell said. "Miss Atkinson and I are ever so interested in moral hygiene amongst Anglo Saxon village women."

In commiseration, Alison whispered that she was sorry.

"How delightful," Dolly said sarcastically to Miss Mitchell, "that you have had such a fascinating and useful afternoon."

"Dolly," Alison said reprovingly.

"How delightful," Dolly said, "that you are untroubled by any recent events that might interfere with taking pleasure in such activities."

Her face impassive, Miss Mitchell looked carefully at Dolly. Mick was reminded of how Miss Mitchell used to look at Miss Paisley when Miss Paisley was rude during condy. Miss Mitchell's blank, alert expression hadn't always worked on Miss Paisley, but it had always made Mick want to be very polite.

"How delightful—" Dolly began.

"Very well, Miss Tee," Miss Mitchell said blandly. "Do let's have this discussion. Pray accompany me."

Miss Mitchell gathered her skirts and walked toward the front door, which a porter respectfully held open.

"Miss Tee," she called out before the door closed behind her.

Suddenly looking more like her usual anxious self, Dolly looked around at Gail and the Squad.

"I should go if I were you," Gail said cheerfully. "Miss Mitchell has the patience of Job but also, rumor has it, the wrath of Yahweh."

Dolly looked at Alison, who shrugged blandly.

Dolly sighed, pulled her shoulders back, and briskly followed Miss Mitchell's path.

"Any notion what all that signified?" Leech asked Alison.

"Yes," Alison replied. She turned her gaze to Gail. "We were told to find you here, but not why."

"That," Gail said, "is regrettably a discussion to be held outside of these warm, dry walls." After a pause, she grinned and imitated Miss Mitchell by saying, "Pray accompany me" and sweeping grandly toward the front door.

They chit-chatted about the weather and the Crimea until reaching the green edge of Hyde Park, where they turned north. At that point, Gail interrupted herself to say quietly, "I believe Miss Mitchell and I have much the same information to relay to you, but if there is anything solely within her ken, we shall have to trust her to tell Miss Tee."

"Miss March," Gail asked Alison, "is anyone taking a particular interest in us at this moment?"

"I see no one," Alison said.

"Mr. Charles? Gunner?"

Leech and Mick both said no.

"Very good, then," Gail said, keeping her voice just loud enough to be heard over the birdsong from the park and the hum and clatter of carriage wheels from the lane. "Miss North asked me to relay certain descriptions of recent alleys affected by the Rumness. Miss March, I believe you and I can better discuss that when we return to the Institute, where I may consult my notes. However, there is more pressing news, which both Miss North and the Vicar wanted me to relay to you, Gunner. You have been summoned to attend upon her ladyship tomorrow afternoon at Demeter Manor."

Mick's stomach sank. He'd been hoping it wouldn't actually happen.

"Eliza Richardson will be in town from Demeter and will escort you there," Gail said. "You know her? Blonde mechanical with a sweet face and a wicked wit?"

Mick nodded.

"You are to meet her at the Boys' entrance at eleven tomorrow morning," Gail continued. "Miss North was quite emphatic that I remind you that you and Miss Richardson are at risk of being overheard and that you therefore must not discuss any of the Palladians' ... concerns ... about Lady Penbrook, even obliquely."

"Is anybody else going?" Mick asked.

"Not to my knowledge," Gail said.

"We could go," Leech said. "The Squad."

"We weren't invited," Alison said. "It would be rude for us to presume upon her ladyship's hospitality."

"A fig's end for her ladyship's hospitality," Leech said. "Gunner might be in danger."

"He'll be in more danger if he arrives with a bodyguard,"

Alison said. "That would tell Lady Penbrook that we suspect her, which would encourage her to move against us, including Gunner."

"And if she already knows we suspect her?" Leech said.

"I very much doubt Miss North and the Vicar would send Gunner into mortal peril," Gail said. She grinned. "Well, the Vicar wouldn't."

"What about peril of getting maimed?" Mick asked. "I don't want to get my legs torn off and have to get my wheelchair pushed around by someone who hates me." It was supposed to be a joke, but it turned into a serious question partway.

Gail looked at him oddly.

"Just something I saw on the way here," he said lightly. They passed the Grosvenor gate to the park. "I guess if she wanted to get me in town," Mick said, "it wouldn't be that hard. We're only a quarter mile from her townhouse right now, and we sleep a mile from it."

"And her thugs will snatch a person off the streets if they've a mind," Gail pointed out. "Traveling to Demeter at Lady Penbrook's invitation is likely safer than being on patrol in the city at large because, with an invitation, Lady Penbrook is known to be involved."

Mick nodded, as did Alison and Leech.

"Mind," Leech said, "that is only comforting for Gunner's trip to Demeter. I am now *less* at ease. Fortunately," he added, as they walked beneath the triumphal arch at the corner of the park, "St. Clare's is just up the road. I shall say a prayer for Gunner and the rest of us before returning to the Institute."

Mick smiled, thinking Leech was joking. But when the rest of the group turned onto Oxford Street, Leech continued onward.

"He's really going to say a prayer, isn't he?" Mick asked.

"Or buy a baked potato," Alison said.

"Both will keep a body warm on a chill day," Gail said cheerfully.

Dolly didn't make an appearance at dinner that night. Alison said she was lying in bed, staring at the ceiling. "I believe Miss Mitchell gave her a few things to think about," Alison said.

Not long after dinner, Alison, Leech, and Mick reconvened at their usual table in the tory common room, trying to revise for their tutorials without discussing secrets where they could be overheard. Alison was the only one who was able to concentrate. Mick mostly sat there with his eyes shut, alternating between enjoying the warm glow of the fireplace on his face and imagining various bloody deaths awaiting for him at the hands of Lady Penbrook and her minions.

At one point he opened his eyes to see Dolly walking toward them. She took her seat quietly.

Before the others could say hello, Dolly said, "I wish to apologize to all of you. I have been out of sorts for quite some time now."

"None of us noticed any such thing," Leech said with insincere shock. "We haven't noticed any such thing, have we?"

"I wish to apologize to Gunner and Alison," Dolly said, deadpan.

Leech laughed and patted Dolly's forearm. To Mick's surprise, Dolly laughed too.

They waited quietly for Dolly to say more. For a moment, it seemed like words had failed her, but eventually she said in an even quieter voice than usual, "I was fond of Miss Jennings. The

Collapser," she added, unnecessarily. "Our friendship was not especially close, but I admired her a great deal, and I thought what she did for Miss Mitchell was heroic. To lose her, to lose all of the Collapsers, on the same day we lost Owl, it was..." She paused, clearly struggling to keep her cool.

Mick and the others nodded sympathetically.

Dolly took a couple deep breaths. "Owl's fate was terrible, but at least we know it. Why and how he died. But for Miss Jennings, for the Collapsers, we know nothing. They may have died without ever reaching 1767. They may have dropped outside a thieves' den in some filthy back alley in 1767 and had their throats slit before the aperture finished closing. They may have become knights and baronesses in Cornwall and lived to see a hundred. Not knowing," she said, "it haunts me."

"And so you've been searching the histories for traces of the Collapsers," Alison said.

Dolly nodded. "I know the Collapsers were modern, disciplined rats not likely to indulge in connans, especially not boasting like the shuttlers before the Collapse. But, if they survived, surely they would have left some record for those who mourn them? Some consoling tidbit?"

She sounded so sad it was hard to know what to say.

After a long silence, Alison said, "I cannot be sure that they would not have left such a record. But all alley rats, at least those old enough to remember their lives before their alleys, leave people behind. Most of us left somebody who cared for us, somebody we for whom we cared. And most of us do not leave messages for those we lost to our alleys."

"Not openly, at any rate," Leech said.

Alison looked at him sharply.

"I'm not saying that I did," Leech said. "But some of us—alley rats—must have. Sure, and it's a natural impulse."

"I have left no message for the future," Dolly said, "nor shall I. For many reasons. But above all because I would have to somehow get a message from 1854 to specific people in 19—" She broke off. "In the future. And that message would have to convince the recipient that time travel is possible and that the message is not simply a hoax or the words of a long-dead madwoman. But the Collapsers would be speaking to people who *know* that time travel is possible *and* that the Collapsers traveled back in time. And they could send it through the Project, or even the Institute itself."

That made sense to Mick, who could tell the others were thinking it over.

Dolly continued. "So I searched and searched. Through all the books I could. But there are certain books restricted to dons and professors. I became convinced that Miss Mitchell must have found a message from Miss Jennings in one of the restricted books, and I asked her several times to tell me what it was. Or at least to admit that it existed. I begged her."

"And she said no?" Mick asked.

"She said she had received no such message. I couldn't believe that. Miss Jennings sacrificed herself for Miss Mitchell. If she was willing to do that, surely she would have been left a message somehow. So I continued to ask." She paused. "I fear that I became ... accusatory." She sighed. "I slowly began to convince myself that Miss Mitchell simply didn't care for Miss Jennings enough to look for the message. And then this afternoon... Well, I..."

"Said a few foolish things to her," Alison said gently.

"Oh, lord," Dolly said, embarrassed.

"What did she say this afternoon?" Alison asked.

"She asked me not to tell anyone what she told me, save that she is confident she has seen no message from the Collapsers, even though she has spent long hours seeking one. And I am certain she does care greatly for Miss Jennings." In a small voice, with her shoulders slumped, she said, "I am ashamed I said otherwise."

"You were distraught," Alison said.

"That is precisely what she said," Dolly said. "But…" She waved her hands helplessly.

Mick was trying to track what was going on. It sounded like Miss Jennings and Miss Mitchell had been in love. But Victorians didn't admit to non-straight love publicly. That was part of the blanket of silence. So sometimes they couldn't even admit to themselves that they were in love. And he couldn't tell if Dolly had been crushing on Miss Jennings, or if she had just admired her. Maybe it didn't really matter right then. Dolly had really liked Miss Jennings and then lost her and didn't even know what had happened to her. And then she'd been a jerk to Miss Mitchell, who was going through the same thing, but worse.

Leech reached out and patted Dolly's hand. "Did you apologize?"

Dolly nodded.

"Did she accept?"

Dolly nodded again.

"Good," Leech said. "Now, simply stop being an utter mudworm to poor Miss Mitchell, and you'll be right back to not-half-bad Dolly, you will."

Dolly raised her head and looked at Leech, her expression inscrutable.

He grinned insolently back.

"I can continue being an utter mudworm to you, yes?" she asked.

"I'd be sorely confused if you didn't," he replied.

It surprised Mick that his carriage trip to Demeter with Eliza Richardson only took about an hour and a quarter. He usually went to Demeter by Tilling omnibus, canal boat, or rickety wagon, all of which took much longer. Suddenly, he remembered that he had taken a cab directly from Demeter to the Institute at least once. After Gail and Stephen had been kidnapped by Lord Harrowgrave's thugs, who might actually have been Lady Penbrook's thugs, Mick and Alison had been summoned back to the Institute. There had been two dons to protect them: Miss Jennings and Harold Bateson. Both had ended up being Collapsers. That was how he'd met Miss Jennings, now that he thought about it.

Poor Dolly. And poor Miss Mitchell.

After stepping down from the cab at the entrance to the Scythe, the narrow, pointed wedge of Demeter Farm separated from the main farm by the public road, Mick and Miss Richardson walked along the tree-lined drive. They soon turned into the southern third of the Scythe, which was occupied by the mechanicals and their workshops. That part of the Scythe was thoroughly screened by trees and hedges, which blocked views from the outside. On a foggy winter's day, it felt oppressive, almost eerie.

Which is probably why Mick jumped a foot up and back when Ward Carlton materialized from the fog to greet them.

"Begging your pardon, Mr. Gunn. Hello, Miss Richardson," Ward said.

"Call me 'Gunner,' Ward," Mick told him. "Really."

"Mr. Anderson said I was to tell you both that Lady Penbrook has been detained in the city and will not be available to speak with Mr. Gunner"—Ward paused as if trying to decide whether to correct himself and then pressed on—"at the scheduled hour. She will speak with him, you, at her earliest convenience. Mr. Anderson will send someone here to escort you to Lady Penbrook. Oh, and I've a sandwich for you, Mr.— for you, Gunner," he said, handing him a parcel wrapped in cheesecloth.

News of the delay filled Mick with relief, worry, and any number of other confusing emotions. He wasn't confused about feeling hungry, though. He'd been too nervous to eat much breakfast, so he unwrapped the sandwich and dug in. It was chicken, with some of the gross bits, but the brown bread was nice, and he was too hungry to be fussy.

Miss Richardson had to change into her working clothes and report to her workshop, so she took her leave.

Ward had to return to lookout duty and invited Mick to join him. "I told Mr. Anderson that you might be up there with me, so whoever he sends will know to shout us up."

Mick was happy to join Ward in the Crow's Nest atop the warehouse. Even on a foggy day, it offered some pleasant views, and it felt safe from the claustrophobic menace of the world below.

Afterward, with the sun very nearly set, Mick followed Ward down the ladder from the Crow's Nest, wondering when he would hear from Lady Penbrook. As if summoned by that thought, a scullion from the Manor younger than Mick and Ward ran up to them as they were exiting the warehouse, announcing in a carefully rehearsed singsong that Lady Penbrook had been further detained and would speak with Mick in the morning.

That sent Ward urgently knocking at the workshop doors until a prentice reluctantly opened a door and even more reluctantly retrieved Miss Richardson, who decided that Mick should sleep in the Foundation that night. Ward thanked her as if she'd rescued his puppy from a fire.

"The Foundation?" Mick asked Ward after Miss Richardson had gone back inside.

"That cottage," Ward said, pointing catercorner across the narrow wagon path.

Mick was about to ask why it was called the Foundation when he realized he knew the answer. He'd stayed there with Miss Jennings not long after they'd fought off an attack by Lord Harrowgrave's thugs. It had been the first mechanicals' workshop at Demeter, but the rest of the original building had been wood and had burned down, leaving only the foundation.

Ward showed Mick into the Foundation. Before hurrying off to dinner, Ward lit a small wood fire in the hearth, hung a cheerful oil lamp from a hook hanging from the ceiling, and showed Mick where the matches and candles were kept.

Once alone, Mick's first action was to bar the cottage's door and shutters. Part of him wanted to light everything at once to keep the dark and the dark thoughts at bay, but he managed to talk himself down. It wasn't too much past six o'clock, and the night was only going to get darker and heavier.

Eventually, Ward returned just long enough to drop off Mick's dinner: bits of bread, cheese, and some cold, boiled mutton. Mick ate everything, even the sheep lumps. Mick occasionally remembered his future self, how picky he'd been and how he'd taken for granted that there would be a lot of food to pick from. By Victorian standards, Mick was kept warm and well-fed, and he was grateful for that. Listening to Alison's stories of life on the streets, or just walking past all the bony street kids with waxy skin and wary eyes, he knew how much worse it could get. He knew he was lucky. But he was also almost always a little hungry and a little cold.

And that night, he was also more than a little scared. Lord Harrowgrave and Lady Penbrook had both been trying to time-travel on purpose. But Lady Penbrook had also been secretly working to undermine Lord Harrowgrave so that she could control time travel, and he probably had been trying to do the same to her. So it was hard to know which of them had been responsible for which horrible thing. Still, it seemed pretty obvious that Lady Penbrook was willing to let people die, probably even to have them killed. And now he was on her turf, at her summons. And at her mercy, if she had any.

Mick again resisted the urge to toss all the wood on the fire and light all the lamps and candles at once. Instead, he lifted the oil lamp off the hook and inspected the cabin again. It was a simple, one-room house with one door, three windows, and a low ceiling. The door and windows were barred. The floor was rough stone. The walls were thick, smooth stone, darker in the original wall, lighter in the newer wall atop it. Mick didn't see any way in or out that wasn't sturdily blocked off from the inside. He knew from experience at the Institute that people could build secret doors that blended beautifully into the surrounding walls, but it didn't make sense to put one in here, where anybody walking by could see you using it.

Even so, he found himself checking the pair of extra thick foundation stones on either side of the doorway. One stone had the founding date (May 5, 1771) carved into it in Roman numerals. The other had a weird set of small carvings that covered nearly the entire face of the stone. He remembered seeing the carvings the last time and having no idea what they meant.

To distract himself from his dread, Mick sat down to try to figure out the carvings. Turning up the flame of the oil lamp until the marks were clear, he looked at everything a couple times just to make sure he was correctly seeing the worn and darkened carving. There were three chunks, separated by large blank spaces. He had no idea what to make of the bottom two chunks, but the short one on top felt familiar. It read:

S
8mine (100+F&IReconq)
2Not XX–III.67
III.6until bat.palcocstr
7◉ V◉◉◉panthawk12th◉◉◉
iJanet AscDr

_____

3xVSay 1invaterivplate
Jealous/Age 2xX.XX,2x2

At first, he was sure it was a coded message from the dons. He'd seen plenty of those during the time lightning emergency. The dons encrypted many confidential messages on two levels. The first level was what Mick thought of actual encryption that required cipher keys, like knowing that "107.2" meant "the 107th word on page 2 of the secret cipher text." The second level was basically in-jokes—little shared slang phrases and insider references. So somebody who was good at cryptography might be able to break the first level of encryption. But then they'd have to also basically be a don to get the inside jokes. Sometimes, using true ciphering would make it impossible for the recipient to decipher the message, and then the dons used only inside jokes.

Except for the eyeballs, this definitely felt like a don's message. Almost all dons' messages started with either "S" (meaning "sinister," meaning "left") or "D" (meaning "dexter," meaning "right.") Those referred to the dons' unofficial motto, which you were supposed to picture written out on a single line:

Count every second. Consider every instant.

If a message started with "S," that meant to use the left-hand statement, "count every second," which in turn meant to include every second item. If a message started with "D," it meant to use the right-hand statement, "consider every instant," which meant to include every item.

If this really was a dons' message, then he was actually supposed to be deciphering every second line. And if he ignored what came after the divider for now, the relevant lines would be:

2Not XX–III.67
7👁 V👁👁👁panthawk12th👁👁👁

The first line, at least, looked like a date to Mick, especially since the date of the Foundation's construction was carved on the matching big stone on the other side of the doorway.

In dons' slang, "Not" meant "November." So if the first line was a date, it was probably "2 November" something. "XX" meant twenty, and "III" meant "three." So "2 November 20–3." November 2, 2003? If so, then what could the "67" stand for?

Then he realized that "XX–III" probably was "twenty minus three," or seventeen. Which gave "November 2, 1767."

The date of the Collapse.

Wait…

The cottage had been built, or at least finished, in 1771, just a few years after the Collapse. And Miss Jennings and Mr. Yardley had known its foundation would survive until at least 1853. What if this was the message from the Collapsers that Dolly had been looking for? Not written in a letter or a book, but in stone.

It was an exciting thought, and Mick was sure it was right. Or at least he had to be right that the message included the date of the Collapse.

That meant the other relevant line was probably a date too. The only problem was that he had no idea what that line meant. He poked and prodded his brain for a half hour, trying to come up with halfway plausible meanings. But the eyeballs were throwing him off. Still, he was pretty sure that the first relevant line was the date of the Collapse. And the timing was definitely right for it to be a message from the Collapsers. So he pulled his notebook and pencil from his satchel and copied all three chunks of the message. Hopefully, somebody else could decode it.

He was just checking his copywork when there was a heavy series of knocks at the door followed by a woman's voice saying loudly, "Mister Gunn? Are you within, Mr. Gunn?"

That was Lady Penbrook's voice. His heart started racing.

"I have just now received an urgent summons to attend

upon Her Majesty on the morrow, so our conversation must be now."

Mick shoved his notebook and pencil back into his satchel and tried to think what to do. He'd never escape the cottage without Lady Penbrook seeing him. And escaping wasn't the right play anyway. It would just confirm that he was suspicious of her. Besides, if she was really planning to hurt or kidnap him, she wouldn't be pounding on his door and shouting where a dozen mechanicals could see and hear her.

He put one hand on the bar for the door, summoning the courage to lift it out of the way.

"Mr. Gunn, do open the door, naturally being sure to first remove your trousers."

What?

"Mr. Gunn, you are to immediately remove your trousers, open this door, and step forth singing 'Down Among the Dead Men' with all due gusto whilst keeping audible time upon your nancy."

Mick started laughing uncontrollably. Miss Richardson. He'd already heard her impression of Lady Penbrook and marveled at how good it was. He lifted the bar out of the way and opened the door to find Miss Richardson grinning at him. She was wearing a plain gray dress that, like her face and hands, was heavily smudged with something, presumably grease.

She looked him up and down, adopting a stern expression. "You were instructed to remove your trousers and sing, Mr. Gunn," she said, still flawlessly impersonating Lady Penbrook's voice. "If you cannot obey your betters in the simplest of matters, one despairs for your prospects."

Still laughing, Mick stepped out of the way and gestured that she should come in.

"I cannot stay, alas," she said in her own voice. "My bed calls to me after many nights of too little sleep. I just popped by to encourage you to learn morally uplifting hymns and to inform you that you will have the Foundation to yourself this evening. In recent months, it has become a guest-house with infrequent guests."

"Oh," Mick said. "Thanks for letting me know. And sleep well."

"You too," she said. "In future, if you hear Lady Penbrook's voice near the workshops, you are surely hearing an impostor. Her ladyship does not condescend to visit us rude mechanicals in our huts of grease and clamor."

Mick stepped back to the cabin and carefully barred the door again. Miss Richardson had raised his spirits, and he no longer felt half-convinced he would be murdered in the night.

That didn't stop him from shoving the heavy chair away from the little secretary desk and up against the door, but it did keep him from lying awake too long in the darkness after he snuffed the oil lamp.

Mick woke with the sunrise feeling fairly confident he hadn't been murdered in the night. Miss Richardson and then Ward separately knocked at his door. Miss Richardson brought him greetings, and Ward brought him hard-boiled eggs and news. The hard-boiled eggs were runny but welcome. The news was that Lady Penbrook's carriage was departing in an hour, and she wanted him on it.

So, after dry-washing himself and combing his hair, Mick was standing in crisp morning sunshine on the Manor drive beside Lady Penbrook's gleaming town coach and four. The coach stood empty, its doors open and the steps on the Manor side lowered. The big horses stood placidly in harness, and the coachman in his gaudy navy-blue livery stood a few feet from them, savoring a stubby cigar. Mick watched the Manor's front door while trying not to imagine being murdered and dumped in the canal.

Lady Penbrook appeared at the front door, and the coachman's cigar disappeared into the gravel beneath his foot. Like an idea of water, Lady Penbrook flowed down the front stairs in a bright, cobalt blue dress, trimmed in whites and lighter blues. As usual, Mick was impressed by her ability to walk so quickly while her legs gave no hint of motion.

Lady Penbrook stepped up into the coach without looking at either Mick or the coachman. "Do join me, Mr. Gunn," she said from within the carriage.

Mick steeled his nerve before ascending the steps. The coachman shut the door and clacked the steps back up under the coach's belly.

Lady Penbrook was facing forward, her dress filling most of the seat, so Mick settled into the backward-facing seat.

Mick looked around the coach, partly to avoid Lady Penbrook's eye, partly out of curiosity. The shades were up, letting the sunlight display the coach's luxurious interior. Everything—from the upholstered walls and seats to the skirting at the lower edges of the seats to the carpet—was done in a harmonious arrangement of blues, whites, and creams, with the dominant color a bright blue similar to the cobalt of Lady Penbrook's dress. What wasn't velvet, embroidery, or tooled leather was polished bronze or gleaming ivory. Mick had been in a lot of carriages since dropping into Victorian London, but those had mostly been much more workaday cabs, with the sort of smudges, tears, and stains you would expect expected in a dirty city where a bucket of water was a lot of work and vacuums hadn't been invented yet. But Lady Penbrook's carriage was spotless. It practically glowed.

The coach shook slightly as the coachman climbed into the box and again as the horses began to plod forward.

"Mark is most punctilious of all things regarding the coach," Lady Penbrook said.

Mick silently gave kudos to Miss Richardson. Her impression really did sound almost exactly like Lady Penbrook, except that Lady Penbrook's voice was a bit deeper and more gravelly.

Lady Penbrook continued, "Mark smokes like a McConnell Bloomer and thinks I don't notice. I overlook it because in fifteen years' service, no ash has ever come within arm's reach of the coach."

Mick nodded. In general, a commoner such as himself, especially a child, would not be expected to say much to Lady Penbrook unless directly answering a question from her. And he planned to do the expected. The less he said, the less likely he was to say something dangerous to himself or the Palladians.

For a while, that approach resulted in silence. As the coach rolled along, Lady Penbrook stared out the window as if inspecting her farm and then the trees and hedges separating the farm from the public road. It wasn't until the coach had turned north that she turned her gaze to Mick.

"You have seen the Obliquity, have you not, Mr. Gunn?"

Mick blinked. "I'm— I'm not sure what that is, my lady." He realized he was using his fancy London accent, which felt awkward. But then, she knew he was faking it, so he didn't really have to fool her. And she'd probably been faking her own accent for decades. So he stuck with it.

"I gather it is better known among the students as the Rumness," she responded.

"Then yes, my lady, I have seen it. Only once, though."

"I believe that very few have seen it more than once," she said.

"Yes, my lady," Mick said, not finding anything better to say.

"You also saw the time lightning, did you not, and described it to me in the autumn?" she asked, her tone entirely casual. "You and the clever girl, Miss … Miss Marsh, was it?"

"Miss March, my lady."

"Ah, of course," Lady Penbrook said.

Looking at Lady Penbrook's sharp, alert expression and bright alley rat eyes was making Mick nervous. He turned his gaze to the window.

"Have you any observations about the Obliquity, Mr. Gunn?"

"I'm afraid, my lady," Mick said, trying to figure out how to say as little as possible, "that I can't remember my specific observations about hue and dimension and the like."

"Nor should I expect you to, Mr. Gunn. I am more interested in your analyses or intuitions."

Mick decided to play dumb, which was easy given that he felt dumb and didn't really know what she was after. "Forgive me, my lady. I don't entirely understand."

Lady Penbrook stared blankly at him for a moment. Mick felt himself blushing. "Allow me to be clearer, Mr. Gunn. I suppose I'm curious to know whether you believe the Obliquity to be a serious matter."

Mick's mind raced. There were so many things he could say that would invite more questions, and more questions meant more risk of saying something wrong. "I couldn't say, my lady. That is, the Rumn— the Obliquity *is* unusual, of course. But then, so is…" He trailed off. Mark didn't have alley rat eyes, so Mick wasn't sure he was supposed to talk about time travel. But Lady Penbrook had already mentioned the Rumness and time lightning, so maybe it was safe.

"This coach is surpassingly well-constructed in a number of ways," she said, "including as to the dampening of sound. You may speak freely without fear of being overheard."

Mick realized that he wasn't really hearing much noise from the outside.

"Thank you, my lady. Time travel is confusing. Every time I think I understand a formula or a rule, something happens, and then I'm not so sure. The Rumness is unusual, to be sure, but nothing bad is happening. The droppers are healthy, and the formulas are working. Or at least they're working as much as usual. It's just the colors that are unusual."

Lady Penbrook nodded. "A fair answer."

They rode without speaking for a while. Mick avoided eye contact by looking out the window at smoke rising from the muted engine of a train keeping pace with them on the nearby branch line. Lady Penbrook mostly seemed to stare at the upholstery a few inches above Mick's head.

Not long after they turned onto New Kent Road, Lady Penbrook turned her gaze back onto Mick. "Tell me, Mr. Gunn, have you any thoughts on whether the realm, or the Empire, is a just place?"

Where did that come from? Mick asked himself. "It's not my place to say, my lady."

Lady Penbrook laughed. "Your tutors have taught you well, Mr. Gunn. And that is the correct answer whenever anyone asks you that question, unless you are asked by someone who has your best interests at heart, in a setting where you cannot be overheard." She waved one hand at the interior of the carriage.

Trying not to let his face show that he was pretty sure she didn't have his best interests at heart, he said, "I suppose it could be more just, my lady."

She nodded encouragingly. "Do tell."

It was hard to figure out a safe way to describe to a Viscountess how stupid and wasteful Victorian England was, even if she was a semi-fake Viscountess who occasionally monologued on injustice. Especially since he was trying hard to say as few words as possible. "Only a small group of powerful people matter here, it seems. And the powerful people send powerless people to other countries to fight powerless people from those countries and take stu— valuables from the powerful people in those countries and bring them back to the powerful people here."

"And how do you plan to fight that injustice, Mr. Gunn?"

Mick shrugged. "I'm not certain," he admitted. He remembered something Tía Verónica had once said. "One needs power to change things. But the more power one gets, the less one wants things to change."

Lady Penbrook nodded as if he'd said something wise. After that, it seemed like she'd gotten what she wanted from him, and for a long while the conversation drifted between small talk and silence.

After crossing the Westminster Bridge, the coach turned onto King Street and rolled along the congested road for a few minutes before coming to a halt. "I must leave you here, Mr. Gunn. I trust you can make your way back to the Institute safely?"

She took his hand and pressed a coin into his palm, and Mick closed his hand over the coin automatically.

"To hire a cab," she told him.

"Thank you, my lady," he said.

Mick could hear Mark lowering the steps outside, so he gathered himself to rise, but Lady Penbrook tugged at his wrist and he settled back into his seat.

"One does indeed need power to make changes. And I now have considerable power," she said, staring into his eyes. "But I have not let power make me forgetful or timid. I intend to make changes. Indeed, as opportunities present themselves, that is precisely what I have done and shall do. I hope I can trust you to assist me, Mr. Gunn."

Mick gave the only answer he could think of by nodding.

"Good, good," she said with a smile.

She flicked the door handle, and Mark opened the door. Careful not to tread on Lady Penbrook's dress, Mick got down. He nodded to Mark and stepped onto the pavement. By the time he looked up again, Mark was already clambering back onto the box.

Soon, Mark was urging the horses up King. Curious where they were going, Mick followed the coach until it reversed direction at Parliament Street. At that point, the coach was headed away from the Institute, so it would have been suspicious to keep following.

It felt like Lady Penbrook had given him sixpence, which would have been just about enough for a cab to the Institute. He opened his fist enough to catch a glimpse of gold rather than silver. Nervously re-closing his fist, he walked to the nearest building and stood with his nose nearly pressed against the stone before looking closer at the coin. A half-sovereign. That was more money than Mick had held, total, since dropping into Victorian London.

Careful to hide what he was doing from pickpockets, cutthroats, and everyone else, he opened his satchel enough to slide the half-sovereign into an inner pocket and button that pocket closed. In doing so, he brushed his hands against his notebook, which reminded him he needed to tell Dolly and the Palladians about the possible message from the Collapsers.

He sighed, realizing he probably also needed to tell the Palladians about the half-sovereign since it was probably a bribe. Being one of the good guys really sucked sometimes.

8

RHYMES WITH COTTON

Miss Emmet let Mick keep the half-sovereign as long as he promised not to flaunt it to other students, and over the next two days, Mick started to feel like he was earning every farthing. He spent most of his free time, and a lot of other time, answering questions from Miss Emmet, Miss North, Mr. Victor, and Chris about his conversation with Lady Penbrook.

Sometimes, the questioning was one-on-one; sometimes they ganged up on him. As far as he knew, he gave the same answers each time, but a lot of the time the answer was "I don't know," which was probably why they kept asking questions. More than once, he'd suggested just asking Catherine Collins what she was doing. The first time it had been a joke. But after he'd thought about it, he actually liked the idea and made the suggestion a couple more times. Sure, she was working for Lady Penbrook, but so were plenty of good people, including other people in the Undertaking. Lady Penbrook had convinced a lot of people she was on the side of angels.

In fact, Catherine Collins actually had a lot of reasons to help them, even if she didn't know it yet. When she had seen Owl get killed, she'd been angry and sad. Mick had seen that clearly on her face. And when she'd seen Mick hurt and lying on the bridge, she'd stopped and dragged him to safety even though it increased her risk of getting caught. And she'd been friends with August Blake, who had died in the alley, apparently because Lady Penbrook had lied to Lord Harrowgrave so that he would die.

Mick could tell the Palladians thought he was biased because she was his sister. Maybe he was. But that didn't mean he was wrong.

Partway through the third day, it seemed to Mick like the professors had decided they'd gotten everything out of him they could, except Mrs. Emmet, who couldn't seem to get over the fact that Lady Penbrook hadn't threatened to mount his head on a pike above her townhouse if he didn't confess everything.

"I mean, it's a *good* thing she didn't come after me harder, isn't it?" Mick asked, standing up to move a chair leg off the book that had been making the chair sit extra unevenly on the floor of Miss Emmet's office for the past quarter hour. "I mean, that she didn't, oh bother, whatever the Victorian is for 'come after me harder.' It means she doesn't think I'm onto her, right?"

"Or perhaps that she does think you are 'onto' her but that she can nevertheless turn you to her cause," Miss Emmet said, exasperatedly trying to make sense of it. "Or feed you scraps of seemingly useful information that in the end merely distract and vex us."

"Or that," Mick said, tiredly slouching in his chair.

Miss Emmet smiled, also tiredly. "Yes, I think we can definitely say that your encounter with Lady Penbrook was X, not X, or partially X."

In a singsong voice, Mick said, "'Not X' means 'Not ten,' which rhymes with 'rotten,' which is cockney rhyming slang for, um, 'cotton.' So this cipher stands for the date that cotton was invented." He'd been spending the last scraps of his free time trying to help decipher the code he'd copied off the Foundation wall, and he wasn't making any progress. As far as he could tell, if it was a message from the Collapsers, the message was, "We're trolling you."

"I rather believe that cotton was not invented, Mr. Gunn," Miss Emmet said with a grin. She was just drawing in breath to ask more questions when there was a knock at the door.

It was Gail, who took a seat next to Mick and told them there had been three separate Rumness episodes that day. "Nothing harmful, so far as we can tell. But spectacular, I'm told. It seems that two of the alleys were fairy paths that glowed so brightly even children with indifferent alley sight were obliged to shut their eyes. And the third was a whirlpool in black with a gray frame."

"Black?" Miss Emmet asked. "That's surely not common, is it?"

Gail shook her head. "*Broome's* specifically says that there has never been a recorded alley of any kind with black as a primary hue. Students are having a delightful time devising names for it. 'Plague alley' is the leading candidate."

"That's preferable to certain alternatives," Miss Emmet said wryly. "I take it you did not observe any of these alleys yourself?"

Gail shook her head again.

"But there were no fatalities?" Miss Emmet asked. "No obvious signs of danger?"

"None," Gail said. "Still, it likely will become dangerous, won't it?"

"If not in itself," Miss Emmet said, "then quite possibly in some terrible power it confers on someone, likely Lady Penbrook."

Gail nodded and placed her hands on the arms of her chair as if to rise, but then checked herself. "Gunner, did you mention something to me recently about a man in a wheelchair? I feel certain that you did, but I cannot remember what or when."

"There was a gentleman in a wheelchair on the steps of the Learned Society," Mick answered. "Another gentleman was helping him down."

"Did you see the gentleman in the wheelchair?"

Mick shook his head. "There was some kind of canopy. But he sounded pretty old. Like, white-hair old. Why?"

Gail frowned slightly in thought. "One of the greets at the black whirlpool said that she saw an old man in a wheelchair who seemed to be watching the whirlpool closely. She said he was being pushed by a much younger man, about the age of a don, who also seemed to be watching."

"Was the young guy blond and thin?" Mick asked. "The one at the Learned Society was."

"He was, I believe," Gail said. "Most interesting. But, truly, I must be off." She rose and started toward the door.

At the door, she paused and added, "By the by, sweet, darling Gunner, one of the reasons I didn't see any of those Rumness alleys in person, and the reason I owe you a debt of grim and terrible vengeance, is that Miss Mitchell and I—and your very clever Miss Tee—have spent the past days helping

Mrs. Cutter decipher those hideous squiggles you brought back from Demeter."

"Cotton," Mick said solemnly. "The key is cotton."

"I'm sure that's ever so droll," she replied. "But I rather think we actually have found a key, though only one of several. I'll let Miss Tee explain." She exited, closing the door behind herself.

About a half hour later, Miss Emmet gave up debriefing Mick and told him that Dolly was probably in the Room of Future Present, where the Institute kept all the time journals from alley rats once the present caught up to the future. For decades, the Institute had been requiring every alley rat who could write to record everything potentially interesting about their future lives in time journals and then locking the journals deep in the ultra-secure Vault buried in steel and stone somewhere in the Institute's sub-basements. Once that future became the present, or more technically, the recent past, the journals came out of the Vault. They were then analyzed, and copies were shelved in the Room of Future Present. So, since it was March of 1854, the journals by rats with 1853 late points had started appearing on the shelves.

March of 1854. It was weird to think that his drop anniversary, March 8, was only about a week away.

Mick knocked on the door to the Room of Future Present and waited for Dolly to let him in, which she did with a nod and an almost imperceptible smile before re-locking the door. Technically, students weren't supposed to be there unsupervised, but Miss Emmet sometimes let students use the room when they needed somewhere private. Which Dolly clearly did. The room was smallish, with just one library table, which was big enough for two people to do serious work. By the looks of it, Dolly was doing the serious work of at least two people. The table was covered with books (none of them time journals, as far as Mick could tell) and, even more, with paper.

"You've been busy." Mick said.

Dolly responded with an expression blending exhaustion, pride, and sheepishness. "I waited so long and so angrily for a message from the Collapsers that I felt obliged to try to decipher the one that finally arrived. Miss Mitchell and Miss Atkinson have been kind enough to let me assist them."

"Gail wouldn't mind if you called her 'Gail,'" Mick said. "Especially since if you decipher the messages, she can stop looking at them." Dolly shook her head, as he'd known she would. "You're getting along with Miss Mitchell now?" he asked.

Dolly nodded. "Quite well." She gave a small, wry grin. "It would seem that to get along, being well-mannered is better than being hateful."

"Sounds fishy to me. *Gail*," he said, leaning into the first name, "said that you had deciphered the Foundation message."

"We believe we have deciphered the first part of it. Here," she said, leading him to the table and placing between them a piece of paper covered with her neat, blocky handwriting:

2Not XX–III.67 = 2ND OF NOVEMBER 1767. (COLLAPSE)
7◉ V◉◉◉panthawk12th◉◉◉ = 7TH OF OCTOBER 1853. (COLLAPSE TRIGGERED)

_____ = _____. UNKNOWN (SHROUD TRIGGERED?)

**Jealous/Age 2xX.XX,2x2 = July or August of 2024.
Shroud (?)**

Even knowing the solution, he didn't fully understand how Dolly and the others had gotten there. "So what do those emoj — eyeballs mean?"

Dolly permitted herself a small, wry smile. "Confusingly, they have two completely distinct meanings. First, they invoke things ocular, which gives us 'OC.' Which is dons' slang for—"

"October," Mick said, kicking himself. "So the first part of the eyeball line is '7 October.'"

Dolly nodded. "The other meaning for the eye is simply 'i,' as it is in the rest of that line."

"So," Mick said, "the 'v' plus three eyes is 'viii,' which is probably Roman numerals. So, it's eight, right?"

"Indeed."

Mick stared for a while. *So then "panthawk" must mean… Nope.* He still had no idea.

Dolly smiled apologetically. "Once we knew the first part of that line was the seventh of October, we felt sure the rest must stand for '1853' because that's when the Collapse was triggered. We eventually discovered that there is a breathing disorder that causes hawks to pant called the 'teine.'"

Okay, so that's "eighteen." "What's '12th'?" But then he saw it. "The twelfth letter of the alphabet. L."

Dolly nodded. "Which is fifty in Roman numerals."

"And then three more eyes is three, so eighteen fifty-three." He rolled his eyes and caught himself wondering what an eyeroll meant in dons' slang. "And the line after that is actually a blank, not a divider?"

Dolly nodded. "It had to be. The four entries not written here, the ones to ignore, all decipher as dates relating to important foundings in Undertaking history—the founding date of the Refuge School, of the Society for Chronal Fancy, of the Undertaking itself, and of the Forsyth Institute. Once we realized that—"

Mick groaned. "*Found*ing dates chiseled into the workshop's *found*ation. At least we know it really was a message from the Collapsers. Only they would have known all of those founding dates, and only they would have thought carving them into a foundation was funny."

Dolly chuckled. "Yes, Miss Atkinson nearly hurled an inkwell out the window. In any event, once we realized those four dates all went together, we felt confident they should all be ignored. That let us devote our attention to these four entries," she said, pointing to the paper, "and eventually we managed to make some sense of them."

"So the blank is the day the Shroud was triggered?" Mick asked.

Dolly shrugged. "We suspect so. We think the Collapsers believed there must be such a date, only they didn't know what it was. Likely because it hadn't happened yet when they went back in time. At least, that all makes sense provided that the fourth entry is indeed the date of the Shroud."

Mick thought that over. He remembered how interested the Vicar and Miss North had been when they talked to him just after he'd dropped into 1853. A lot of their interest seemed to come from learning that his late point was after 2020. He'd long known that his August 2024 late point was probably close to the Shroud, and this was another reason to believe it.

"So," he said. "We know it has to be a message from the Collapsers. We probably know some of the dates. Do we know why they told us those dates?"

Dolly shook her head. "No. We're hoping the remaining two-thirds of the message will tell us."

"So we still don't know what those say?" Mick asked.

"They're double-ciphered," Dolly explained. "This part," she said, tapping her index finger on the paper, "is only single-ciphered. I believe the Collapsers made it more easily under-stood so that someone from the Undertaking would be able to immediately realize that it was a ciphered message and then take the time to understand all three parts. Miss Mitchell says that if the Collapsers did what dons usually do, there will be some agreed-upon text that helps us to break the code for the remaining parts of the message."

"But we don't know what that text is?" Mick asked.

Dolly gave a long, tired sigh. "No, and unless we find it, we shall never understand the message. And all of this," she said, gesturing at the mass of papers in front of her, "will be so much kindling."

Although Mick and Alison couldn't tell Leech and Dolly that Catherine Collins was probably Mick's sister, there was plenty of other Palladian business for the Squad to discuss. Since that required privacy, the Squad started spending more time in the Room of Future Present. To make that less obvious, they arrived separately, even using different entrances to the library since Miss Emmet had loaned them a key to its back door.

Although Alison and Dolly had apparently decided that Miss Emmet had loaned *them* the key and that it was very rude of Mick or Leech to ask for it. No matter who had the key, Miss Emmet tended to put them all to work for a bit when they came by. She claimed it was to help them maintain their cover, but Mick was pretty sure she just wanted help organizing books.

One afternoon, a cold, gloomy insult of a day, it was a good time to be inside, though the Room of Future Present wasn't particularly cozy, with no coal in the fire and little sunshine from the high windows. Still, a little gossip warmed things up a bit, and Alison had just returned from a talk with Gail that gave her plenty of tea to spill. Metaphorical tea, of course. They weren't allowed to have actual tea in the Room. Mick realized that he'd started to go native. Not only was he using his London accent more often than his American one, he was starting to get genuinely irritated if he couldn't cadge an afternoon cup of tea. If he was ever going to get back to his future life, he needed to do it soon, before he developed opinions on cricket and Tsar Nicholas.

"This was in the salon?" Leech asked Alison.

Apparently, Lady Penbrook and an old gentleman had gotten into the posh Londoner equivalent of a screaming fight at the Ladies Society, and Gail had reported on it first to the Palladian adults and then to Alison.

"In the lobby afterward," Alison said. "The old gentleman kept saying, 'The time to act is now' and something about hunting. Lady Penbrook kept telling him to moderate his tone, and eventually he did. After that, Lady Penbrook and the old gentleman were at the center of the lobby whispering at each other like words were daggers. Gail says the young gentleman pushing the old gentleman's wheelchair just stood there the entire time pretending not to be aware of any of it."

"Wait—an old gentleman in a wheelchair?" Mick asked. "The same one Gail was asking about a little while ago? The one we saw at the Learned Society?"

"Well," Leech said, "you and I saw him, Gunner. These two were too busy spitting daggers of their own."

"Shut up, Leech," Alison and Dolly said in unison.

Mick wondered if they practiced that.

"Gail did say something about its likely being the same gentleman," Alison said.

"I think Gail thinks the old gentleman is an alley rat," Mick said. "The young gentleman too. She said some rats saw them at a Rumness alley, and they both seemed to be watching the alley."

"They're all Rumness alleys these days," Leech noted.

"So they say," Mick said, a bit grumpily. The Palladians hadn't exactly benched him, but he only went out when the Squad had its regular patrol. And he suspected that the Palladians were making sure that the Squad only got the alley signs unlikely to turn into real alleys.

Miss Emmet had told him that until the Rumness alleys themselves turned out to matter, the Palladians didn't want to send Mick galloping around half the city, drawing attention from Lady Penbrook and her allies. It made sense but still felt like a demotion compared to what he'd done for the waylaid alleys and the time lightning. It also felt like an excuse to keep him away from Catherine Collins, who reportedly was showing up near more and more alleys, usually a day or two after they closed. And she wasn't the only one. There was a young blond gentleman, maybe the wheelchair pusher, who was also appearing at the sites of alleys after they closed. This was worrisome because it suggested that Catherine Collins wasn't the only person causing the Rumness.

Not that anybody understood any of it. At least, nobody on their side.

Which is why they were all proud of Dolly when she announced that she'd helped to crack the code for the rest of the Foundation message.

"We don't yet understand it, mind," Dolly said. "But we've found the cipher texts. Miss Mitchell seems quite confident we shall soon understand the rest."

"Dolly's the one who found them," Leech stage-whispered.

"Oh, that's marvelous to hear," Alison said. "Well done, Dolly."

"How'd you find them?" Mick asked.

"The Society for Chronal Fancy," Dolly said with a wry shrug.

"What?" Alison asked incredulously.

"We were having so little success, you see, and Miss Atkinson became most ... intemperate with the Collapsers for including the founding of the Society on their list of important dates in Undertaking history. Why not the founding of Young Scholars? Or the drop date of the Nye twins?"

That was a good point, Mick realized.

"Then it occurred to me," Dolly said, "that the main reason the Society for Chronal Fancy exists is that the Project needs a publishing house for certain books and a way to ensure that those books would seem harmless if any arrows were ever to find them."

"The Disclaimer," Alison said.

"And the silly lectures," Mick said.

"Yes," Dolly said. She smiled faintly. "Miss Jennings was amused and exasperated by the Society and its nonsense."

Mick smiled too. "The 'Society for Knothead—' No, 'the Society for Knotty-Pated Numbskulls,'" he said. "She called it that once."

"And some other things," Dolly said. "But she understood that the numbskulls were an alibi for the books the Society's press publishes."

"Oh, clever, Dolly," Alison said.

"The cipher texts are Society books?" Leech asked.

Dolly nodded. "The Society was founded in August of 1805 and began publishing books at the end of that year, in preparation for the Institute's opening in 1806. I asked the Vicar to consult the Society's publishing catalog from 1805 when he next went to the Society. He did so yesterday."

"But the message Gunner found was carved in *1771*," Leech pointed out.

"There were six books published in 1805," Dolly said. "Three of them were first editions, and three reprints."

Alison made a happy 'oh' sound.

Dolly smiled. "Indeed. The three reprints were identical in every way to the original editions, where were all published between 1765 and 1768."

"Identical save the Disclaimer," Alison said.

"Save the Disclaimer," Dolly acknowledged. "Those three books were part of a child's introduction to time alleys, and Miss Emmet says that in 1771, they were being read by every new dropper who could read, and being read to those who couldn't. And decades after writing the message, the Collapsers must have ensured that the Society for Chronal Fancy republished those texts to make them easier to find. After we identified the texts, we noticed that there were several other clues in the Collapsers' message that could also have pointed us to those same texts. The Collapsers had several years to craft their message, and they hedged their bets. Or so I believe." She paused before adding. "I shouldn't be surprised to discover that, if we were to search the Seat, the Institute, and possibly other Project buildings, we would find other carvings of the message that Gunner found."

"My brain hurts," Mick said.

"Your fault for finding the message in the first place," Leech said.

"Miss Atkinson is still most vexed with you for that," Dolly told Mick.

Back when Cassandra Halliwell had been turning a lot of alleys that should have been full alleys into fawkes alleys, Institute students had started calling uneventful patrols "fawkes hunting." Now that the Palladians were giving the Squad nothing but hopeless alley signs, every patrol was fawkes hunting for them. So, over the next few days, they finished patrol early each day. The others took advantage of the extra time before dinner to go back to the Institute. Leech played footie. Alison helped Miss Emmet conduct research that she refused to tell them about. Dolly spent every second she could with Gail and Miss Mitchell trying to understand the Collapsers' message, though she confessed that they had probably deciphered it as much as they could, and the important part turned out to be equations that Mrs. Cutter was studying with Miss Richardson.

During his time off, Mick found himself wandering the neighborhood near the Institute, maybe drifting to watch a bit of a Punch and Judy show, and then drifting to Cavendish Square to sit on a bench beneath the statue of Lord Bentinck and watch the self-serious young men entering and exiting the Royal Polytechnic.

One improbably pleasant late afternoon, he looked across the square and saw Catherine Collins.

She was pushing a wheelchair.

The same wheelchair. It had to be. There was the canopy, hiding the face of the occupant, though this time Mick could at least see the man's legs, torso, and arms. There, laid across the man's thighs and clutched firmly in both gloved hands, was the cane with the big silver handle. And, as they drew closer, there was the querulous old man's voice.

Not knowing what else to do, Mick pulled out his pocket watch and looked down at it as if all the world's winning lottery numbers were engraved on its face.

As Catherine Collins and the old man passed within five or ten yards of him, Mick risked lifting his head slightly to get a look. Catherine Collins looked almost perfectly like a wealthy young woman enjoying the easeful airs while half-listening to her elderly uncle's stories about battling the Turks. But Mick noticed a faint hardness to her eyes and slight clenching in her jaw that reminded him of his mother when he had gotten on her "second-to-last nerve" and it was time to shut up or lose wifi privileges. The man's facial features were regular and strong and might have been what Tía Julieta called "old man handsome" if it hadn't been for the permanent scowl. But his eyes! Mick had never seen such a bright alley rat glow. Catherine Collins' eyes were extraordinarily bright, and the old man's outshone hers like an oil lamp eating the light of a dying match.

Mick realized he was staring and tilted his face back down.

When Catherine Collins and the old man had continued on twenty yards or so and had their backs to him, Mick stood and followed them at a distance as they crossed the square and then the street to the pavement in front the west side of the Royal Polytechnic. They were met there by a slender blond gentleman, who replaced Catherine Collins pushing the wheelchair. Hanging back behind the partial protection of a tree trunk, Mick couldn't be sure that it was the same man he'd seen pushing the wheelchair the last time. But if not, they could be brothers.

The young gentleman pushed the old gentleman a ways before turning out of sight. Catherine Collins stood motionless, still staring at the direction in which the two men had gone.

Mick tried to decide whether he should follow the old man or Catherine Collins.

Catherine Collins solved his problem by retracing her steps, which meant she was coming right at him. He pressed his back against the tree, trying to ooze into the bark. When she was perhaps twenty paces from him, she called, "You, young fellow, be an angel and rescue a maiden plunged into woe."

Her accent made her sound like she gave elocution lessons to the Queen.

Mick stopped trying to meld with the tree. "I, miss?" he asked in his best London accent.

"Indeed, you," she said, closing the gap between them and thrusting something at him.

Half-expecting to feel a sword sliding through his guts, he looked down and felt a mixture of relief and embarrassment to see the handle of a carriage parasol hovering a foot in front of him.

"I simply *cannot* coax it open," she said. "It was a gift from the Marquis, and I should be forever outraged with myself if I have done it damage."

Mick looked at the parasol handle, at Catherine Collins' simpering expression, and then back at the handle. Overwhelmed with a sense that he was either in mortal peril or about to follow a rabbit into Wonderland, he slowly reached out and took the parasol.

"I see the alleys sparkle in your eyes," she told him quietly in a brisker and flatter tone than she had been using. "Just as I did that wretched day on the footbridge. Let us hope there is a spark of intellect there as well. I believe that you or people known to you wish to speak with me. I shall attend a soirée the day after tomorrow at the Ladies Society and shall slip away at half seven to the first-floor office of Lady Eloise. You may come alone, or you may bring others. But if you bring the wrong people, I shall not speak words that bring you any profit."

She looked sharply at him to make sure he'd understood. Apparently satisfied, she took back her parasol, pushed it open, and said loudly in her bubble-headed tone, "Young sir, you are my unerring knight errant. My complexion and I are forever in your debt."

And with that, she bustled from the park beneath her lustrous pearl parasol toward several Polytechnicians, who competed to help her to hail a cab.

Mick watched with bemusement as she was handed into a hackney whose driver turned his trotting horses away from the square.

"Well," said a voice behind him, "that was an utterly fascinating turn of events."

After crawling back into his own skin, Mick turned to look at the person who had appeared out of thin air behind him. The person looked for all the world like a junior secretary in some prosperous concern, an open-faced, amiable young man in a tidy woolen suit with spectacles on his nose and a twinkle in his eye.

"Chris, *please* don't do that," Mick said.

Strolling quieter streets nearby, Chris got the details from Mick. She then condescended to tell him a few of the things that she knew, including that she and a few trusted helpers had been investigating the man in the wheelchair since he'd argued with Lady Penbrook at the Ladies Society.

He turned out to be a gentleman named Arthur Aurelian Ambrose, who had begun rising to wealth and influence not long after the turn of the century, though his fortunes had somewhat declined in the past ten or fifteen years, after he had lost the use of his legs. Mr. Ambrose lived a secluded life in an apartment with, according to Chris, a cleverly counter-weighted lift at the rear entrance that allowed him to raise and lower his chair into his apartment without help. Chris was interested in the fact that Mr. Ambrose's apartment was basically at the center of Little Cadogan Cluster as well as a short distance from Catherine Collins' apartment. Catherine Collins had made the short walk twice that week, once to pay a call, once just now to join Mr. Ambrose in a hired coach and four to Cavendish Square.

"I managed to procure a calotype photograph of Mr. Ambrose that I have been showing to the Palladians," Chris said. "So far, nobody remembers his face. Since you are lately in the habit of idling the last of the afternoon at Cavendish Square, I sought you out there. Which, by the by, is likely how Miss

Collins knew to find you there. It would be wise to vary your habits, especially the habits you have when you are alone."

"You think she wanted to see *me*?" Mick asked.

"Very possibly it didn't have to be you in particular. But she did make a point of pushing Mr. Ambrose past you and, as soon as she was satisfied Mr. Ambrose was out of sight, she did come slap at you."

They had reached Paradise Street at the cemetery that extended north to the workhouse, the two of which combined to give Work to Death Cluster its name. Chris led Mick into the burial ground and to a set of lonely headstones with identical dimensions. Owl's grave was in the same cemetery, Mick realized, though toward the other end.

Chris halted at one of the headstones and reached into her jacket pocket. She handed Mick a few calotype photographs. When he didn't recognize any of them, Chris made him learn the faces. She particularly made him study the somewhat blurry photograph of John Harris, a balding man with a grim and tired expression. As she returned the photographs to her jacket pocket and they started walking again, Chris explained that Mr. Harris was a former Eye who worked at the Seat and probably was running Lady Penbrook's extensive and secretive spy network.

"He is a cold and clever man who taught me much of what I know about turning observation into information, and he has the loyalty and respect of many Eyes. Too many. Avoid him if you can. I would not be surprised to learn that his hand and his orders have added a half-dozen headstones to various burial grounds."

They walked in silence a while before exiting the burial ground and turning back toward the Institute.

Clearly worried, Chris told Mick, "Do tell Miss Emmet, Miss North, or Mr. Victor what passed between you and Miss Collins today. I shall also tell them, but I haven't the time to return to the Institute until tomorrow evening, and time is of the essence." Without waiting for an answer, she patted his shoulder and departed at a trot.

9

FAMED SHUTTLER

The next day in tutorial, after the other students had left, Mrs. Cutter told Mick that he was expected to attend an urgent meeting of the Palladians that evening. It would be a full meeting in the solarium, which was increasingly rare. Meeting together gave Lady Penbrook's spies chances to confirm that the Palladians existed and even to deduce who they were. The Vicar and Miss North had been trying to muddy the waters by insisting that various overlapping groups of professors, dons, and older students meet more often than usual, but that only went so far.

For now, Mick wasn't even supposed to tell the rest of the Squad about the meeting. "Tell them I've instructed you to join me for a vespertine on secondary approximations," Mrs. Cutter said. "Goodness knows you've need of one."

. . .

That afternoon, the Squad dutifully went on patrol in the usually quiet sequences of Gray's Corrections Cluster, despite knowing it was probably going to be yet another nothingburger barbecue. At least Mick still had most of Lady Penbrook's half-sovereign to spend on snacks for the Squad. Not long after three o'clock, Mick, Alison, and Dolly stood on Clerkenwell Green opposite the sessions house. While waiting for Leech to return from drinking his coffee, they were eating roasted nuts and reminding each other that they had a duty to finish their last patrol stops, even though it would be a waste of time.

After handing his tin cup back to the stall's owner, Leech trotted back to the group. "The sheet says there are alley signs by the Charter House, does it not?" Leech asked.

Alison nodded, her always vigilant eyes scanning their surroundings. "Or thereabouts. Why?"

"I might have sensed a stirring in that direction," Leech said.

"At this distance?" Dolly asked.

"It's in that direction," Leech said. "It needn't be so far as the Charter House."

They followed Leech's sense far enough for Mick to hear the faint sounds of alley song that led them to a square not far from the Charter House. They occupied a bench, all pretending to consult a copy of *Wilson's London Guide*, except Leech, who was staring raptly at a beautiful girl a few years older than he was while she arranged a display for the second-hand clothes store across the square.

"You will scald that poor girl with your gaze," Dolly told Leech without looking up from *Wilson's*.

Leech was still protesting his innocence when Alison grumpily reminded them that they were there to observe alley phenomena.

A few minutes later, Mick started to be able to see alley phenomena in a corner of the square about twenty-five yards away. Soon, they had enough data to predict the alley's size and opening time (a whirlpool Seven opening in roughly a half hour). Mick was proud that he managed to pick the correct formulas. He messed up the actual calculations, but he was quickly able to figure out what he'd done wrong. Given his struggles with formulas, that was nearly as satisfying as being right.

The whirlpool continued to develop at the usual size and pace, but it had peculiar secondary characteristics. It was a nearly monochromatic dark gray, which was odd in itself. Odder still, it was dividing into concentric rings, each spinning in the opposite direction from the ones it was touching, although the uniform, contrastless gray made that hard to spot until there was only about a quarter hour left. And the alley still showed no signs of framing up.

"Rumness," Leech whispered, getting nods of agreement.

The alley song was as enticing as ever, but by then Mick knew to brace himself against the urge to drift toward the alley.

The whirlpool's rings were spinning faster and faster and gradually turning slightly different shades of gray, some lighter than the initial monochrome, some darker. There didn't seem to be a pattern.

When the rings were spinning so fast that they appeared motionless except for a faint flickering, Mick closed his eyes against the impending explosion of alley light. Soon, even though his eyelids, a white wave of light washed over him, leaving floating spots of color hanging before him when he dared to open his eyes.

The others were already standing, and Mick realized there was a dropper. A toddler.

A gentlemanly arrow of early middle age was crouched down, talking to the toddler, who fortunately appeared to be more or less fully dressed, although not in one of the shapeless little dresses Victorian kids usually wore. Leech and Alison dashed toward the toddler, and Mick and Dolly followed at a more casual pace.

"Henry!" Leech called in his maximally posh London accent, "Henry, you remain just where you are, you naughty scamp!"

The dropper, who appeared to be awake but dumbfounded, simply gazed about in wonder, making no protest as Leech picked him up and handed him to Alison, who walked away briskly, while issuing a torrent of relieved scolding prominently featuring the words "mama," "naughty," "fright," and "home." Leech paused long enough to thank the gentlemanly arrow and shake his hand with hearty firmness. Then he jogged to catch up with Alison, joining his voice to her gentle scolding of poor "Henry."

Her eyes on the gentlemanly arrow, Dolly put a restraining hand on Mick's forearm to keep him from following their friends. The arrow was watching Alison and Leech thoughtfully. Eventually, however, he shrugged, brushed off his hat, and walked away. Mick and Dolly watched him go until they were confident that he wasn't going to try to follow Alison and Leech.

Dolly and Mick crossed Red Lion Street. Reaching the far side, Dolly turned right to follow their friends, but Mick stopped and turned around, trying to figure out why it felt so familiar. Then he spotted a window painted with the words "John Reed & Sons, Tobacconists."

Of course. He was standing almost exactly where he'd been when he'd seen his first alley, other than his own drop alley. Where he'd first (unknowingly) seen Cassandra Halliwell, or, more accurately, an echo phantasm of Cassandra Halliwell entering the alley to waylay it. She'd been wearing a puffy dress and moving slowly because—

Because she'd been pushing a wheelchair.

And whoever had been sitting in that chair had been holding a cane with a big silver handle.

"We have to get back to the Institute," he told Dolly.

Mick and Dolly got to Clerkenwell Green just in time to see Leech help Alison and the dropper into a cab and climb up after them. It was almost two miles back to the Institute, so Mick spent a little of Lady Penbrook's half-sovereign on another cab. He and Dolly caught up to Leech and Alison at the warden's nook, where Leech was holding the dropper while Alison dealt with paperwork. Mick told Dolly he'd have to skip the debrief and then took off for Miss Emmet's office as briskly as he could without drawing too much attention to himself. After hustling up back stairs and down dusty corridors, he strolled through the library casually, nodding at the don on duty at the circulation desk. As soon as he was out of sight, he rushed to Miss Emmet's office and burst in without knocking.

He found Miss Emmet sitting with a student, who turned to face him with a startled expression. Angela Paisley.

"We can enroll you in a tutorial in the uses and customs of knocking, if you wish, Mr. Gunn," Miss Emmet said sternly.

"Sorry," he said. "I'll come back."

"No, do stay. Miss Paisley and I are just concluding our discussion. Miss Paisley, you understand what you must do?"

"Yes, Miss Emmet," Miss Paisley said in a quiet and surprisingly polite tone.

"And you believe yourself capable?"

"I— Yes, miss," Miss Paisley said. "Though..."

"Though it will be difficult?" Miss Emmet asked. "Yes, it very likely will. Still in all, I do believe it is one of those things one feels easier for having done."

"I hope so, miss."

"Very well. You may go, Miss Paisley. And you, Mr. Gunn, may remain."

Miss Paisley stood and walked toward the office door with her eyes down. Mick stepped awkwardly out of her way, almost tripping over a pile of books on the floor.

"Mr. Gunn," she said quietly.

"Miss Paisley," he said.

Miss Paisley opened the door carefully and closed it behind herself gently.

"Bolt the door, Mr. Gunn, and take a seat," Miss Emmet said.

Mick did so. "I'm sorry I forgot to knock."

Miss Emmet waved her hand. "No need to apologize. My sternness was largely play-acting for Miss Paisley's benefit."

Mick waited for her to explain, but she didn't. "Is Miss Paisley well?" he asked. "She seemed..." He trailed off, unsure what word he was looking for.

"Emptied," Miss Emmet said. "I'm afraid our Miss Paisley has had an *annus horribilis*, as the Queen once said." She smiled at Mick conspiratorially, but he wasn't sure why. "Not that any of us have had an *annus mirabilis*, of course." She paused. "Horrible year and marvelous year," she translated. "But you didn't thrutch through my door for Latin lessons, I assume?"

Mick quickly explained what he'd realized after that afternoon's whirlpool alley.

After asking a couple questions, Miss Emmet sucked her lips in and pressed them out exaggeratedly a few times in thought. "You did well to apply your battering ram to my door, Mr. Gunn. This is clearly important. Though what we should do with this important knowledge, I cannot for the life of me say. Fortunately, we have our clandestine assembly"—she consulted her wristwatch—"no earlier than twelve minutes hence. I am to enter through the Vicar's office at nine past." A smile flickered across her face. "The fact that it is nine minutes precisely is all the proof one needs that Mr. Victor hatched the plan. And you?"

"The antechamber door at five past."

She stared at the wall behind Mick's head for a little while. "As we have a few minutes to spare, I wish to tell you a bit more about Miss Paisley. I think it may help you soon, and also more generally. To be clear, I am telling you this as a Palladian, not as a member of the faculty of this Institute. A faculty member is not supposed to discuss these things. Yes?" she asked, with her eyebrows raised.

Mick nodded. "I won't snitch."

"I know that you and your friends—and indeed most of the students at the Institute—dislike and distrust Angela Paisley because she, albeit unknowingly, conspired with a madwoman who was killing children to prolong her spiteful and misguided life."

"But except for that, she's totally great," Mick said, exaggerating his American accent.

Miss Emmet chortled. "And I suspect that you and your

friends—and, again, most of the students here—believe bringing Miss Paisley back was foolishness."

Mick shrugged.

"Possibly it is foolish. But I think not. First, I believe in redemption. Despite her flaws and errors, Miss Paisley is a very young person in a terrible situation, like all alley rats. You children have lost families, friends, ways of life, and even the right to speak freely about what you have lost. You and your 'Squad' are remarkably resilient of spirit, but you know how crushing the pain of loss can be."

"We didn't try to murder a bunch of kids," Mick said.

"True," Miss Emmet said. "But neither did Miss Paisley. She merely helped a woman who petted and flattered her at first. And when Miss Paisley became suspicious of the links between the disorder in the alleys and the secret tasks Cassandra Halliwell set for her, Cassandra Halliwell blackmailed and menaced her. And it was not only Cassandra Halliwell who manipulated Miss Paisley. There were, in particular, two young women from Lady Grenville's and another from the Ladies Society. I rather suspect we shall find that they served Lady Penbrook, perhaps unwittingly. And, of course, setting aside hopes of redemption for Miss Paisley, bringing her under my supervision, first at Orphans and then here, has given me the opportunity to draw this information out of her, which has helped Chris and others to understand the scope and nature of the forces moving against us. And, indeed, it has given us a chance to dangle Miss Paisley before Lady Penbrook and her allies to see if any of them would attempt to regain control over her."

"Maybe they already have control over her," Mick pointed out.

"A real possibility," Miss Emmet admitted. "Which is why I

have made quite sure never to provide her with information that would harm us if it were to fall into hostile hands. I have even provided her with a number of apparently important but identifiable and inaccurate pieces of information, and there is no hint that she has breathed a word of those to anyone."

"I guess that's good," Mick admitted. "But she knows that you're up to something, right?"

"A necessary drawback," Miss Emmet said. "But she doesn't know what I am doing or with whom. In any case, we risk disturbing Mr. Victor's meticulous schedule if we linger further. I shall see you shortly."

By quarter past six, the Palladians attending the meeting had drifted in, and there were a couple trusted dons keeping watch on the corridors outside. The usual people were there: Chris, Miss Emmet, Miss North, Mrs. Cutter, Mr. Victor, Miss Mitchell, and Gail. They all looked much the same as always, except Chris, who appeared to be dressed as a governess for a wealthy family. To Mick's surprise, the Vicar was also there, also looking much the same as always except for the dark circles under his eyes.

Once Miss North and Mr. Victor returned to their seats after checking that the doors and windows were locked, everyone was seated around the large oval table. Mick was sitting next to Gail near the foot of the table, looking out the long bank of east-facing windows, watching the soft orange light fade slowly from the world as the sun fell below the earth behind him.

"I believe we are ready to begin, yes?" Mrs. Cutter asked. She and the Vicar were sharing the head of the table, with Miss North at the foot and the rest spread out along the longer arcs of the oval. "Miss Mitchell and Miss Atkinson, please report on the Collapsers' message."

Gail raised her eyebrows at Miss Mitchell, who sighed and said, "As most of you know, the Collapsers' message came in three parts. The first part was single-ciphered. The second two were both double-ciphered. As to the first part, Mr. Gunn correctly realized that one of the four relevant lines was the date of the Collapse. We were able to determine that another line was the date on which the Collapse was triggered. Another line appears to be the estimated date of the Shroud, and the remaining line is a blank, which we take to stand for the date on which the Shroud was or will be triggered."

"And that analysis is entirely based on the first part of the message?" Mr. Victor asked.

"Not entirely," Miss Mitchell answered. "We have now deciphered the second and third parts of the message, and they further corroborate it."

Mrs. Cutter said, "Miss Mitchell, pray tell us the relevant contents of those second and third parts."

Miss Mitchell squared her shoulders. "With help from Miss Tee—"

"Damned clever girl," Mrs. Cutter interjected.

Miss Mitchell continued. "We were able to find the cipher texts for the double-ciphered portions of the message. One portion gave the date of the message's composition—April 21, 1771— and a list of all eight Collapsers. It also contained a short note saying that all the Collapsers survived their trip to 1767. Although one, Mr. Bateson, died in 1770 of an ague. The other seven were 'hale and optimistic' when the message was written."

Mick had barely known Mr. Bateson, but he'd liked him, in

part because Mr. Bateson had looked like Mick's cousin Mateo. Gail had tensed slightly at the mention of Mr. Bateson's death. Mick turned to look at her face, which was impassive but rigid.

"The other double-ciphered portion," Miss Mitchell continued, "was primarily a message from Mr. Yardley to Mrs. Cutter—"

"To anyone with sufficient mathematical knowledge," Mrs. Cutter said.

"So I just said," Miss Mitchell noted with a small smile. "Mrs. Cutter?"

"The message from Mr. Yardley," Mrs. Cutter said, pausing to clear her throat, "was a set of calculations related to undoing the Collapse. Apparently, in the years after he and the others dropped in 1767, they began to worry that Lord Harrowgrave or someone else might again seek to undo the Collapse."

"Prescient," the Vicar remarked.

"Indeed," Mrs. Cutter said. "Mr. Yardley's questions and calculations strike me as sound and serious, and Miss Richardson agrees."

"None of us being half so blessed by Urania as you, Mr. Yardley, and Miss Richardson," Miss Emmet said, "we shall trust your assessment. What does Mr. Yardley's message signify?"

"It suggests three ways that one might undo the Collapse," Mrs. Cutter said. "One of them would, I believe, cause symptoms that looked just like the Rumness."

"Then it is as we feared," Miss North said.

"And in some ways worse," Mrs. Cutter said. "We have always feared that some villain or cabal might hope to seize a great deal of power by restoring the ability to shuttle the alleys. But we now also understand that the act necessary to seize that power would require a staggering discharge of chronal energy through the threads of time. Such a discharge would kill dozens, even hundreds of alley rats in every time alley between now and the Shroud."

"Are we," the Vicar asked, "reasonably convinced that Lady Penbrook intends to perpetrate this monstrous act?"

Mrs. Cutter said, "Someone does, at any rate."

Breaking her silence, Chris said, "I am quite confident it is Lady Penbrook. Some of you know my reasons."

Miss North, Mr. Victor, and Miss Emmet all nodded.

"Then the question," the Vicar said, "is how we may prevent it."

"I have no answer to that," Mrs. Cutter said. "Not as yet."

"I might have some notions," Miss Emmet said. "And I believe they relate both to tomorrow's conference with Miss Collins and with a discovery that Mr. Gunn made this afternoon. Mr. Gunn, if you please."

Mick walked them through passing the tobacconist's and remembering that he'd seen an echo phantasm of Cassandra Halliwell pushing a wheelchair like Mr. Ambrose's into a glow orb.

"Was she an old woman in that one too?" Gail asked. "Or was that only in the one by the Foundling Hospital? The one I saw?"

"She didn't look that old at the tobacconist's," Mick said. "Her actual age, I think."

Mick felt Gail's attention shift.

"Was there something, Mrs. Cutter?" Gail asked.

"Yes," Mrs. Cutter said, with a puzzled look, "but I'm damned if I know what it is."

"You're certain that Cassie Halliwell was pushing a wheel-chair identical to Mr. Ambrose's?" Mr. Victor asked Mick.

"I'm not sure about identical," Mick said. "But definitely close."

"He's right," Miss Emmet said. "For some time now, I've had Miss March compiling all of our observations of the alley waylayments and the time lightning. The former category includes the various notes taken during and immediately after the alley in question. At the time, Mr. Gunn described Cassandra Halliwell as pushing a wheelchair with an occupant whose face was covered by a canopy and who had a walking stick with a silver handle."

"So this Mr. Ambrose," Miss North said, "knew Cassandra Halliwell. And he knows both Miss Collins and Lady Penbrook. That cannot be a coincidence."

"I continue to wonder how Cassandra Halliwell and Miss Collins learned to manipulate alleys as they do," Miss North said. "I must believe none of the faculty here would be so wicked as to teach them. More importantly, I am quite certain none of the professors here knows *how* to do it. Perhaps the old gentleman in the wheelchair taught Cassandra Halliwell and Miss Collins?"

"Old though he may be," Mrs. Cutter said, "perhaps even so blighted by the snows of eld as I, but surely he is not old enough to be a pre-Collapse shuttler. And they were the last people whose deeds reveal such knowledge."

"So far as we know," Mr. Victor said. "However, if someone knew but acted discreetly—"

"Vicar," Mrs. Cutter said with a peculiar look on her face, "without calling undue attention to the fact of our gathering here in conference, could you arrange for someone to fetch me a copy of Hinch-Cowlings' *Apertural Novation and Innovation?*"

"No need," the Vicar said, rising and crossing to the small bookcase built into the wall near the sitting area. He extracted a book and handed it to Mrs. Cutter before settling back into his chair.

Mrs. Cutter riffled the book impatiently until finding something promising. She flipped the pages slowly and then settled on one, appearing to read it over at least a couple times. "H.A. Braithwaite," she said decisively.

"Mrs. Cutter?" Miss Mitchell asked.

"When I was a mere slip of a girl, perhaps Miss Mitchell's age, I went to a soirée at the Society for Chronal Fancy when it was but newly founded. I was on the arm of an arrow. A remarkably handsome and formidably clever man. He was, however, not a pleasant companion. A terrible monologist, for one thing. Proud and thin-skinned for another. He fell to quarreling and departed early, in a deep dudgeon. I remember that clearly because his departure freed me to spend the evening in a fascinating conversation with Mr. Cutter, which began our courtship."

Mick remembered the story but had no idea where it was going.

Apparently Miss North didn't know either. "And how might this relate—"

"Just now when Miss Atkinson asked whether Cassandra Halliwell appeared to be an old woman when she was pushing the wheelchair, it made me wonder whether I would have recognized a picture of her disguised as an old woman. I then realized that, as a girl, if shown a photograph of my own current face, I shouldn't have recognized myself. And I thought about that photograph of the gentleman in the wheelchair, and started to wonder how he might have looked as a young man. Was he, for example, remarkably handsome? And then I asked myself, what was that handsome arrow's name? I tried to recollect it for Mr. Gunn not too long ago, thinking it was perhaps Amos or Abrahms."

"But it was Ambrose?" Miss North asked.

Mrs. Cutter slapped the open book in front of her. "Correct. And then, I happened to remember something Mr. Ambrose said to me at least a half-dozen times that evening, that it was his intention that 'one day the name of A.A. Ambrose be every bit as celebrated as the name of H.A. Braithwaite.'"

"Who?" Mr. Victor asked.

"Well, indeed," Mrs. Cutter said. "I asked the same question when Mr. Ambrose first mentioned the name. Mr. Ambrose was appalled by my ignorance and delivered a lengthy hagiography of H.A. Braithwaite, 'famed shuttler of the Pre-Collapse Era.' There is an entry in here in Hinch-Cowlings that lists Braithwaite's various accomplishments before noting that 'Braithwaite took umbrage at criticisms of his theories and at the praise bestowed upon Earnest Witherstrop Putnam after Putnam traveled almost five years backward in time, very nearly four full months further than Braithwaite's famed voyage documented in Braithwaite's own *Principia Aperturarum*, which treatise had been published not a month before Putnam made his claim. On the first of November of the year 1767, before beginning a chronal journey in the clear view of reliable witnesses, Braithwaite proclaimed that he would that very day travel not only a full half-dozen years, but a half-dozen years into the future. His fate is a mystery.'"

Mrs. Cutter looked up from the book. "The entry also provides a rather nice etching of Mr. Braithwaite. And unless time is playing puckish with my memories, he looks uncannily like young Mr. Ambrose."

Everybody looked at one another in bafflement.

After a moment, Mr. Victor asked, "To be clear, your conclusion is that the present-day the gentleman in the wheelchair is the same person as the arrogant young Mr. Ambrose you met in — what year?"

"1806," Mrs. Cutter said.

"And," Mr. Victor continued, "that Mr. Ambrose is also H.A. Braithwaite, who disappeared in 1767?"

"One day before the Collapse," Mrs. Cutter said, nodding. "Yes, quite possibly, though I am aware that it sounds utterly mad. A more sensible explanation might be that our Mr. Ambrose is, say, a grandson of H.A. Braithwaite. In truth, I suspect that the utterly mad explanation will also turn out to be the correct one, time-travel being what it is."

"I haven't had time to turn every stone," Chris said, "but so far, I have found no real trace of Mr. Ambrose before 1806. I have heard stories about his life prior to that year, but each contradicts the other, and I suspect to find that it is all a pack of lies."

"Another point in favor of madness," Mrs. Cutter said with a crooked grin.

"If indeed, the present Mr. Ambrose is one of the great alley shuttlers," Miss North said, "that would certainly explain how Cassandra Halliwell and Miss Collins learned to manipulate the alleys."

"Though it invites an infinity of other questions," Mrs.

Cutter said. "How he managed to travel this far forward, or forward at all. How—"

"Indeed," Miss Emmet said. "But I think the question that we must confront, in this moment, is what does he mean to us today? Does he serve Lady Penbrook, or she him? Or are they perhaps rivals?"

Everyone nodded.

"And I believe," Miss Emmet said, "that an important way to find answers to those questions is to meet with Miss Collins as she requested. Are we comfortable with the plan as agreed, or does this discovery about Mr. Ambrose suggest the need for amendments?"

The others looked at one another and shrugged.

"I see no reason not to proceed as agreed," Mr. Victor said, "provided that our representatives feel able to play their roles."

The others nodded their agreement.

"I feel confident in my ability," Gail said.

"I have spoken with Miss Paisley," Miss Emmet said. "She is willing to proceed."

Miss Paisley? Mick thought. *What plan did they come up with?*

"With my sincerest apologies to our third representative," Miss Emmet said, "I have not yet been able to speak with Mr. Gunn."

Me? Seriously, what kind of plan did they come up with?

"Mr. Gunn," Miss Emmet said, "we shall explain the plan to you now. I feel quite confident that you are capable of playing your role, but the choice is naturally yours to make."

They spent another half hour in the conference, mostly explaining Mick's role but also debating the finer points of meeting with Catherine Collins. In the end, they asked Mick whether he felt able to do what would be required of him, and he said that he did. He even thought that he did. But mostly what he thought was, *What kind of weird-ass plan did we come up with?*

10

THE POINTED CORNERS

The Palladians had actually come up with a fairly simple plan. They didn't think they could con Catherine Collins into revealing information during the meeting. Or frighten her. If they kidnapped her, it would be difficult to hold her somewhere Lady Penbrook couldn't find her. Also, they'd be kidnappers. The smartest plan seemed to be to listen to what she had to say while not revealing much about the Palladians or even, hopefully, that there was such a group. So they decided to send kids.

Everybody knew that Gail was smart enough to listen carefully and report back better than most adults. And she, like Miss Paisley and Mick, could tell Catherine Collins some personal experiences that raised questions about Lady Penbrook's motives. True, going to the meeting might mark them for special attention from Lady Penbrook. But it was pretty clear that Lady Penbrook was already paying Gail and Mick special attention, and she had to know about Miss Paisley's involvement with Cassandra Halliwell. Besides, the mere fact that they went to talk to Catherine Collins wouldn't prove anything other than someone had told them to go, and it was their job to pretend they didn't know why.

Sure, if they got kidnapped and tortured, they could reveal all sorts of secrets. But that was why Chris would have a half-dozen trusted operatives, including her formidable lieutenant Mr. Ferness, in and around the Ladies Society to make sure nothing went wrong. And why Miss Mitchell would have a half-dozen trusted dons there too. Besides, if she'd wanted, Lady Penbrook could already have had them kidnapped and tortured.

Mick was surprised that he hadn't been more bothered by people repeating the phrase "kidnapped and tortured" so many times. Maybe he was just too dumb to think it through. Maybe he was too excited about the chance to talk to his sister.

Miss North, Miss Emmet, Chris, Miss Mitchell, and Gail would all attend the same lecture as Catherine Collins. Gail was a frequent visitor to the Ladies Society, so it made sense for her to sneak out of the post-lecture soirée to meet with Catherine Collins. Mick and Miss Paisley were too young to attend lectures at the Ladies Society, so they had to wait upstairs in a dinky, dusty room where the Society stored thirty years' worth of unread pamphlets and other forgotten junk. They had been smuggled into that room at half four that afternoon and had been killing time since.

When there had still been daylight to read by, they had sat on the floor a few feet apart, facing each other with their backs against cluttered shelves and reading old pamphlets. Sadly, the Ladies Society was apparently doing for women's rights what the Society for Chronal Fancy was doing for time travel: making them so boring that nobody would ever wonder if something important was going on.

Still, it had been easier to pretend to read pamphlets than to try to make conversation. What would they even say to each other? "Hey, Miss Paisley, sorry I got you busted for trying to steal time journals." "No worries, Mr. Gunn. Sorry the woman I worked for tried to gut you in the garden." "LOL, 1853 was super crazy, right?"

But then the sun disappeared from the dusty windows, and the storage room fell dark, making it impossible to pretend to read. After about a half hour in darkness, when the bells rang seven o'clock, Mick and Miss Paisley discovered that sitting in the darkness somehow made it easier to talk. Well, to whisper.

"Did Miss Emmet tell you to know the hour by the Farm Street bells?" Miss Paisley asked.

"Yes," Mick said as flatly as possible.

"I see," she said, hesitantly. "When she told me that, I wondered if she might... Well, if it mightn't be a test of sorts. The church being Jesuit, you see."

Mick didn't see, so he just made a "hmm" noise.

"Miss Emmet has been... I am grateful for her, you see. Sometimes people are not as they seem. And sometimes they only seem as they do because we are taught to see them a certain way and so do not see them as they are."

Mick made another "hmm" noise.

"Your London accent is much improved," she said.

"Thanks," he said, trying not to be annoyed.

"I don't wish to say that your American accent is wrong, you understand. I meant merely that your London accent is rather good now. I had to learn a London accent too. Twice. The first time was when my moth— When we moved to London from Londonderry. But then I dropped from that London to this

London and had to learn a new accent. An East Croydon accent not being quite what is desired at the Institute."

Miss Paisley had just said more to him in two minutes than in the rest of the time he'd known her. It was a shame that he didn't really understand it. "Your accent sounds good to me," Mick said. "For what it's worth."

She thanked him, and they sat in silence a while.

"Are you acquainted with Miss Collins?" she asked.

I used to change her diapers and dangle her teddy bear over her crib while she tried to grab its legs. "I spoke with her a couple of days ago, but we haven't been formally introduced," he said.

"It's only that Miss Greigheye—that's what Cassandra Halliwell called herself when I knew her. Miss Greigheye, she could be cruel. She frightened me, especially at the end."

Mick thought for a minute. "Catherine Collins doesn't seem cruel."

"Miss Greigheye seemed most kind, at first," Miss Paisley said darkly.

The bells rang a quarter past seven. Mick pulled his matchbox and pocket watch from different pockets, opening the watch and then striking a match. It was indeed a quarter past seven.

"Ten minutes until we go downstairs," Mick said.

Miss Paisley didn't speak, but he could sense her nod her head.

After a long pause, Miss Paisley said, "I'm frightened."

That irritated Mick. He remembered being afraid of the Mysterious Interloper, not yet knowing it was actually Miss Paisley. He'd been afraid of Cassandra Halliwell when she'd been trying to stab him. He was pretty sure those kids who'd

died in the alleys because of Cassandra Halliwell had died terri-
fied. What right did Miss Paisley have to be frightened now?

"Frightened of what?" he asked impatiently.

After a pause, Miss Paisley said matter-of-factly, "Everything." After another pause, she said, "I suppose, most of all,
being foolish again and causing pain again."

That deflated Mick's irritation. "It'll be all right," he said,
wincing at how unconvincing he sounded.

After several more nervously struck matches, Mick
confirmed that it was time to go meet Catherine Collins.

Hoping that the dons who were supposed to be protecting
them were actually doing so, Mick snuck downstairs with Miss
Paisley. They lurked around the corner from the office they were
going to until Gail appeared near its door. She motioned to
them to join her.

Feeling painfully exposed, Mick turned the corner and
started to walk toward Gail, with Miss Paisley following just
behind. Gail unlocked the door and stepped inside, leaving the
door ajar. Mick and Miss Paisley picked up the pace and
followed her inside. After closing the heavy door, Gail lit a
match and then a candle stub, which she used to locate a
hanging paraffin lamp, which was soon filling the office with
warm light.

All three of them stood awkwardly for a moment until the
handle turned and the door opened, allowing Catherine Collins
and her elegant dress to pour through it.

After latching the door, she looked at them carefully.
"Should I be insulted to find only children?" she asked
neutrally.

"I'm not a child, Miss Collins," Gail said, "and I think you
are unlikely to take offense at caution and precaution."

Miss Collins smiled tightly. "Very well. This must be brief. If I am powdering too long, I shall arouse suspicions. First, the Rumness, as they are calling it, is not natural, whatever 'natural' may be for time alleys."

Gail said "duh" with her eyebrows.

"Quite," Catherine Collins said. "I am ... familiar with its origins and properties, and I fear that it may portend mischief and even great peril and suffering."

Gail's eyebrows were a little less sarcastic.

Catherine Collins continued, "I still consider myself bound by oath and conscience not to say so much as you might wish, or indeed so much as I might wish, but you must be alert to the danger and contemplate it with the utmost seriousness. I once thought it a bold and perilous undertaking," she said, emphasizing "undertaking." "But I believed the perils would threaten only those bringing it about. But lately I have come to fear that far more people, innocents, could be in danger. With potentially horrific results."

"And you have summoned us here to warn us of this danger?" Gail asked.

"I have rather been hoping that you are already aware of it. And I had rather hoped to speak about it with whomever sent you." She stared at Gail, who kept her face blank. Mick tried to do the same.

After staring a little while longer, Catherine Collins said, "But if you and those who sent you are not yet aware of the danger, then I most certainly *do* wish to warn you." She paused. "I wish I knew whether I can trust your intentions, or the intentions of those you serve, or whether this world is naught but lies and grasping." She shook her head firmly. "No matter. If it indeed be the case that the conduct of ... others is such that I am no longer bound by oath and conscience, I shall contact you again. My heart hopes that it will not be necessary, but my reason increasingly warns me that it will. And if indeed I must contact you, it will be with gravest urgency." She thought for a moment. "Miss Atkinson, would a message delivered to the Gee Street Outpost reach you?"

"Yes," Gail said, "but it might reach others as well, and might not reach me the same day unless the subject impressed the duty don as important. But the more important it seems…"

"… the more likely that others will take notice," Catherine Collins said, nodding. "Very well. If you receive a note in a gentleman's hand saying that the press of business prevents him from the stroll he had so longed to share with you that evening, it will signify my intention to present myself at All Souls the following morning at eleven o'clock. You may send whomever you please, but know that I may be watched."

"All Souls at Langham Place?" Gail asked.

"Indeed. I shall arrange for a door to be open on the north-east side and shall meet you within. Now, my time grows short," she said. "May I be so bold to presume that you, Miss Paisley, came to tell me of your role in the evil deeds of Cassandra Halliwell, and that you, Miss Atkinson, came to tell me of the time that ruffians kidnapped you and put you in fear for your life? And that both of you have good reason to believe that these evils were not done in service of Lord Harrowgrave alone, but also, or even solely, in service of another powerful person, a woman you had long believed to be a champion of progress and humanity?"

Gail and Miss Paisley looked as surprised as Mick felt. Gail recovered quickly. "I do not believe we wish to dispute those points."

"And you, my fine fellow?" she asked Mick.

Mick froze. During the planning session, the Palladians had given Mick permission to tell Catherine Collins she was his sister, but only if Gail believed it would be helpful. Gail was shaking her head at him. He knew she was right, but he also knew that he desperately wanted to say it, so much that he was trembling from the effort of restraining himself. In the end, what helped him hold his tongue wasn't wisdom but possessiveness. He didn't want to share that secret with Miss Paisley. She didn't deserve to know.

Mick fell back on his prepared answer. "I can vouch for both of them, is all," he said.

"And doubtless your word is bond," Catherine Collins said, looking at him. "But no bond is required in this instance." She turned her gaze to Gail. "If you would kindly extinguish the light before I open the door?"

Gail turned off the lamp.

"Oh," Catherine Collins said in the dark, "and I have changed my mind. If we do meet at All Souls, do send whomever you deem it wise to send, but be sure that this boy whose word is bond is of the party." With that, she opened the door and slid into the dim hallway.

Mick wasn't at all surprised that he and Gail and, to a lesser extent, Miss Paisley got grilled by Miss Emmet as soon as they returned to the Institute, or that he and Gail got grilled again by Miss Emmet, Miss North, Mr. Victor, and Chris the next day. Nor was he surprised that, during patrol, the Squad also had a lot of questions for him about where he'd been or that they got a little surly with him when he couldn't answer the questions.

After patrol, they left him to himself in the Great Hall as a gesture of reproach.

And he was getting ready to sneak off again to meet with Gail and Chris, so the Squad was going to be even surlier when they noticed that he'd disappeared again.

To his surprise, he noticed that Miss Paisley was approaching him.

"Miss Paisley," he said.

"Mr. Gunn." She glanced around and sighed.

Mick realized that she was getting side-eye from passing students. And he was included in some of the glances because he was talking to her.

"Might I speak with you in the garden?" she asked.

"I have to meet with—" At the last second, he managed to avoid saying "Chris." "With a professor. A vespertine, you see."

She seemed so disappointed that he looked up at the silver hands of the Great Clock. "But I have a few minutes. We could talk in the garden." He was supposed to use the garden gate to sneak out to meet Chris anyway.

She smiled gratefully. He was startled to realize that he'd never seen her smile.

In the garden, sitting on his favorite stone bench in the shade of a London plane, he waited a while for her to speak. At last she said, "I wanted to thank you. For listening to me yesterday. You haven't any reason to like me or trust me."

Which is why I don't like or trust you, he thought.

"But you did listen to me, and I'm grateful. I hope my part in … whatever took place yesterday and whatever is happening with the Rumness—" She cut herself off. "All of it. I hope my part in all of it is over, or at least will be soon." She paused. "I disliked Orphans at first, but I would gladly return now. They have never heard of time alleys there. Here, I shall always be known as the girl I was, forever condemned for the things that girl did. I think a braver girl, someone like Miss March or Miss Tee, might be able to front the whispers and the stares. But I," she sighed again, "am afraid of everything, and I cannot see how anything here will make me any braver. In any case, thank you, Mr. Gunn."

Mick told her she was welcome. They sat in silence for a couple minutes, with Mick getting increasingly antsy and struggling to conceal it. To avoid having a record of Mick's signing out with the warden, Chris had arranged for the gate to be left unlocked for him at five to the hour, and it was very nearly time. But Miss Paisley thought he was going back into the Institute for a vespertine. If he went the opposite direction toward the gate, it would be obvious that he'd lied, and just as obvious that he was leaving the Institute without permission.

Fortunately, Miss Emmet appeared in the garden from the faculty wing and told Miss Paisley to come with her. Once Miss Paisley was safely back inside, Mick went toward the gate, making sure to stroll casually. En route, he spotted young Mr. Davies and his delivery wagon stopping outside the gate. Mr. Davies ran a stick back and forth across the iron bars of the gate to attract a scullion, distracting the poor girl with questions and antics, allowing Mick to slip out unnoticed, patting the flank of one of Mr. Davies' elderly mares as he left.

For a moment, Mick felt lucky that Miss Emmet had happened along. Then he realized that there had been nothing lucky about it. She'd made sure to be there in case he needed help.

Mick took a long, zig-zagging route to the Grosvenor Square home under renovation that Chris used to spy on Lady

Penbrook. As before, he entered from the alley and snuck up the backstairs.

Looking like a young gentlewoman dressed soberly for a daytime outing, Gail unlocked the sitting room door at Mick's gentle knock and then locked it again as soon as he was inside. Gail led him to Chris, who was sitting by the window at the fake surveyor's transit, wearing her Mr. Samuel suit.

"May I present my dearest cousin, Estelle Langhorn," Chris said, gesturing to Gail. "Miss Langhorn has surprised me and delighted me with her presence. Her papa, the colonel, has made a rather impromptu trip to the city."

"Mother is with Lady Sylvia in Bath, you see," Gail said, "and Father can be so hasty when Mother isn't there to rein him in. Still, it does give one a chance to visit one's most dashing cousin." She lowered her voice and whispered theatrically, "And one's favorite dressmaker. One looks like such a frightful frump when one's father decrees the tone."

Sometimes, people were too impressed by their own cleverness, and it didn't do to encourage them. Mick simply stared at them blankly.

They both started chuckling, but Chris broke off to peer through the disguised telescope.

"The gentleman in the beautiful frock coat?" Gail asked. She explained to Mick, "There is a gentleman who often stands on Charles Street just below a window of Lady Penbrook's townhouse. Chris is convinced that he is there to receive orders from Lady Penbrook."

Still peering through the telescope, Chris said, "He's there every day, including Sundays, at half-eight in the morning and again at half-five in the evening. Always alone, almost always wearing the same frock coat, which is indeed most beautiful.

He stands in his accustomed spot for ten minutes often making a show of winding his watch or lighting his pipe. I have yet to see him speak, so he must, in the main, be there to listen."

When Mick had first dropped in Victorian London, he would have asked why the gentleman didn't just go inside. But now Mick knew a fine lady like Lady Penbrook would have at least a half-dozen servants about her townhouse at all times, including a butler at the door. The servants could see any visitor and might overhear any conversation in the townhouse. In some cases, it would be more discreet for Lady Penbrook to close the door to the room she was in and speak softly to someone on the street outside.

Chris looked up from the telescope. "I believe the gentleman is one of Mr. Harris' lieutenants. Whatever information or instruction the gentleman receives from Lady Penbrook is likely to be of consequence. But that isn't why I've asked you to meet me here."

She raised her eyebrows at Gail.

"Ah, yes," Gail said. "Gee Street just relayed a message from my fictitious suitor saying he is unable to stroll with me this evening."

"Catherine Collins wants to meet?" Mick asked.

Gail nodded. "Tomorrow at All Souls. Eleven o'clock."

"I have conferred with the others," Chris said. "You two are to meet with Miss Collins. Some dons who normally worship at All Souls will be spread about the place, and some trusted Eyes will be on the streets."

"I doubt that Miss Collins intends us harm," Gail said.

"Likely not," Chris agreed. "But very possibly Lady Penbrook does, and I cannot tell whether she suspects Miss Collins of disloyalty. Perhaps she has just now told our friend in the beautiful coat to have Miss Collins watched at all times."

Gail nodded to acknowledge the point.

Chris said, "Gail, if speaking proves necessary, that task will be yours in the main. But both of you should endeavor to listen, not speak."

Gail nodded. "Miss Collins clearly has a great deal she wishes to say."

"Gunner," Chis said. "As to your belief that she is your sister, the same instructions still apply. Speak of it only if you can be certain that speaking will aid our cause, and, even then, only if Gail does not forbid you."

Mick nodded. He really hoped he could stick to the plan and not just blurt it out at the worst possible time.

"Now," Chris said, "let us ingratiate ourselves to the gods by making careful plans for them to disrupt."

The next morning, as Gail had instructed, Mick lurked in the lane near All Souls until Gail entered a side door to the church and then beckoned him to join her. Inside, he found Gail in a narrow hallway with Catherine Collins, who led them just past the vestry to a room not much bigger than a broom closet. There was a small bookshelf, filled largely with odds and ends, a small desk and a small chair. Mick and Gail stood shoulder to shoulder, facing Catherine Collins, who also remained standing.

"I worshiped at All Souls until I left Lady Grenville's," Catherine Collins said, "and even now I return on occasion. The senior warden graciously fails to ask me questions when I make use of this room."

She smiled charmingly, but the smile soon fell away,

replaced by a look of exhaustion, dismay, and anger. She drew in breath a couple times as if to speak but remained silent.

Gail nudged Mick with her elbow, reminding him to keep quiet.

After drawing another heavy breath, Catherine Collins said, "Honor no longer compelling my silence, I may say now what I could not when we last met. I have been deceived and betrayed. I can no longer convince myself that Lady Penbrook is the woman she pretends to be, nor that her plans are what I thought them."

Gail nudged Mick again.

"Are you familiar with waiting alleys?" Catherine Collins asked.

Gail and Mick shook their heads.

Catherine Collins nodded. "Few are. For decades Mr. Ambrose—" she nearly spat the name— "was the only person who knew much about them." She paused to look at Mick, then Gail. "I paraded Mr. Ambrose past this young gentleman, so I hope you now have learned something about him."

"Something," Gail said. "But we are always willing to learn more."

"As perhaps you know, much about him is vile in workaday ways," Catherine Collins said. "But there also are hidden things, things that strain credulity. If I were to tell you, I fear you might doubt my honesty, or even my sanity."

Trade you, Mick thought. *You tell us about Mr. Ambrose, and I'll tell you about trying to get you back asleep after Uncle Dan accidentally turned on the light over your crib at two in the morning.*

"For now," she continued, "please believe me when I say that Mr. Ambrose is both an extremely capable and an extremely selfish man, and that his ability to manipulate waiting alleys makes him immensely dangerous. It also threatens to give power to Lady Penbrook that would make *her* immensely dangerous. One can find scraps of good-for-nothing grimgribber about waiting alleys in quite a few dusty books, but there are somewhat more useful passages in Blake's *Disquisitions* and," she paused slightly, "Braithwaite's *Principia Aperturarum*."

Mick tensed up at the mention of Braithwaite and felt Gail do the same. Catherine Collins gave no sign of noticing.

"Both accounts," she continued, "are incomplete and often inaccurate, the *Principia* deliberately so. But they do show that I am not simply inventing waiting alleys. It is essential that you know that they are real."

She paused, gathering her thoughts. "The events on the Hungerford Bridge made it impossible to weave the alley threads as alley rats had long done. To simplify, perhaps excessively, they rendered the alley realm between the second of November, 1767 and the seventh of October of 1853 a desert for secondary time travel. The live alleys—"

"Live alleys?" Gail asked.

Catherine Collins frowned while framing her reply. "The alleys that spontaneously appear, by unknown means and for unknown reasons, in the future and drop alley rats into the past when they are still fully charged with chronal energy. That is essentially the time—'time' is misleading, but so are all other words—when the alley is 'live,' which is to say when it is expecting to carry or actually carrying its intended alley rat." She held up her hand to cut off a question from Gail. "Understand that the time in the alley realm does not—and obviously cannot—function as it does in the tritical."

"The 'tritical'?" Gail asked.

"The everyday world," Catherine Collins said, gesturing

vaguely at London, the Earth, and the universe before continuing. "Once an alley has served its purpose, as time and purpose are measured in the alley realm, much of its energy dissipates. But its thread remains. With patience and luck, the thread can be used to shuttle the alleys. You know this from the events of last October."

Gail nodded.

"The events of last October, as I say, have made the alley realm a desert for shuttling the alleys. So far as I, or Mr. Ambrose, or his dead-eyed minions can tell, live alleys continue to form as they always have and to anchor themselves in the past as they always have, leaving threads as they always have. Some of those threads can even be moved about and reanchored. But, thanks to the Collapse, their vestibules cannot, in the main, be persuaded to open into the tritical before the seventh of October of last year."

"Vestibules?" Gail asked.

"Where the alley connects with the tritical. When an alley is live, the vestibule becomes the aperture itself." Catherine Collins paused. "I don't wish to give offense, but I do hope that there are those among you who understand these matters better than you seem to do."

Gail said flatly. "There are some, yes. And there were more before 'the events of last October.'"

A sad look crossed Catherine Collins' face. "Yes, I helped cause a great deal of pain. Such was not my intent, I assure you, but the pain remains. For me as well. I did not, of course," she looked at Mick, "anticipate or desire the death of your young friend. For that I am deeply sorry." She returned her gaze to Gail. "The murderer in that case was Lord Harrowgrave's creature, and I trusted Lady Penbrook to baffle and hamper Lord Harrowgrave such that his callousness would not endanger innocents. She manifestly did not. Though I do suspect she ultimately hampered Lord Harrowgrave quite thoroughly by having a knife shoved into his neck." She took a deep breath. "That day on that day on the bridge, however, she allowed him free rein. Worse, I believe that she deliberately used him as an instrument of murder by misleading him as to what needed to be done in the alley realm so that, in turn, he would mislead August Blake to his death."

She paused, her jaw clenched and her fingers and her fingertips pressing hard at one another beneath the high waist of her gown. "August served Lord Harrowgrave loyally, but I believe that he was blind to the man's true nature. August had many extremely fine qualities. Sadly, the ability to consider with due skepticism those who showed him favor and preferment was not among those qualities. In the end, Lord Harrowgrave also showed himself lacking in that quality, which is how Lady Penbrook managed to use him to kill August and then managed to end Lord Harrowgrave's life as well. She may also have intended that I die in that alley."

She paused again, her jaw and fingers still tensing. "But I digress. With the alley realm a desert through the seventh of October of last year and, to a lesser extent, for years to come, it is a practical impossibility to shuttle the alleys using the threads. But Mr. Ambrose has devised an alternative."

"Waiting alleys?" Gail guessed.

"Just so," Catherine Collins said. "Live alleys are fully energized alleys. The threads are their flickering ghosts. Waiting alleys are, let us say, the possibility of live alleys. They are not yet live alleys, but instead await a quickening that will bring them fully into being. Before the Collapse, shuttlers and scholars speculated on how they might be used for time travel, but, until Mr. Ambrose, no one ever found an approach with any promise."

"How promising is his approach?" Gail asked.

"He will succeed unless stopped," Catherine Collins said. "For months, at Lady Penbrook's urging, I have helped him explore the alley realm, learning how we might partially quicken waiting alleys. What I did not know, until recently, is that Mr. Ambrose has progressed well beyond studying. With Lady Penbrook's blessing, he used my labors and discoveries to train a platoon of fair-haired, dead-eyed young men. Those young men have been weaving waiting alleys into 'toils,' which are, let us say, nets of waiting alleys capable of channeling chronal energy in certain directions, instead of simply evenly filling the background space of the alley realm."

She paused.

"Does this sound like gibberish? Likely so. In many ways it must do until one has been in the alley realm and experienced the things to which I am giving these inadequate names. But what they are doing will let them shuttle the alleys. It is already affecting the alleys."

"The Rumness," Gail said.

"Indeed. Remember, the alley realm can only be accessed by a vestibule connected to a thread. But once one is in a thread, one can weave waiting alleys into toils. If a source of sufficient chronal energy can be summoned, the toils can be used to channel that energy to revivify what is now a desert. Mr. Ambrose has begun to call it the 'Summons,' and the Summons will allow alley rats once again to shuttle the alleys." She paused. "At least, it will allow Lady Penbrook and Mr. Ambrose to shuttle the alleys. They will not share the ability freely with others, of course."

"What source of energy could accomplish such a thing?" Gail asked in a carefully neutral tone.

Mick was pretty sure that Gail knew the answer, that this was the danger that Mrs. Cutter had alluded to and that she and other Palladians had feverishly been trying to understand.

"An excellent question," Catherine Collins said, "and the one that perhaps most horrifies me about Lady Penbrook's and Mr. Ambrose's plans. Those plans require finding a sufficiently long and live thread that an alley rat may step into and stretch into the future beyond the rat's birthday, thereby triggering the birth flame."

The birth flame was how Cassandra Halliwell had died. If alley rats went far enough into the future, they would burn to death at the very instant their infant selves were being born. This happened to very few rats because time alleys usually dropped rats a century or more in the past. But Cassandra Halliwell's alley had dumped her only thirty-five years in the past, as a five-year-old girl. She had spent her entire life from that point forward knowing that the birth flame would kill her well before she turned forty. She had been willing to hurt and kill people, including little kids, to avoid that fate, although that fate had come for her regardless.

"Do we know," Gail asked, "that the birth flame can be triggered within the alley realm? The only known cases involve people aging normally in the real world."

"Also an excellent question," Catherine Collins replied. "And the answer is probably that the birth flame can only be triggered in the tritical."

"Then, how," Gail asked, "is there a danger? Alley rats

cannot travel forward in time, certainly not a long way forward in time."

"So I long believed," Catherine Collins replied. "And that belief blinded me to the danger. The answer is the vestibule. A rat need not entirely leave the vestibule to touch the tritical. Much as an alley rat can stand in this world and reach a hand into the vestibule as the first step of opening the vestibule, an alley rat can stand in the vestibule and reach a hand into this world. We had all assumed this must be part of a complete transition to or from the alley realm—entering or exiting it altogether. But Mr. Ambrose now believes otherwise."

"Would that rat not simply burn to death horribly?" Gail asked.

Mick was really glad that Gail was there. She was putting her finger on a lot of big issues that he wasn't catching.

"That's the rub," Catherine Collins said. "Mr. Ambrose is convinced that having only a hand in the tritical is the difference. And, no, it needn't be a hand precisely. A human is a self. A soul and a body. It seems that the vestibule, at least, serves to translate the self into and out of the alley realm. But our bodies at least, are not at all the same thing in the alley realm as in this world. I'm told you will know that, if you remember your journey through your own alley. Having been but an infant, I remember nothing of mine."

Mick shuddered, remembering his trip through the alley, where his body had felt like a chew toy pulled in different directions by all the world's angry dogs.

"So," Catherine Collins continued, "when I say 'reaching a hand' into or out of the vestibule, what I really mean is having only just begun the process of transition. In any event, Mr. Ambrose is convinced that if one is only very slightly in the tritical, one will not burn to death. He believes, and has reams of equations to support him, that the birth flame consumes a person in the tritical so utterly because, if one is in the tritical, one is suddenly made the vessel for an unutterable amount of chronal energy." She paused, looking them both in the eyes in turn. "It is a truly *staggering* amount of energy. And, in the tritical, that energy cannot spread beyond one's body. So one's body burns from within as if plunged into the forge of Hephaestus. But if one is almost entirely in the vestibule, one is in contact with a time alley, or at least a thread, which exists in order to carry just such unutterable energies. With luck and skill, those energies will pass harmlessly through the rat and into the thread."

"Which would re-energize the thread?" Gail asked.

"Yes," Catherine Collins said. She opened what had appeared to be a large locket but turned out to be a watch. She frowned but continued talking. "And not just the thread, if the thread is attached to the toils. Waiting alleys, by their very nature, are able to connect with a specific thread. But they are also always and already connected to the alley realm more generally. I don't think the human mind will ever truly grasp how the alley realm functions, but it is quite clear to me, and to Mr. Ambrose, that the alley realm in some way consists of every alley that has ever existed or will ever exist. Some of those connections are stronger, some weaker. But the strongest connections will be with live alleys closest in time—as time is measured in *our* world—with the vestibule connected to the birth flame. So, in Lady Penbrook's and Mr. Ambrose's plan, enough of the chronal energy from the birth flame would go into the thread connected to the vestibule to achieve their aim of reanimating that thread. But far more of it would go into the alley realm, and most of that would go into the closest live alleys."

"With what effect?" Gail asked.

"Death," Catherine Collins said grimly. "Death for some or all of the alley rats inside. Unlike threads, which have very little chronal charge remaining, live alleys are maximally charged. Adding any additional charge would be enormously disruptive, and what disrupts an alley often kills its rat."

This matched Mrs. Cutter's worst fears. Mick and Gail looked at one another. Gail's face was serious but otherwise unreadable. Mick tried to keep his the same.

"In theory," Catherine Collins, "one could avoid the risk of so much killing, but that won't be possible for Lady Penbrook and Mr. Ambrose."

"Why not?" Gail asked.

"To reanimate a thread using the birth flame, the thread's anchor point must be sufficiently far in the future. The further in the future, the more powerful the birth flame. The more one has to stretch a thread to make it reach the future anchor point, the less efficient it will be at absorbing the birth flame. The ideal circumstance would be reanimating the thread of the alley that brought one to the past in the first place, but—"

"Those have all been lost to the Collapse, at least for anybody who dropped before the seventh of October of last year," Gail said. "Including Lady Penbrook and Mr. Ambrose."

Catherine Collins nodded. "Essentially, yes. Of course, the scorching of the alley realm resulting from the Collapse seems to have originated from the year 1767 and spread through the alley realm forward to October of last year. As I said, live alleys continue to form in the future and drop rats throughout that scorched period, but one cannot otherwise exit an alley during that period even if one re-anchors its thread to a date within that period."

She checked her watch again. There was a moment of indecision before she continued. "However, Mr. Ambrose and I discovered quite recently and quite by accident that this is not *entirely* true. Because the scorching originated in 1767, its effects are less absolute the later in time one goes. One could, with the right thread and with the blessing of the Goddess of Time, potentially re-anchor an alley and travel back a year, perhaps even two. But only Mr. Ambrose and I have the skill, and neither of our drop alleys are within the last two years. Besides, if one doesn't scruple at murdering many dozens of children, the plan that Mr. Ambrose and Lady Penbrook have devised is simpler and thus more likely to succeed." She checked her watch yet again, frowning even more deeply.

Mick did everything he could to look calm.

"And," Catherine Collins said, "I fear that Lady Penbrook and Mr. Ambrose are very close to success. Indeed, Mr. Ambrose has boasted to me of how close. I don't think Lady Penbrook would wish him to tell me such things. But he has always been bitter and contemptuous about having to obey her commands, and as his sense of urgency increases, his sense of discretion dwindles. I believe, however, that his indiscretion has given me, given *us*, a real chance to stop them. As he was boasting of his genius and of his inevitable success, he waved about certain papers, which, I believe, lay out his plans. Because he is so incapable of believing that anyone can understand his genius, he does not properly cipher his writings. He keeps them under lock and key, but I can get the key."

Gail looked at her for a long moment. "And how do you believe we can help you?"

"You can help me steal the plans," Catherine Collins said. Before that could sink in, she added, "And you can tell me that Chris Biggs is on your side. We shall need her."

After dropping her bombshells, Catherine Collins declared that she had to go and that she would arrange the next meeting by contacting Gail in a similar fashion, though using a different fake message from a different fake sender. Gail nodded, and Catherine Collins bustled off.

Mick and Gail returned to the Institute separately. Mick made it only as far as the warden's nook before being told that Mr. Phillips wished to see him. Mick correctly interpreted that to mean that Miss Emmet wanted to see him.

He found Miss Emmet in her office with Gail, who began summarizing the meeting as soon as Mick appeared. That afternoon and evening, a series of Palladians swore him to triple-cross-his-heart secrecy about everything Catherine Collins had said and everything related to it. Later that evening, the Squad glared grumpily at him because he couldn't tell them anything he was up to, not even that he'd talked to Catherine Collins. He got more grouching from Leech when they went to bed.

The next day was more of the same—endless questions from various Palladians followed by silent surliness from the Squad. The day after that was mostly the same, except that the Palladians started asking him more questions about his contacts with Catherine Collins that all seemed designed to find out whether he'd secretly been in contact with her, or maybe even with Lady Penbrook. Miss Emmet asked those questions neutrally. Then Miss North asked them suspiciously. Then Mr. Victor asked them accusingly. That was when Mick snapped.

"Put on your brass knuckles and punch me for a while, if you want," Mick said. "I'll say the same thing I just told all of you. Because it's the truth. I'm just a kid, and I shouldn't have to do all this anyway. But I'm doing it, and I think I'm doing a pretty good job, and... and saying that I'm lying is just ... stupid. Ungrateful. Stupid ungrateful."

"Mr. Gunn, do control yourself and—"

In a red mist, Mick jerked to his feet and stamped to Mr. Victor's office door. "I'm done," he snapped. "Even if you don't believe anything else I say, believe *that*." As he reached to open the door, his brain dug up something his mom had occasionally said when somebody pushed her too far for too long, "And if you don't like it, fold it until all the corners are pointy and shove it up your ass."

He then stormed out, slamming the door and stomping down the hallway, automatically navigating to Tory Six. In his room, he pulled down the rope ladder and climbed up to the roof, where he sat on the gravel with his back against the leg of a cistern.

For a while, he was too angry to worry about what he'd just done.

Then he was too angry to admit that he was worried about what he'd just done.

Then he was just worried. He'd slammed the door on a professor and told him to shove something somewhere *rude*. A Victorian professor. A Victorian Mr. Victor, who really did have brass knuckles—and knew how to use them.

So either they were going to throw him out on the streets to join all the starving match girls, sickly mudlarks, and chain-smoking baby pickpockets or Mr. Victor was going to accept Mick's invitation to smack him around for a while.

Mick wrapped his arms around his shins even harder and leaned his forehead on his knees.

"You know," Chris' voice said from above him, "I cannot recall the last time I heard Jordan Victor genuinely laugh."

Chris settled onto the gravel beside him, her ribcage lightly touching his shoulder.

"Laugh?" Mick asked.

"Laugh," Chris repeated. "Tears in his eyes, even."

"Why was he laughing?" Mick said, irrationally offended to be laughed at instead of expelled.

"He said something about having a field marshal's tantrum in a child's body," Chris said. "But also, I suspect that he was simply relieved to find that he believed you entirely."

"Why did I have to throw a tantrum for people to believe me?"

"Accompany me for your answer, young sir," Chris said, rising and leading him across the roof to the Turret. Miss Mitchell was standing watch, and waiting inside were Miss North, Miss Emmet, and Gail. And Mr. Victor.

Mick looked at Mr. Victor and then looked down awkwardly.

"Yes, Mr. Gunn," Mr. Victor said dryly, "you do owe me an apology. But we owe you one as well. Let us consider the scales balanced, shall we?"

Mick nodded and managed to raise his gaze to look Mr. Victor and the others in the eye as he sat down. Chris took over standing watch at the gate as Miss Mitchell excused herself.

"Miss Mitchell," explained Miss Emmet, "is assisting Miss Richardson and Mrs. Cutter in attempting to confirm that our understanding of time alleys matches what Miss Collins described to Mr. Gunn and Miss Atkinson."

"Does it?" Chris asked.

"We shall see," Miss North replied. "Thus far, it would appear that our understanding is cruder than Miss Collins', but not fundamentally different."

"Mr. Gunn," Mr. Victor asked, "I take it you haven't any idea why we have been so, ah, persistently asking you about Miss Collins?"

Mick started to tense up again and tried to make himself count to ten. He got to seven. "No."

"Chris and Miss Atkinson spoke with Miss Collins again yesterday evening," Miss Emmet said. "We are still considering Miss Collins' plan to steal Mr. Ambrose's notes about knitting the toils. To our dismay, it increasingly seems necessary if we are to have any chance to stop Lady Penbrook and Mr. Ambrose."

That didn't explain the interrogation Mick had gone through, so he waited.

"Miss Collins cannot steal the plans alone," Chris explained. "The best chance to steal them is when Mr. Ambrose is out of his apartment, but Miss Collins can be sure that he will leave his apartment only when he leaves it with her. They often go out together, essentially on patrol. Occasionally, Lady Penbrook will accompany them in the guise of some sort of distant relation."

"Patrol?" Miss North asked in surprise.

"His apartment is very nearly at the center of Little Cadogan Cluster," Chris said.

"But Little Cadogan is nearly inactive," Miss North objected. "The Eaton Square dons seldom have any need to patrol it."

"The Eaton Square dons have many other responsibilities," Miss Emmet pointed out, "and must rely on the Eyes for much of their intelligence about alley phenomena. And most Eyes are arrows and thus must rely on caterwaulings, which are more easily missed or misunderstood than the signs and stirrings that alley rats can perceive."

"Perhaps more to the point," Chris said, "the Eyes may not always tell the dons everything. Or certain dons may tell Mr. Ambrose or Lady Penbrook's operatives but not the other dons. I suspect that Little Cadogan Cluster will turn out to be rather more active than we have long believed."

"To return to the point," Mr. Victor said, "Miss Collins cannot steal the plans unassisted. But she has no one to assist her, at least no one whom she can trust. Most of the alley rats she knows well are loyal to Lady Penbrook or Mr. Ambrose, and it is not certain that an arrow could identify the plans, even if an arrow could be permitted to see sensitive plans for time travel."

"So she needs our help," Gail said.

"And she has specifically requested *your* help," Chris told Mick.

"Mine?" Mick asked. "Why?"

"Our question precisely," Chris said with a wink. "You might begin to see why we wondered whether your connection with Miss Collins—"

"Who may also be your sister," Miss Emmet observed.

"Who may also be also your sister," Chris echoed. "We feared your connection might be closer than you had admitted. After all, she approached *you*. She insisted on conferring with *you*."

"And now she wants you to commit burglary," Miss North said.

"Housebreaking," Chris corrected with a grin. "It's only

burglary if it happens by night, and we'll have to do it by day. Anyhow, Gunner, you can perhaps understand our concern."

Annoyingly, Mick could understand. "I don't know why she wants me," he said. "You know everything about us that I do. I mean, except stuff that happened in the future, when she was a baby."

"Is there some way she could know of the familial connection?" Miss Emmet said. "You're absolutely certain you didn't tell her, Mr. Gunn?"

"I really wanted to," Mick said, "but I didn't."

"I think we must ask her forthrightly why she is so interested in Mr. Gunn, and why she is so resolved to have a child go housebreaking." Miss North said. "Unless she can provide an excellent explanation, I refuse to permit Mr. Gunn's involvement."

Chris sighed. "It goes against my principles as a sneak and a cheat, but I suppose I could ask honest questions and demand honest answers. Are we so resolved?"

The others looked at each other and, slowly, nodded.

"Mr. Gunn," said Miss North, "if Miss Collins' explanation for desiring your assistance is not compelling, we shall proceed no further with this plan. And even if it is compelling, the housebreaking plan will have to be a very good one indeed. And we shall not force you to do it if you do not think yourself capable. It is too much to ask of you, in truth, and I feel that I have failed as a professor for even contemplating it. But then I imagine a world in which Lady Penbrook is successful, and, God help me, I am willing to contemplate far worse."

11

THE TIME TO ACT

Catherine Collins' explanation for wanting Mick's help with the housebreaking did turn out to be compelling, though anticlimactic. While attempting the Realignment, after falling out of the time alley in a daze, she had seen Mick rush toward her and try to drag her away from the dangerously misbehaving alley. (Although she really had been hurt, she had exaggerated her injuries in hopes of finding a moment to escape, which had worked out nicely for her.) So she trusted him, both his bravery and his morals, and that trust comforted her because she trusted so few people.

Mick discussed this with Chris the following afternoon, when he snuck away from patrol for a few minutes to meet with her in an alleyway near University College London. Chris didn't like it. It would be better to send someone older, ideally an experienced housebreaker. Ideally, it would also be someone Chris trusted completely but not known to be a person she

trusted. And, since the task required going through Mr.
Ambrose's papers, it ideally would be an alley rat who could
read. Unfortunately, very few people checked all those boxes,
and none of them could do it the following day. And Catherine
Collins said it had to be that day because it was the last day she
knew for certain she would be taking Mr. Ambrose out of his
apartment before he and Lady Penbrook might be ready to start
the Summons. Besides, the few people who would be available
the next day and who checked some of the boxes were needed
to run interference and protection outside the apartment to
keep the housebreaker from being seen.

So, as much as Chris didn't like it, Mick probably actually
was the best option. And it was true that whoever went inside
didn't actually need to be a good thief. Catherine Collins knew
where Mr. Ambrose kept his spare keys, and she could arrange
to stash them where Mick could easily find them. If they were
lucky, she would even be able to stash a front door key so that
Mick could sneak out that way and thus avoid Mr. Ambrose,
who used only the rear door because it had the wheelchair lift.

And so, early the following afternoon, Mick found himself
lurking in a carefully chosen spot in the sprawling cobblestone
yard behind Mr. Ambrose's apartment, sitting on a low brick
wall and hoping the broadsheet newspaper on his lap made him
seem respectable and law-abiding. He looked, and felt, alone,
but he knew that Chris and her people were nearby, working
behind the scenes to get him into and out of Mr. Ambrose's
apartment, unobstructed and unnoticed.

Mick couldn't see or be seen from Mr. Ambrose's apartment,
but he did have a clear view of an important set of curtains. One
of Chris' people had broken into an empty apartment that

looked across the wide cobblestone courtyard at Mr. Ambrose's back door. That person was using the curtains to signal Mick. So far, the curtains had moved only once—three quick tugs to one side to let Mick know somebody was on the job. As soon as the coast was clear at Mr. Ambrose's apartment and Catherine Collins gave the signal that she had left the keys for Mick, the curtains would open and close three times.

Mick checked his watch and then the curtains, as he had been doing every thirty seconds for the past ten minutes. He was trying very hard not to freak out. Knowing he would have to sneak into the apartment while Mr. Ambrose was patrolling with Catherine Collins had shattered his sleep with nightmares. And then, just as he had been readying himself to take up his current position, Chris had warned him that Lady Penbrook had been spotted at Catherine Collins' apartment. So there was a pretty good chance that Lady Penbrook would be joining Mr. Ambrose and Catherine Collins.

Mick checked his watch and the curtains several more times, amazed at how much he needed to pee even though he'd already gone three times that morning. Then he heard women's voices. He recognized Catherine Collins' voice immediately, but it took him a moment to recognize the other voice as Lady Penbrook's. She was using an accent that made her sound like one of the social-climbing women at the Ladies Society who always sounded like they were about to chew out a maidservant for impertinence.

He couldn't make out most of what they were saying, but he did hear Lady Penbrook call Mr. Ambrose's name a few times. Eventually, Mick heard a man's voice, followed by some squeaking that Mick assumed came from the pulleys on Mr.

Ambrose's wheelchair lift. The voices continued for a little while and then fell silent.

After an infinitely long ten or fifteen seconds, the curtains opened and closed three times. Cautiously, Mick poked his head around the corner to confirm that the yard was empty. Keeping his hat brim as far down over his face as possible and trying to look casual, he crossed the yard and, to his great relief, found a key hidden in a recess of a cartouche on the stone doorframe, right where Catherine Collins had promised. He quickly unlocked the door, stepped inside, and locked the door.

The first room Mick passed was a kitchen. As Catherine Collins had promised, there was no sign of the maid, whom Mr. Ambrose had sent away for the day. Next was a small back parlor with drapes over all its windows except two dim lunettes at the top. Almost directly opposite the small parlor was a bedroom. Next, on the same side of the hallway, came a larger bedroom, probably Mr. Ambrose's. Then, to the left, a large front parlor and, to the right, a locked door that had to be Mr. Ambrose's study. The hallway ended at the front entryway.

Mr. Ambrose's apartment looked to Mick like what you'd expect from a moderately affluent Victorian gentleman with old-fashioned tastes, except that it was wheelchair-friendly like Tía Julieta's apartment—no furniture cluttering the hallways, no interior doors blocking the common rooms. Otherwise, nothing seemed out of the ordinary. There were definitely no open time alleys or steampunk neon signs flashing "Time-Travelling Villain."

Mick backtracked a few paces to an alcove next to the study. He gently ran his fingers over the top of the frame of a small portrait of Henry VIII until he found where Catherine Collins had left the key to the study. So far, so good.

Unlocking the door, he entered an airy study pleasantly lit by two large bay windows looking across the street at Cadogan Square. The desk was between the windows, beside a short, wide bookshelf.

Crossing the room, Mick worried that he might be visible from the street, but he'd have to rely on the sheer curtains and the fact that it was brighter outside. Among the several dozen leather volumes on the bookshelf were a few with no writing on their spines, including a thin volume bound in slightly cracking red leather. It was a copy of Mr. Ambrose's own *Principia Aperturarum*, written back when he'd been H.A. Braithwaite. Someone, presumably Mr. Ambrose himself, had filled the margins with spidery notes in pencil and inks of various shades. Mick briefly considered sticking the book in his satchel but decided against it. Mr. Ambrose would surely notice if his own book disappeared.

Besides, Mick told himself, he had to focus. He had—he checked his watch—as few as thirty-three minutes until Mr. Ambrose, Lady Penbrook, and Catherine Collins returned. Since he needed a cushion to make sure he got out undetected, he had only twenty minutes to find and steal the right notes. He ran through the description mentally: a few loose sheets with writing on both sides and an ink-splotched front page with a large diagram that looked like the strings of a warped tennis racket.

The obvious place to start, of course, was the desk. Mick carefully searched its drawers and cubbies, finding no sign of the pages he needed. Next, he searched for obvious signs of hidden compartments without any luck.

His stomach started to complain, and his hands trembled a little bit with stress. If Catherine Collins was right, this was his only chance, and so far he hadn't found any papers related to time travel, much less the ones he needed.

Then Mick realized that he *had* found something related to time travel: the *Principia Aperturarum*. He pulled the book off the shelf again and held it over the desk while riffling its pages. Toward the end, some papers fell out. Mick held his breath slightly as he unfolded them. And there they were—ink-splotches near the top, with a diagram on the first page that indeed did look like the strings of a warped tennis racket. There were three more pages, all densely covered with spidery notes. Mick placed the pages in his satchel and buckled the satchel shut. After returning the book to the shelf, he checked his pocket watch again. He still had a quarter hour until Mr. Ambrose and the others were supposed to come back.

Sighing with relief, he quietly locked the study door behind himself. After restoring the key to the top of Henry VIII's portrait, he tiptoed to the front door. He was kneeling beside the hat rack to see if Catherine Collins had managed to leave the front door key for him when he heard a clatter at the yard door followed by loud, surly scolding in a man's voice.

Mr. Ambrose's voice.

Mick froze everything but his right hand, which he let continue to grope beneath the hat rack for the front door key. An eternity passed without his fingers finding anything promising.

During a pause in Mr. Ambrose's scolding, Mick heard the horrifying sound of feet on the back stairs. Realizing with a jolt of panic that Lady Penbrook might enter before Mr. Ambrose, Mick scuttled to the back hallway to hide in the kitchen pantry. But then he saw the doorknob of the rear door starting to turn, so he had to duck into the small bedroom and drop to the floor.

He slid beneath the bed and hoped the flimsy lace bed skirt would shield him from sight. It did, but it also blocked his own view.

Mere seconds later, he heard Lady Penbrook's quiet voice and footsteps from the hallway. She soon stopped speaking and was wearing something soft-soled, so it was hard to tell where her confident strides were taking her. But it sounded like she might have turned into the small parlor directly across the hallway.

There was a soft squeaking sound that Mick assumed came from the winch and pulleys of Mr. Ambrose's wheelchair lift. After some clunking of wood and metal and a few phrases from Mr. Ambrose that sounded like he was probably saying something grouchy, Mick heard the sound of Mr. Ambrose's wheelchair thrumming across the wooden flooring.

"In the family parlor, Mr. Ambrose," Lady Penbrook called, still using her social-climber voice.

"Family," Mr. Ambrose snorted.

Mick heard the yard door being closed and locked, followed by Catherine Collins' quiet footsteps down the hallway, turning the same direction that Lady Penbrook and Mr. Ambrose had gone.

"And here we are," Lady Penbrook said in her regular voice.

"Bloody unnecessary that is, too," Mr. Ambrose said. "The toils are knitted, awaiting only the Summons, which is not my labor. Then you may shuttle the alleys as far as your dainty feet will carry you, Lady Penbrook," he said, placing more than a hint of sarcasm on "Lady." "And I shall avoid burning like the Chambermaid of Orleans and live out my allotted span in pacific rustication. Provided, of course, the girl is equal to her task."

"I rather think you have already exceeded your allotted span, dear Mr. Ambrose," Lady Penbrook said in a cheerful tone, "though by reason of strength you may claim more years, I suppose."

"*My* strength assuredly will not be an issue," Catherine Collins said, a slight edge to her voice. "I am more than equal to my task."

"I am buoyant with delight," Mr. Ambrose said. "Yet, Lady Penbrook," he said, again coating "Lady" with sarcasm, "my hour *does* draw nigh. The guards are dragging me toward the hangman even as we speak. I should perhaps not object to that fate quite so much if I could but watch my dear, drunk papa go to the gallows before me. But his fate must wait a few years yet, and I cannot do so if I wish to live. And I do wish, and deserve, to live, and I shall not accept death, particularly not death by delay."

"It is several days yet, my dear Mr. Ambrose." Lady Penbrook cheerfully. "We are in the palm of Providence and must trust it will see us through."

"Faith without works is a bowl without stew," Mr. Ambrose said sharply. "I have done all that you asked, and more, Diana. I await your fulfillment of our bargain. I shall not die roasted on time's spit like that slobber-chops Cassandra Halliwell. Nor shall I stand, alms bowl in hand, begging for what is mine by right." He paused. Mick pictured him quivering in his chair, maybe shaking a fist. "The time to act is now," he continued. "The fox is in the thicket, so cast your bitch to hunt."

Victorians sometimes used the b-word to actually mean female dogs rather than as an insult, but Mick didn't need to be in the room to know that Mr. Ambrose had meant it as an insult.

"I assure you, Mr. Ambrose," Lady Penbrook said, "that you will not share your protégée's fiery fate. Nor," she added, her tone taking on a slight edge, "do I think you are in any peril of finding yourself standing, whether to beg or otherwise."

Mr. Ambrose spluttered. "Woman, I shall not be mocked, not by—"

"No," Lady Penbrook interrupted calmly. "I shan't mock you. Thank you for that reminder." She paused. "As you say, the toils are knitted, and your work is done. So, I've no need to mock you. And no need to keep you."

Mick heard a faint gasp followed by a louder one. The first gasp might have come from Mr. Ambrose. The second definitely had come from Catherine Collins. Mick had heard the same gasp from her when she'd watched Owl die.

All Mick's muscles stiffened, and his already racing heart accelerated further.

"No," Lady Penbrook said crisply. "Let him be. It is done." After a pause, she continued, "I take it, dear Mr. Ambrose, that, unlike the tabloid journalists, you never marveled that Lord Harrowgrave's killer contrived to escape detection after brazenly stabbing him in the neck in a public building during daylight. Oh, do stop pawing at my hand," she said, "My hand is holding the knife in place, and the knife likely is the only thing keeping your death at bay. If it is removed, I daresay the blood will simply *fountain* forth."

Wait, Mick thought, *did she just—*?

"The solution to the invisibility of Lord Harrowgrave's killer is sadly prosaic," Lady Penbrook continued. "There was no clever use of time alleys or secret passages. Or even daring feats of wall-scaling and rooftop dancing. No, I simply went to Lord Harrowgrave's borrowed offices dressed much as you see me now. A respectable woman of middle-age, marked neither by great wealth nor great poverty, neither by great beauty nor great ugliness. That is to say, invisible, so long as I stood in the right places, with the right demeanor. No one took close note of me, not when I entered the office to kill him, not when I left the office with his corpse slumped forlornly in his chair. Rather like yours will be."

There was a short, awful pause before Lady Penbrook spoke again. "Thinking to offend me just now, you used not my title but my Christian name," Lady Penbrook said. "But then, Diana isn't really a *Christian* name is it? Pagan goddess of the hunt. My dear Mr. Ambrose, the bitch has hunted, and her fangs are in the fox's throat."

There was a sickening gurgle followed by silence.

The silence lay heavy and total for a while before Mick once again heard the sounds of the outside world: cries from the street, the clatter of carriage wheels, even the impossibly cheerful trills of birdsong.

"My dear," Lady Penbrook said, presumably to Catherine Collins, "your compassion does you credit, but it is misplaced. He had only days to live in the present, and under no circumstances could he be permitted to return to the past. Don't delude yourself for one instant that he planned to voyage to the past merely to raise his wrinkled face to the sun and wait for flights of angels to sing him to his rest. At best, he would have gone back to conspire with his earlier self to accumulate power and treasures like a bronze age kinglet piling up a hoard. At worst, well... Perhaps he would have found a way to murder Prince Albert and marry the Queen. Or murder them both and crown himself King Arthur II. Such mortal anachronisms would have meant nothing to him. As far as this wretch was concerned, he was the universe entire. If he was burning, then all the universe burned. And if all of creation had burned *except* him, then, in his eyes, nothing and no one would have been harmed."

"Did you say 'protégée'?" Catherine Collins said. "Did he teach Cassandra Halliwell…"

To waylay all those time alleys and kill all those kids, Mick thought.

"He did indeed train Miss Halliwell," Lady Penbrook said. "I disapproved, naturally. Unlike you, she had neither the alley sight nor the intellect required. But Mr. Ambrose insisted that the fervor to survive was paramount, and Miss Halliwell certainly had that in abundance. Besides, he so delighted in dangling before her the time journals describing useful lift alleys that he had stolen so many decades ago. Carrots in front of a slowly starving donkey, they were. Cruel and, in the end, inadequate." She paused. "Still, Miss Halliwell's efforts, however clumsy, did yield some useful information, and I have been grateful for that of late."

After a long silence, Catherine Collins said, "My lady, should we not leave this place?"

"Momentarily, my dear," Lady Penbrook replied.

During another long silence, Mick lay breathless beneath the bed, screened from murder by only a thin layer of slightly dusty cloth. The ordinary sounds of the world reached his ears but seemed to come from impossibly far away.

Then came a series of muffled crunches. "Broken during his struggle with the burglars, you see," Lady Penbrook said. "Remain here a moment."

Lady Penbrook's feet padded quietly into the bedroom where Mick was hiding, stopping near the head of the bed. He held his breath and made sure not to twitch even slightly. There was a rustling of fabric from above, and then the feet left the bedroom. They continued to pad about the apartment, occasionally falling silent. Eventually, the footfalls returned to the family parlor and fell quiet again. "I've gathered some valuables here," Lady Penbrook said. "Oh, don't look so stricken. This isn't common thievery. It's storytelling. We must give the police a Sunday school tale of good and evil, with all the characters easily identified. Poor Mr. Ambrose, I fear, was killed by housebreakers, who are prone to such atrocities. It's their inherent criminality. Nothing to be done with such men but the gallows, I'm afraid. Hand me his purse, if you will. The burglars took that too, naturally."

Catherine Collins mumbled some reply.

After a silence, Lady Penbrook said in a soothing tone, "My dear, there is a lesson here. I hope you will be able to learn it, after your current very understandable and, indeed, commendable horror and shock have faded away. Pray attend my words now so that you may reflect upon them at some calmer time. Do promise me that, yes? Yes?"

"I promise," Catherine Collins said quietly.

"The lesson, my dear, is that ruthlessness, mere ruthlessness, is not in itself a problem. The problem is ruthlessness in the service of cruelty or solipsism. Mr. Ambrose was quite cheerfully— Well, not cheerfully. He hadn't the faculty for cheer, I fear. He was quite *blithely* preparing to travel to the past to change things with only one purpose and to only one principle—he would have his own way. His mental faculties were remarkable, his genius for time alleys unrivaled. He had been given so much in this world, had seen untold marvels. And yet, he burned with a fury more elemental and more fatal than perhaps even the birth flame. He was aflame with rage that he could not have absolutely everything he wanted, precisely when he wanted it." She paused. "What could be keeping them?"

After another pause, Lady Penbrook laughed grimly. "Ah, I am ahead of my time. The story of my life, as they will one day say. Still, that permits me to finish my sermon. Consider Mr. Ambrose's legs, for example. He lost their use rather late in life and therefore was forced to drink his gins and tonic while seated in a wheelchair at his gentleman's club, rather than while seated in one of the club chairs. A dreadful inconvenience, naturally. A source of considerable physical distress, assuredly. A blow to his independence, beyond doubt. And yet, so many young British men have lost their legs to wasting diseases or industrial machines. Or battling the Taiping Heavenly Kingdom or the Koossas. Or the Burmese, the Sikhs, the Russians, or any of the Empire's endless cast of foes."

After a brief pause, Lady Penbrook continued, "And then, of course, there are the Russians and the Chinese and the rest who lost their legs fighting our young men. Few of those maimed young men, of whatever race, will ever enjoy the luxury of a gin and tonic on ice, much less admission to the famously comfortable salons of Mr. Ambrose's gentleman's club. So too all the women without legs, all the women without voices. Even after all his losses, Mr. Ambrose had far more remaining to him than most people have ever dreamed of having."

After a pause, Lady Penbrook continued. "Mr. Ambrose could have regarded his woes as a test of his character or his faith, like Job. Or he could have taken them as opportunities to forge common bonds with his fellow man—and woman. He could have taken them as one of Fate's endless supply of random cruelties, shaken his fist at the skies for a season or two, and then sought the grace to carry on with some measure of dignity, some scruple of compassion for the suffering of others. Did he do those things, my dear?"

Catherine Collins answered softly.

"Correct. Not one of them. I doubt he even tried. No, he rolled in the fiery gulf, confounded to be held in bondage by his body like a common mortal. Such men are mere boors when their rage turns into tedious maundering about the lost potency of their youth. They are perils when they beat wives and children in order to feel themselves masters of their fists, if not their fates. And they are pestilence itself when they decide that they will set fire to the world in the faint hope that the blaze will nurse them back to health like the hot springs of Bath. And in the face of such all-devouring solipsism, ruthlessness is no vice. It is often a prudent option, even the only option. In the face of destructive selfishness like Mr. Ambrose's, the needle-pointing twittering of the Ladies Society and the feckless whitter-whattering of the Seat are not merely useless, they are wicked. Do you see that?"

After a pause, Catherine Collins said hesitantly. "I ... I believe so, my lady."

Lady Penbrook laughed mirthlessly. "I rather suspect that you don't, dearest Catherine. But such men are all too common in this world, so I rather think that you *will* understand, likely all too soon. Men like this will not hesitate to use you and everyone you cherish as sharpening stones. Or as sheaths. I have spoken now in hopes that, when the time comes, you will do everything possible to be the one holding the knife. But enough of that," she said. "Let us stand by the rear door, if you please. We should make ready our departure."

Their footfalls came close and then moved away from him down the hallway.

"I should think," Lady Penbrook began, "that any moment —" She fell silent at the sound of a voice crying out from the direction of Cadogan Square.

In a deep bellow, the voice called out, "Bottle of gin, fifth of November. Quaff to forget, scream to remember." The voice repeated the same rhyme twice more and then fell silent.

"The time to act is now," Lady Penbrook said. "Do let's go."

"Should we perhaps leave the yard door unlocked, my lady?" Catherine Collins asked. "So that the police will think the cracksmen forced their way in?"

Mick silently thanked her. If she and Lady Penbrook locked the yard door behind themselves, he'd still be trapped in the apartment when the police got there.

"You've kept your wits about you," Lady Penbrook said approvingly. "Yes. That would help the other authors of our tale. Now, let us depart so that they may commence their labors."

Mick heard the door open. In her Victorian social-climber voice, Lady Penbrook called into the apartment. "We shall certainly hope to see you when you are returned from the country, Mr. Ambrose, God willing. Farewell, and thankee for a delightful stroll."

The door closed, silencing any further speech. Mick lay under the bed for a moment, frozen with fear and uncertainty. But the phrase "so they may commence their labors" played on repeat in his mind. It meant that somebody working for Lady Penbrook was coming to Mr. Ambrose's apartment, probably soon. Mick was pretty sure that getting caught by them would be worse than getting caught by the cops.

He pulled himself out from under the bed, making sure his satchel was still buckled.

At the bedroom door, he hesitated, not wanting to look at Mr. Ambrose. At the body.

But in the end, he didn't feel like he had a choice. Partly, it was horror movie curiosity. Partly, he felt that the murder wouldn't be real if he didn't look. And it seemed to him that a murder deserved to be a real thing. So he took a couple steps into the room. The unblocked arcs of window above the closed drapes shed enough light to let him see Mr. Ambrose's slumped form and the dark pool of blood forming around the wheels of his chair.

And suddenly it felt sickeningly real.

Choking back the urge to vomit, Mick turned and hustled to the rear door. He paused there, his hand on the handle, worrying that he would be seen by Lady Penbrook's unknown accomplices. But being seen in the yard would be better than being seen in the apartment. In the yard, he could make a run for it. And maybe Chris and her people could help him.

Pulling his cap down as far as it would go, he lowered his head and slid out the door. Not looking up or around, he forced himself to move at a normal pace while descending the short stairway and crossing the yard's uneven cobbles. Still keeping his cap and his head down, he crossed the street and turned a corner before stopping.

He listened carefully for a while. There were no shrieks of horror, no cries of alarm.

He made himself resume walking, still at a calm pace, until the far end of the block, when he turned right and gradually picked up speed until he was trotting briskly. He held that pace for a couple miles of mostly random motion, steering a course only enough to avoid dons' outposts and Eyes' lookouts and, after realizing that he still had Mr. Ambrose's backdoor key, to toss it into Grosvenor Canal. Once he began to work his way back toward the Institute, he realized that he would have to pass dangerously close to at least one of the Eyes' lookouts to get there. To avoid being seen, he hired a cab, keeping the shades drawn and his head low.

Once the cab had carried Mick far enough away from Mr. Ambrose's apartment, he got out and walked until he needed to stop and concentrate on not completely losing his mind. He stood, leaning his shoulder blades against the cool gray stone of an unseen building until his hands stopped trembling.

He made it very nearly to the Institute before he had to stop again, this time leaning his forehead against more cold stone while his legs trembled. Once the trembling mostly stopped, he resumed walking. By the time he pulled the bell at the Boys' School door, he thought he might even look mostly normal. Fortunately, the warden didn't really look at him when he signed in. He made it to Miss Emmet's cramped, messy, and blessedly safe office and Miss Emmet's worried, safe face before he began to cry.

After Mick pulled himself together enough to explain what had happened, Miss Emmet summoned Gail and whispered urgently to her. Gail rushed off, and Miss Emmet hung the kettle over her little fire to boil water for tea. She allowed Mick to bring his second cup with him when she led him to the Turret.

They were the only ones there, so Mick spent a few moments concentrating on the heat of the tin mug in his hands and the jumbled clamors and clatters rising from the surrounding streets.

Then others trickled in. Mr. Victor was first, then Miss North. Mrs. Cutter arrived with Miss Mitchell. Then Alison, then Gail.

"Chris?" Miss Emmet asked Miss North, who was standing watch at the Turret's gate.

Miss North shook her head. "She is at large, and I thought it inadvisable to send an urgent message without knowing whose hands it would pass through."

Miss Emmet nodded. "Then I believe we may commence. Mr. Ambrose has been murdered," she said bluntly. "This very afternoon, not two hours ago."

There were shocked expressions and murmurs. Mrs. Emmet raised her hand to cut off questions. "Mr. Gunn witnessed the murder, so let us proceed with deference to his overstrained nerves. Mr. Gunn, if you are quite ready?"

Mick pulled his attention back from the tea warming his palms and tried to organize his thoughts. Idly, he noticed that it was chilly despite the honeyed light, which was actually a blessing because it would discourage others from being on the roof. Clever of Miss Emmet, he thought.

"Mr. Gunn?" Miss Emmet prompted gently.

"Sorry," Mick said. He told the story as best he could, sometimes having to circle back and explain something he left out, sometimes having to answer questions.

When he finished, Alison rose from her seat across the table, walked over to stand beside him, and took his hands in hers. "That must have been dreadful, Gunner. I hope, well..." She paused. "I hope that it wasn't *too* dreadful," she said with an apologetic shrug.

He held her hands for a moment before they realized that everybody was staring at them. Alison let go of his hands and returned to her seat.

"And Lady Penbrook said nothing to indicate precisely when she would initiate the— what did Mr. Ambrose call it? The Summons?" Mr. Victor asked.

Mick shook his head. "She didn't really talk about that. Or alleys, even. Just that she didn't need Mr. Ambrose anymore."

"One wonders—" Mr. Victor began before falling silent at a sharp gesture from Miss North. They heard the quiet crunch of feet on gravel.

After a tense moment, Miss North said, "It's Chris."

Mick relaxed a bit, as did the others.

Soon, Chris stepped through the Turret's gate. She wore a plain, clean country dress and bonnet, the sort of outfit worn by the wife of a moderately successful farmer. "Hail and well met," she said with a grin that didn't disguise her fatigue. She focused her gaze on Mick, giving him a compassionate look that suggested she already knew about the murder.

She remained standing at the gate, as usual. "I relieve you, soldier," she told Miss North.

Miss North nodded and took a seat next to Alison.

"Out of purest curiosity," Mrs. Cutter asked, "how on earth did you find us? Miss North said she didn't send for you."

"I guessed where I would go if I desired to convene a secret conclave at short notice. And," Chris added, raising her eyebrows, "I suspected you might desire such a conclave because I just had a fascinating conversation with Miss Collins, who told me of witnessing a murder most foul. She said she rather suspected that our Gunner was also forced to witness it." She looked at Mick. "I take from your face that you were?"

Mick nodded.

"What a terrible thing," she said. "In any case, I shall be happy to answer questions about my conversation with Miss Collins as best I can and to shed any light upon whether we may trust what she told me, but I must begin by saying that she is convinced that Lady Penbrook plans to begin the Summons in four days' time."

12

RED FOR ARTERIES

Mick spent the next morning in tutorials that were basically excuses for Mr. Victor and Miss North to ask him follow-up questions and to give him a few scraps of information. The adult Palladians obviously were holding a lot of things back, but he didn't mind. That afternoon, he and the rest of the Squad received a greet sheet that was basically a permission slip to take a lap around Regent's Park, which is exactly what they did.

As they walked, Mick and Alison tried to catch Dolly and Leech up on the stuff about Lady Penbrook and Catherine Collins that they were allowed to talk about, which wasn't much. Mick still couldn't tell them that Catherine Collins might be his sister, and he and Alison weren't even allowed to say that Mr. Ambrose had been murdered, much less that Mick had witnessed the murder. But Mick could tell that Alison had already warned Leech and Dolly that Mick had recently gone through something terrible and told them not to ask him any questions about it. Mick was grateful for that.

As the Squad was crossing the Great Hall lobby after dinner, Miss Mitchell wandered casually past them and, without stopping, said, "Miss North's office now, all of you."

They reported as required to Miss North's office. Mick sat in one of the small chairs across from her desk, under the sober scrutiny of portraits of Miss North's predecessors as Headmistress of the Institute's now mostly fictional Girls' School. After Miss North emerged from the small study attached to her office and took a seat at her desk, they came under equally sober scrutiny from Miss North herself.

"I must be brief," she said. "Something of great significance might happen in just under three days' time. We must prevent it. Mr. Gunn, your assistance will be required, and you must sleep outside the walls tonight and possibly beyond."

Mick sighed and nodded.

"The rest of you will also have roles to play, and, indeed, those roles will begin with play-acting," Miss North said. "Presumably, tomorrow, if not this evening, others will notice that Mr. Gunn is outside the walls. Miss March and Miss Tee, if anyone at the Institute, whether student, don, or professor, asks you where Mr. Gunn has gone, say that you're not certain but that he did say something about Rumness alleys and spending some time at Oddy's Outpost. Mr. Charles, if asked, you are to say that at first Mr. Gunn said something about the unusual alley phenomena in Tower's Shadow Cluster and perhaps staying at Orphans for a few nights but later said he had been mistaken and probably would be spending some time at Oddy's."

"Mr. Charles," she said, making eye contact with Leech, "master your impulse to embellish. The object is to be believable, not to be amusing. Understood?"

"Yes, miss," Leech said.

Miss North looked carefully at all of them for a moment. "Miss March, Miss Tee, and Mr. Charles, in children of your age, envy is a common failing. I would not be surprised if, in some quiet cockle of your heart, you envy the attention Mr. Gunn has received from the faculty of late."

"We gave up on envying one another some time ago," Leech told Miss North with a wink at Mick.

Dolly and Alison nodded.

Miss North studied their faces for a moment. "And have you likewise given up resenting Mr. Gunn for being unable to satisfy your curiosity about unfolding events because he has been instructed to remain silent?"

"We've agreed to abstain from such resentment for Lent, haven't we?" Leech asked Dolly and Alison, who both smiled slightly in response.

Miss North surprised Mick by smiling slightly as well. "I'm gratified to learn it. The purpose that we all serve is more important than our sensitivities, and our success is far from guaranteed. We must, at least for a little while longer, be our best selves whilst enduring perhaps our worst pressures. All of you but Mr. Gunn are dismissed, with my thanks."

After his friends left, Mick sat silently in Miss North's office for a little while until Gail came to smuggle him outside through the dons' wing. Hailing a cab, she instructed the driver to take them to Islington Green. However, less than halfway there, she tugged the string to halt the cab. The cab had hardly rolled away before she began hailing another. In the second cab, as the rough ride reorganized his internal organs, Mick realized that

Gail was laying a trail that suggested they were only pretending to go to Oddy's Outpost but actually going to Orphans.

Of course, they weren't going to Orphans either, so there were a few more cab rides and some walking around randomly to shake off potential tails until they reached the darkened and deserted offices of Alberts & Samuels. There, Miss Mitchell answered Gail's knock and escorted them along the twisting route to the cork-lined room above Longshanks coffee house.

"I must take my leave," Gail told Mick, "long enough to present myself at Orphans to request a cot in the ladies' apprentice teachers' dormitory and then slip out the back way. Miss Mitchell will stay with you until I return."

Mick nodded his thanks to Miss Mitchell, who nodded back. Finding two cots near the center of the room, Mick lay down on the smaller one. He fell asleep before Gail returned, though he woke when she moved her cot to block the door.

He woke several more times in the night, heart racing from nightmares of Mr. Ambrose's dead face coming toward him and of his mother's sad face turning away from him. Each time, the sheer featureless black of the windowless room oppressed him, but he managed not to call out to Gail or even to cry, at least not much.

In the morning, Gail told him where to find a restroom that would keep him out of public view, but other than that, he wasn't allowed to leave the silent room, which was warmed only by a pair of tired oil lamps until someone from Longshanks eventually left some coal by the back door.

Around eleven o'clock, not long after Gail had lit the fire, Palladians began to trickle in, muttering urgently about things

Mick only half-understood. By noon, Mrs. Cutter, Miss Richardson, Mr. Victor, Miss North, Miss Emmet, Miss Mitchell, and Gail were all there, speaking with one another in small and shifting groups. Mick got the sense they were waiting for something.

It turned out they were waiting for someone, specifically Catherine Collins, who arrived with Chris not long after half-twelve. Catherine Collins was wearing a dress one might find on a rector's daughter, and Chris was dressed like a rector's son who read law at one of the nearby Inns.

At that point, the entire group rearranged the chairs to form an oval so that most people could sit. Gail stood guard near the front door, Chris at the back door. Because there weren't enough chairs, Miss Mitchell and Mick stood with their backs against the middle of the longer walls, facing one another across the oval.

Nobody bothered with introductions, and Miss Collins obviously knew everybody from the Institute and the Ladies Society and probably also from Lady Penbrook's spies.

At Miss Emmet's request, Catherine Collins began by walking through the non-technical stuff. She explained briefly that she had met Lady Penbrook about six years earlier, when she had been growing tired of having exceptional alley sight because it meant that alley-spotting was the only thing she got to do. During a discussion after a Ladies Society lecture, Lady Penbrook had suggested that she could just pretend to go alley blind, which would let her transfer to Lady Grenville's without hassle. "I thought then it was an idle thought, perhaps even a jest," Catherine Collins said, "but I now realize Lady Penbrook had been watching me since I was a girl of eleven or twelve, with the notion that I might one day be useful to her."

Chris shot Mick a glance, raising her eyebrows. Yes, that would explain the interest Lady Penbrook had taken in him.

Gradually, Catherine Collins had become Lady Penbrook's agent. She provided Lady Penbrook with alley-spotting when Lady Penbrook preferred not to use the Institute. She went to society parties attended by alley rats, absorbing information and gossip. She charmed powerful men, also absorbing information and gossip. And, above all, after leaving Lady Grenville's, she became Mr. Ambrose's apprentice.

Lady Penbrook and Mr. Ambrose had never liked one another, but they had needed one another. He had once been a very wealthy man, but he had squandered a great deal of it in his later years, particularly after injuring himself and losing the use of his legs. After that, he had needed Lady Penbrook's money and position to fund and protect his research. And he had needed Catherine Collins because she was young, strong, and able to see alleys extremely well. And, of course, Lady Penbrook had needed Catherine Collins to learn what Mr. Ambrose knew, so that Lady Penbrook could depend on him less as time went by.

"What Mr. Ambrose can—could—do, and what I also learned to do, it isn't simply seeing apertures," Catherine Collins explained. "It's also being able to understand the alley realm. Usually, if one has exceptional alley sight, one can develop adequate understanding of the alley realm. But that is not guaranteed."

"Did Mr. Ambrose injure himself trying to employ this understanding?" Miss North asked.

Catherine Collins smiled thinly. "In a way. He was so interested in testing a new technique for exiting a vestibule that he forgot that the alley was on a railroad track. After the train struck him, he couldn't stand or walk. Although he was as nimble as ever inside the alleys, he needed help finding them and getting to them."

"He didn't remember that moving trains are dangerous?" Mr. Victor asked. "Was he mad?"

"Well, clearly he was mad," Catherine Collins replied. "But not in the sense of not understanding this world. He understood this world quite well, in his own selfish way. But, in the time I knew him, he concentrated more and more of his will and intellect upon the alley realm, becoming utterly monomaniacal."

"Do you know why?" Miss North asked. "Was it something about his plan for the toils?"

Catherine Collins looked at the blank plaster wall for a long moment and sighed. "I told Miss Atkinson and Mr. Gunn not too long ago that I had information about Mr. Ambrose that would make you misdoubt my honesty and even my sanity. I fear that the time has come to explain it. Because unless you know, you cannot understand the full extent of his obsession with traveling backward in time."

"Does it have something to do," Mrs. Cutter asked casually, "with his also being famed alley shuttler Hubert A. Braithwaite, who somehow managed to defy all that we know about time travel and go forward in time nearly forty years, dropping in 1806?"

Catherine Collins bugged out her eyes and lowered her jaw like a stunned goldfish. Mick laughed before he could stop himself. Partly it was just a funny expression, and partly she looked exactly like his mom had once, when he'd done something really dumb that had resulted in his spilling half a bottle of fruit punch Gatorade on her favorite silk blouse when she'd been heading out the door to work.

Catherine Collins showed no signs of noticing Mick's laughter. She was too busy staring at Mrs. Cutter. "How— What— I thought nobody..."

"Nobody did," Mrs. Cutter did. "Not until you brought him to our attention. And until I realized that the fifth worst episode of courtship I ever endured was in Mr. Ambrose's company, in 1806, when he still looked like the illustrations of H.A. Braithwaite that one finds in old books."

"*Fifth* worst?" Chris asked.

"He did not, for example," Mrs. Cutter said, "drunkenly vomit upon my slippers or set my ball gown ablaze with a thurible that he purloined from St. Paul's and swung about like a mace during teatime." Mrs. Cutter smiled. "One so often longs to be young again, but perhaps only because one's memories of being young decay with age." She tilted her head at the flabbergasted Catherine Collins. "Fill your lungs fully and slowly a few times, dear."

"I infer from what Mr. Gunn overheard during—" Miss Emmet stopped herself. "I infer that Mr. Ambrose was fast approaching the day of his birth, and thus his death by birth flame?"

After taking Mrs. Cutter's advice for a few breaths, Catherine Collins managed to regain most of her self-possession. "Yes. In only a few days. Over the years, as the birth flame loomed ever closer, he became obsessed with finding a way to travel back in time."

"Like his pupil, Cassie— Cassandra Halliwell," Mr. Victor said.

"In spirit, but not in procedure," Catherine Collins said. "I hadn't realized that he had been Miss Halliwell's tutor until Lady Penbrook mentioned it after ... after killing him. Since then, I have thought back to remarks he made to me over the years and realized that the monstrous experiments that he forced on Miss Halliwell eventually convinced him that he would never be able to waylay alleys using her method. Something about traveling forward in time changed his relationship to the alley realm, making it far more difficult for him to travel backward in time than it had previously been."

Catherine Collins paused and looked around. "That was why he helped Lady Penbrook with the Realignment, you see. When that failed, he was forced to put his hopes in the Summons. Given his peculiar difficulties traveling backward in time, the Summons might have been less useful to him than to many. Even so, it would likely have saved his life. At first, he thought the Summons might allow him to travel back only as far as last October, when the Collapse was triggered. But he and I learned that, with luck, some rats already can travel back a bit further than that, perhaps a year or two from the present. At the very least, the Summons would have allowed him to do the same, which would have been enough for him. If he could have traveled backward in time by a year or two, often enough, he could have lived out his full life span. Or perhaps given himself enough time to figure out a more enduring solution."

"Why not simply do what Cassandra Halliwell tried to do at the end?" Mr. Victor asked. "Steal another rat's lift alley?"

Catherine Collins shook her head. "He always said that if an alley rat's time journal describes using an alley, that rat necessarily made the trip successfully, and other rats would be unable to steal the alley for themselves."

"Gods," Miss Emmet said. "He kept Cassandra Halliwell

dancing for those journals, and he never for one instant believed they could help her."

"Perhaps Lady Penbrook was not so wrong to kill him after all," Chris said.

"Certainly many who deserved death less have met it sooner," Catherine Collins said, "But his death was not an act of justice. I saw Lady Penbrook smile." She seemed to be searching for the right words. "Perhaps Mr. Gunn was too polite to repeat the particular insult in the telling, but shortly before she killed him, Mr. Ambrose uttered one of his accustomed vile epithets. On the surface, it was directed at me because he and Lady Penbrook were still pretending that they needed my help with the Summons. But he knew that Lady Penbrook intended to initiate the Summons without me. He meant that insult for her. And when he used it, she smiled a small, quiet smile, like a woman yet again reading an old love letter. The smile broadened slightly when she plunged the knife into his neck. And it was still there as she watched the life drain from his face."

For a long moment, Catherine Collins stared across the room at a bare wall. "Lady Penbrook may truly believe her actions to be in the service of justice. She may sincerely wish to champion the cause of the weak against the strong, the righteous against the wicked. But in the end, more than anything, she is precisely what she despised in Mr. Ambrose: someone who thinks that the ultimate purpose of creation is to manifest her desires."

Mick heard all of that, and he understood the warning. But mostly what he noticed was that the look of horror on Catherine Collins' face was almost identical to the one his mom had gotten when she described especially disgusting, cruel actions. The only difference was that there was something in

Catherine Collins' scrunched eyebrows that reminded him of his dad. Well, *their* mom and *their* dad.

Miss Emmet poured Catherine Collins a cup of wine, and everyone sat in silence for a moment except Chris, who tugged a bell pull before unbolting the door and stepping through it. Mr. Victor rose and secured the door, taking up Chris' post in her absence.

"Do we know how Mr. Ambrose traveled forward in time?" Miss North asked. "Perhaps more to the point, do we think Lady Penbrook or one of her minions might also have learned to do it?"

Everyone looked at Catherine Collins. "To my knowledge," she said, "Mr. Ambrose is the only person outside the pages of fairy tale who ever managed to travel forward in time more than a day or two. I don't believe he ever understood how it happened, and I feel quite confident he never managed to do it again. He told me once—when roaring drunk—that, when he told the world of alley rats in 1767 that he was going to use an alley to travel forward six years, he knew he would be able to travel forward two days at the absolute most. But he started the journey on the first of November of 1767, and the day after that was—"

"The Collapse," Gail said.

"Mr. Ambrose thinks that being in the vestibule of a time alley connected so close to the Collapse somehow subjected him to the full force and chaos of the chronal explosion that burned forward in the alley realm. Through fate, or luck, or what have you, when the chronal energy from Collapse hit him, he was already moving forward. So he bobbed upon it like a scrap of flotsam caught in the curl of a tall wave. He said that he was shunted from thread to thread, all of them burning, dying, and forming anew, and that only his, what was it, 'peerless skill' and 'unequaled alley understanding' allowed him to survive." She saw that almost everybody was getting ready to ask questions. "Please remember that time does not move at all the same way in the alley realm. Mr. Ambrose was in the alley realm at what the alley realm considers the same time as the Collapse."

"You sometimes speak of the alley realm as if it were alive," Mrs. Cutter said.

Catherine Collins shrugged. "The threads often feel like living creatures that communicate with each other—and with us. Whether the threads are ultimately complex but lifeless forms of electricity or whether they are actual beings, even sentient beings, I do not know. Perhaps the threads are nerve fibers of a vast and subtle awareness, and the great pulsations of chronal energy through them are celestial nerve impulses. Perhaps to enter an alley is to touch a tiny portion of a single thought in the infinite mind of God."

The room fell silent for a while, so they all startled at the knock on the door. Mr. Victor checked the peephole and opened the door, allowing Chris to bring in a tray laden with pots of tea and coffee and mismatched porcelain cups.

Mick thirstily drank tea while the others savored their preferred beverages. He was halfway through a second cup when Catherine Collins spoke again. "I do not begrudge you your questions. I would ask them were I in your place. But our time is short, and our adversary began the race long before us. Talk must soon give way to action."

Mrs. Cutter nodded and searched vainly for somewhere to set her teacup. Chris caught Mick's eye, lifted the empty tray, and tilted her head at Mrs. Cutter. Mick cut through the oval of people to take the tray from Chris and put Mrs. Cutter's cup onto it. That led to him doing the rounds so that everyone could put their cups on the tray. He deposited the tray on a small, battered table near the door Chris was guarding. Well, now nobody could say he hadn't contributed to the meeting.

"What action do you propose, Miss Collins?" Miss North asked. "It was my understanding that the toils are already knit and cannot be sufficiently unraveled before Lady Penbrook is likely to act."

Catherine Collins, Mrs. Cutter, and Miss Richardson all nodded.

"Miss Collins is the only person opposed to Lady Penbrook who could make the attempt to unravel the toils," Mrs. Cutter said. "And working alone, it would be a matter of weeks, even if Mr. Ambrose's pallid minions did not undo or prevent her work."

"Could she not train others to do it?" Mr. Victor asked.

"In a matter of weeks," Mrs. Cutter said.

"But the Collapsers were able to learn what they needed without Miss Collins' instruction in less time than that," Miss Emmet said. "With her assistance, could we not—"

"That was a different task," Miss Collins said. "They were manipulating threads, which are... But our work would be with waiting alleys, which are much less..." She looked appealingly at Mrs. Cutter and Miss Richardson.

"It won't work," Mrs. Cutter flatly told the group.

"So," Miss North said, "there may then be no solution *inside* the alleys."

"What solution *outside* the alleys could there be?" Mr. Victor asked.

After a tense silence, Catherine Collins said, "The same

solution Lady Penbrook found for the problem of Mr. Ambrose."

A profound silence followed. It was obvious what she meant, but Mick still couldn't believe it.

"Murder?" Miss Emmet asked. "To be clear, you are proposing murder as our solution?" Her tone was surprisingly neutral.

Catherine Collins took a deep breath. "I am proposing homicide. Whether it is murder, self-defense, or defense of others is a different question."

There was a long, awkward silence.

"With Lady Penbrook," Catherine Collins said, "the difficult and terrible thing is that she is so often correct. She is correct that ruthlessness is sometimes justified, even required. I served her because I thought she wished to do good on a grand scale. Now, I realize that, however sincerely she might once have wished to do good, what drives her now is the grand scale itself. She does not scruple at any deed, no matter how foul, that will increase her grandeur. What she proposes to do will kill dozens of alley rats and put her in a position to place more and more of us, and more and more arrows, under her thumb. This is neither fancy nor conjecture. We know that she is willing to abet murder. To *do* murder. And we know, or at least I know, that, at bottom, in the deepest wells of her heart, she does it *not* to protect herself and not to protect others but to cultivate her power and satisfy her pride."

"But still," Mr. Victor said, "to contemplate the deliberate killing of—"

"If those ranged against you," Miss Collins said, standing up and holding her slightly shaking palms up in front of her, "are capable of murder and you are incapable of self-defense, they will win, and you will lose. Always and forever."

"The rub, alas," Mrs. Cutter said, "is that one woman's self-defense is another woman's murder. No, no," she said, holding up her palms to silence Catherine Collins' reply, "I am not saying you are wrong, necessarily. Do sit, dear," she said kindly.

Catherine Collins reluctantly sat down.

"What I am saying," Mrs. Cutter continued, "is that it is a vexed question, one requiring serious moral consideration and practical analysis, and that it may, in this instance, be an academic question. Chris?" she said in a prompting tone.

"Even if we resolve to stab her more thoroughly than Caesar," Chris said, "I'm damned if I know how we would get close enough. Since murdering Mr. Ambrose, she has been living in seclusion in her Mayfair townhouse. My operatives estimate that at least half a dozen armed men guard her person, another half-dozen the property. They are under the supervision of Mr. Harris—"

Catherine Collins shuddered slightly.

"Just so," Chris said. "Mr. Harris is a man given to neither mistake nor mercy. When he deems it advisable to kill someone, the only serious consideration he gives is to which weapon would be most suitable and where best to dispose of the body." She paused. "For Mr. Ambrose's body, it was a lonely wood beyond Fulham. I'd wager the grave was dug well in advance, though my man didn't dare get close enough to see. That was a very neat operation, as one would expect. Three gentlemen went into the apartment by the front door not five minutes after Gunner scarpered out the back. Fifteen minutes later, two gentlemen used Mr. Ambrose's wheelchair to push the body out the back and into a waiting carriage. They had dressed it in a new coat innocent of blood and placed a scarf about his neck to hide the fatal wound. They lifted the body into the carriage as if merely helping Mr. Ambrose to mount it, all the while chatting about his visiting relations in Weybridge for a fortnight. The third gentleman emerged by the front door nearly two hours later, presumably having wiped up the blood and having placed inconvenient materials about time travel in his paper-case."

"So she planned Mr. Ambrose's murder well in advance," Catherine Collins said. "Cold-bloodedly. This is why she must be stopped."

"And why it will be nigh impossible to stop her with a knife to the neck," Chris pointed out. "She has planned to keep herself safe, and her plans are being carried out by cold and careful men. And, although we cannot be sure that she is aware that Mr. Ambrose's plans for the Summons had been removed from his study, we must assume that she is, which will only heighten her care and strengthen her precautions. Short of sending in a regiment or burning down the entire mews in the dead of night, we cannot touch her when she is so thoroughly guarded."

"She must leave her townhouse to undertake the Summons," Catherine Collins said.

"Doubtless her bodyguards will accompany her," Mr. Victor said. "And we shall not know the relevant particulars until she is in motion. Any assassination attempt under such circumstances could succeed only by dumb luck."

They all sat silently for a while.

"I refuse to accept," Miss Emmet said, "that there is nothing to be done."

"As it happens," Mrs. Cutter said cheerfully, "Miss Richardson and I believe that there may indeed be something."

That got people's attention.

Mrs. Cutter looked around the room, "Now, as you know, with Miss Collins' invaluable aid, Miss Richardson and I have grappled with the pages that Mr. Gunn rescued from Mr. Ambrose's study," she began.

Mick smiled slightly at the choice of "rescued."

"And these papers truly were not ciphered?" Miss North asked.

Catherine Collins shook her head. "When first I met Mr. Ambrose, he was jealous of his knowledge and secrets. He shared them only when Lady Penbrook found means to compel him. But as the birth flame drew nearer and his mania grew all-consuming, he became less guarded. He stopped ciphering his papers and grew indiscreet in his discussions of alley phenomena. And, as you know, he'd lately begun to make scenes in public, though I rather suspect at least some of those were carefully calculated to goad Lady Penbrook into swifter action."

"As indeed they did," Mr. Victor noted dryly.

Mrs. Cutter said, "As Mr. Ambrose's papers confirm, it seems inevitable that any great release of birth flame into alley threads, whether into the toils or otherwise, is likely to cause vast collateral devastation. And it seems almost as inevitable that any such devastation proceeding from alleys anchored in 2024 must be the cause of the Shroud, does it not?"

Catherine Collins and Miss Richardson nodded.

"So, perhaps such an event must take place, or, in the inscrutable alley realm, must already have taken place. Otherwise, how would there already be a Shroud? If that is correct, then—"

"We are doomed, and Lady Penbrook is fated to succeed?" Mr. Victor asked.

"Or we ourselves must do something to prevent the Summons that also causes the Shroud," Mrs. Cutter said.

"I have no intention of murdering dozens of alley rats to prevent Lady Penbrook from murdering the same dozens of alley rats," Miss North said, getting several nods of agreement.

"Ah," Mrs. Cutter said, clearly enjoying herself, "but what if our method of causing the Shroud doesn't require killing anyone? In perhaps overly simple terms, Lady Penbrook intends to cause a chronal energy surge by triggering the birth flame and using the toils to augment that chronal energy manyfold. Thus, an already staggering amount of chronal energy will become inconceivably greater, bringing the threads back to life. And that will once again make it possible to truly shuttle the alleys. Of course, the excess of energy would spread to live alleys, killing the alley rats in those alleys. However," she said, raising a finger for emphasis, "what if one were instead to concentrate the energies not in the threads but in the toils themselves?"

Almost everyone responded with uncertain expressions. Catherine Collins frowned thoughtfully for a while. "It would unknit the toils, I think. Without harming the live alleys."

"And thus prevent the Summons," Mrs. Cutter said.

"*And* thus cause the Shroud," Miss Richardson added happily.

"If we can stop Lady Penbrook without becoming murderers ourselves," Miss North, "we must do so."

Catherine Collins was shaking her head. "To do such a thing, we would need to gain entry to Lady Penbrook's alley, wherever it may be. And, as you say, she and Mr. Harris will assuredly have it surrounded by cut-throat guards."

"We could use another alley," Mr. Victor said.

"No," Catherine Collins said flatly. "Only an alley strengthened and stretched by the toils could reach as far as 2024, and it took months to prepare the toils for Lady Penbrook's alley."

"Not if we have access to an alley that already reaches 2024, correct?" Mrs. Cutter asked. "You told Mr. Gunn and Miss Atkinson that a few days ago, and repeated it to Miss Richardson and myself yesterday evening."

Catherine Collins shook her head again. "No. That is to say, yes, in theory. But to trigger the birth flame, Lady Penbrook will have to breach the vestibule in 2024 and touch the tritical then, and that cannot be done without the toils."

"Unless the alley happens to be the alley rat's own drop alley," Mrs. Cutter said.

Wait, Mick thought. *Wait...*

"Mrs. Cutter, I don't wish to be rude, but we have strayed entirely into academic irrelevancies here," Catherine Collins said. "I would have to be the one to step into this hypothetical alley connected to 2024, which means it would have to be my drop alley."

"Let us say for a moment that it is," Mrs. Cutter said.

"It still would avail us nothing," Catherine Collins said. "I don't know my own late point, but even assuming it were in late 2024 or beyond, it wouldn't matter. I dropped in 1833. The thread of my drop alley is long dead and inaccessible."

"What if you could travel back to 1833?" Mrs. Cutter asked, almost playfully.

"If I could travel back to 1833," Catherine Collins said testily, "we would not be having this increasingly pointless conversation, because it would already be possible to shuttle the alleys more freely than has *ever* been possible, and there would be no need for any of this. As I have told you and the others several times, it might be possible to travel back as far as 1853, or even so far as 1852, but certainly no further."

"Well," said Mrs. Cutter cheerfully, "but let us imagine for a moment—"

"Mrs. Cutter," Miss North said, "perhaps a little more explanation, and a little less Socratic dialogue?"

Mrs. Cutter laughed. "Yes, yes. I apologize, Miss Collins. But Miss Richardson and I had an epiphany in the cab ride here this morning that, I feel deep in my bones is correct, because I refuse to live in a universe in which I am mistaken on this point. But I should stop teasing you, and I should actually confirm my belief lest it turn out that the universe is cruel and I am wasting everyone's time. Mr. Gunn?"

Uh oh.

"Mr. Gunn, I think many in this room, for various reasons, have long known or suspected that you have an uncommonly distant late point. You do, yes?"

Mick looked at Miss North.

Miss North said, "I am inclined to tell Mr. Gunn to consider himself unencumbered by all prohibitions on revealing his late point. Does anyone here disagree?"

Nobody spoke.

"Very well," Miss North said. "Mr. Gunn, please tell Mrs. Cutter your late point."

Mick swallowed and took a breath. "The tenth of August, 2024," he said. Saying it sounded bizarre to him. Part of him still thought of 2024 as home, but part of him now considered it alien and impossibly far away.

There were looks of surprise and even a couple gasps.

"And you dropped when?" Mrs. Cutter asked.

"The eighth of March 1853," Mick said.

"So, Miss Collins, if you could take Mr. Gunn back in time thirteen months, you could use his drop alley to prevent the Summons if—"

"Again, no," Catherine Collins said. "*He* could use his alley to stop the Summons. If he had the skills to do so, which he does not and cannot possibly learn in time to stop Lady Penbrook. And once a thing is done within the alley realm, it remains done. If she enters the alley realm in two days' time, what she does there can never be undone. And I fear that is exactly what will now happ–"

"Mr. Gunn," Mrs. Cutter said, "I think now it is time for you to tell Miss Collins."

Mick almost blurted out, "That she's my sister, you mean?" Instead, he asked everyone, "Is that acceptable?"

"Tell me what, Mr. Gunn?" Catherine Collins demanded.

"It is acceptable," Miss Emmet said. The others who knew the truth all signaled agreement.

"Tell me what, Mr. Gunn?" Miss Collins asked again.

Mick sighed. He wanted to just say it and get it over with, but he was afraid that she wouldn't believe him unless he built up a case. He thought for a moment. "When I lived in 2024, I had a family. Aunts, uncles, cousins. Grandparents. Sort of a dad. Everybody except a mom. She died about a year before my late point. So I had to take care of my sister. She was just a baby. In 2024, taking care of a baby can be a boy's job, sometimes. Anyway, my sister had a teddy bear—that's a poppet— named Swaggy Bear. One of our aunts made it for her. That aunt wasn't great at sewing, so Swaggy Bear was kind of ugly. His head was lopsided, his eyes were too close together. But my sister loved that bear. She cried if you put it where she couldn't see it, and maybe her favorite thing to do in the world was to try and grab its legs when I held it above her in the crib."

He paused. He was mostly keeping his eyes on the blank wall because he was worried he'd lose focus if he looked at Catherine Collins' face. "And our aunt was proud of it too. She wasn't great at sewing, like I said, but she worked really hard on it, and she even worked really hard at finding all-natural, child-safe materials so that my sister could chew on it all she wanted and not get sick. And my sister definitely chewed on it all the time. Anyway, because my aunt was proud of it, she sewed the first letter of her first name—J—into one ear and the first letter of my sister's first name—E—into the other ear."

A quick glance at Catherine Collins told him that she knew where he was going and that she was getting a suspicious furrow in her forehead.

"Anyway, it was a one-of-a-kind bear, especially with the initials, so I was pretty shocked when Chris and I were snooping in your apartment last year. This was right after the fight on the bridge. I found Swaggy Bear on your bed. That's when I realized why you looked so familiar. Back in 2024, I had seen photos of our mom when she was almost as young as you, back when she first met our dad. And you look almost exactly like her." There was definitely a suspicious furrow in Catherine Collins' forehead now. "Including when you think I'm lying. Her forehead used to do that too."

Catherine Collins looked at him. "You admit that you saw the bear in my rooms. Naturally, you know what it looks like. You needn't be my brother to have eyes. And I have never seen your mother, so I have no way of knowing whether we resemble one another."

Mick shrugged. "Nope." He realized that he was using his

American accent. He was pretty sure he'd started off in his London accent. "I guess I can't tell you why *you* should believe I'm your brother. I'm just telling you why *I* believe I am. I know what our mom looked like. I know what Swaggy Bear looked like, every crooked stitch, even the ones where our aunt used red and blue thread on the inside because she was worried she'd hadn't bought enough brown thread and didn't want to run out for the parts that showed. She was pretty funny about that. She said she was giving Swaggy Bear a circulatory system. You know, red for arteries and blue for veins."

Catherine Collins was looking at him weird now.

"I know," he said. "I can't prove it to you. Just to myself."

"Red for arteries, blue for veins?" she asked him, still with a weird expression on her face.

"Yeah, mostly down where the legs connected to the body. Maybe also in the neck."

Her face had gone blank, and her mouth was goldfishing again.

"Look," Mick said. "Maybe we can prove it by trying? You can take me back to 1853, and you can try to get into my lift alley with me. If you are my sister, it's your alley too because that's where you sloughed off. Or maybe I'm the one who sloughed off. But you had to go through the same alley from 2024 to 1853, right?" He shrugged. "I don't really understand that stuff, but if there's a chance it'll stop Lady Penbrook, why not try? We don't have an army to stop her in the real world, so this might be all we've got."

"Her name was simply 'Bear,' for a long time," Catherine Collins said slowly. "I was perhaps not the most imaginative child. When I was, oh, nine or ten, I rechristened her 'Artio.' By the time I was matriculated at Lady Grenville's, she had become quite shabby. Having no friends yet among the girls at Lady Grenville's, and not yet having begun my studies, I spent my first day there alone in my little room tending to Artio. I undid what stitching the years had not already undone, washed her fur, filled her afresh, and restitched her all in brown thread."

She looked at him and saw he wasn't getting whatever she was trying to tell him.

"*All* in brown thread. I remember thinking the red and blue thread curious before disposing of it. Not a soul saw me do this, nor did I ever have occasion to tell anyone. I myself had forgotten it."

Ohhhh, Mick thought. "So the poppet I found on your bed..."

"Had not one stitch of red or blue thread. And yet you knew about it, including precisely where it had been." Her hands started to tremble.

"Fill your lungs fully and slowly quite a few times, dear," Mrs. Cutter advised.

They took a break so Catherine Collins could regain her composure. After that, she gave Mick a profoundly awkward and profoundly satisfying hug. Chris cleared the coffee and tea service and came back with fresh pots and cleanish cups.

After that, Catherine Collins, Mrs. Cutter, Miss Richardson, and Gail gathered by the unlit fire to debate whether they could use Mick's drop alley to stop the Summons. The others simply assumed that it could be done and focused on helping make it possible in the real world. They also, it sounded like, were trying to figure out how they could get at Lady Penbrook to slow her down by a week, a day, or an hour, to give Catherine Collins a better chance to get into the alley realm first.

As five o'clock drew near, Catherine Collins and her group announced that they thought it was at least worth trying.

Noting that Lady Penbrook had killed Mr. Ambrose at least in part because he served no further purpose, Chris pointed out that Lady Penbrook might try to kill Catherine Collins for the same reason. Visibly unnerved, Catherine Collins agreed to remain in the room above Longshanks overnight.

"You too, Mr. Gunn," Mrs. Cutter said. "The room is ours for another two days yet, though I think we must act tomorrow if we are to have any chance of success."

Planning continued well into the evening, lit by oil lamps and a small coal fire. After Alberts & Samuels closed its doors for the evening, Gail brought in some bread, cheese, and water. The meeting broke up around midnight, though Mick only knew that because he woke up when people started leaving. Soon, it was just him, Gail, and Catherine Collins.

At some point, someone had found a third cot, so they each settled in to sleep, and Gail extinguished the lamp.

Mick and Catherine Collins had set their cots within a few feet of each other.

Catherine Collins lay there quietly for a while, and Mick assumed she had fallen asleep until she asked in a whisper, "Mr. Gunn?"

"Yes?" he whispered.

"What was my name?"

It was too late to worry about protecting this little bit of the future. "Emilia."

"Emilia," she repeated. "And our surname?"

"Conway."

"Are we Welsh? Scottish?"

"Well, American. In 2024," Mick said. "But before that, Dad's family was Irish. Mostly. Mom's was mostly Mexican."

"Mexican," she said. "I have often wondered. People sometimes suggest I am Italian or Spanish or even Moorish."

"Our skin speaks of the Mediterranean," Mick said, quoting something Lady Penbrook had once told him.

She guffawed. "We really must stop her, you know."

"I know."

After a pause, she asked. "What was your name?"

"Mick. Mick Nicolás Conway."

"A fine name."

"I liked it. Our dad picked it." He paused. "When Mr. Ambrose... When he said he wanted to see his dad get hanged, what did he mean?"

"He was alone with his father when his lift alley appeared," she said. "Mr. Ambrose sometimes said he hoped the police would assume he had been murdered and that a court would hang his father for the crime."

Mick nodded. When the newspapers ran a story about a kid who mysteriously disappeared, the kids at the Institute would debate whether it was an accident, a crime, or a time alley. Sometimes Mick felt bad for a parent or a governess who was getting blamed for it when the real culprit was probably a time alley. He was appalled that Mr. Ambrose had wanted his own father hanged. Mick's dad had turned into a really lousy parent, but Mick didn't want him hanged.

"Why do you ask?" Catherine Collins said.

Mick wasn't sure why he'd asked or why he felt uneasy trying to figure out why he'd asked. "Just curious, I guess. Um, I didn't understand most of what people were saying today. But basically, the plan is for you and me to go back to my drop alley in 1853 and use it to go forward in time and attach Lady Penbrook's alley to ours so that we can do what we need to do before she can start the Summons?"

"Yes, using the alley realm equivalent of blue and red thread to sew a shunt between the alleys in place," she said.

"And then, we'll need to stick our hands or knees or whatever into 2024 from the vestibule to start the birth flame. And then we come back to 1854, if we're still alive."

"Correct."

"And we do have to come back, right? Because the birth flame would absolutely, one hundred percent kill us if we stepped all the way into 2024?"

"Correct." They were both silent for a while before Catherine Collins said gently, "But you must already have known about the birth flame? That you could never return to 2024?"

After a pause, Mick said. "I mean, I knew, but…"

"But you didn't believe?"

"I time-traveled a hundred and seventy-one years to get here. How should I know what to believe?"

She sighed. "A fair point. Still, you must accept that you cannot return to 2024. The birth flame is very real, very powerful, and altogether unforgiving. Otherwise, Mr. Ambrose would not have become so desperate in his final months and days. For that matter, Lady Penbrook would not be preparing to use the birth flame to trigger the Summons, and we would not be preparing to use it to stop her."

Mick realized why he'd asked about Mr. Ambrose's father, at least part of it. "Poor Uncle Dan," he said.

"What of him?" Catherine Collins asked.

Mick explained how he and Emilia had been alone with

Uncle Dan's apartment in a bedroom with bars on the windows. "They're going to think he did it. Like, sold us to kidnappers or murdered us or something."

He could feel her thinking about that for a while before she said, "Poor Uncle Dan, indeed. And you were thinking that if we could return to 2024, then our uncle wouldn't have anything to explain?"

"I guess," Mick said.

"But you do accept that we cannot return, correct? That *you* cannot return?"

"I know," he said reluctantly.

"But do you *accept* it?" she asked.

He shrugged unhappily in the darkness.

13

A QUALMING ALLEY

The planning resumed early the next morning, and by noon the Palladians were resolved that Catherine Collins and Mick should soon begin the first step of the plan, sneaking into the alley thread still attached to a glow-orb Eight that had closed that morning near Granville Square. To help them do so undetected, Chris would scatter a bunch of impostor Gunners and Catherine Collinses around the city to make it harder for Lady Penbrook's spies and thugs to find the real ones. Then, at sunset, the real Mick and Catherine Collins would make their way to the glow-orb under the protection of Chris and her most trusted people, including Mr. Ferness.

The morning and early afternoon passed with Catherine Collins discussing technical points with Mrs. Cutter, Miss Richardson, and Gail. That afternoon, as the others drifted off to their assignments one by one, Catherine Collins and Mick discussed what they needed to do, first, in the alley back to 1853 and, second, in the alley from 1853 to 2024. She had a lot more to do than he did. Basically, in the first alley, he would just need to help her find March 1853. After that, he would have to help her to cause the birth flame. And that mostly just meant he'd have to do whatever she told him to do.

"You do show every sign of being capable of significant alley understanding, including having navigated such an astonishing number of way-worlds, but we simply haven't the time for you —or anyone—to learn the necessary skills," she told him apologetically.

"It's okay," he said. He'd decided to take a vacation from worrying about every word choice. "I should be old enough for high school before I save the world solo anyway."

Sunset was at almost exactly seven o'clock. By six, Gail was the only other person left in the cork room with Mick and Catherine Collins, and she left not long after that, giving Mick a hug that left him flustered.

"She's a formidable girl," Catherine Collins told him after locking and barring the door after Gail's departure. "I can see why you so admire her."

Mick blushed but otherwise ignored the teasing. As the seconds ticked agonizingly down to quarter till seven, Mick stirred the dying coals with the poker and wondered whether he could trust Catherine Collins. He liked her, but he didn't know her. And now he was going to have to depend on her. Obey her. And the stakes were life and death.

He reminded himself he didn't have any choice. Mr. Ambrose and his creepy assistants had finished preparing the waiting alleys, and Lady Penbrook could step into her prepared thread and trigger the Summons at any moment. She had to be stopped, and they couldn't stop her without Catherine Collins.

Besides, Catherine Collins felt trustworthy. She had tried

hard to make the world a little less awful and seemed genuinely horrified that Lady Penbrook had hijacked her efforts in ways that caused death and devastation. She seemed determined to prevent further death and devastation.

Or maybe she only felt trustworthy because she reminded Mick of his mom. He was having a hard time figuring out what he really thought and felt, much less whether any of it was accurate.

But, trust or distrust, he was going to have to go with her to stop the Summons. Or maybe to die painfully while trying.

"It's time," Catherine Collins said.

Mick chuckled as he hung the poker back up.

"What?" she asked as she rose to her feet.

"For us, it's always time," Mick said, also standing. "The problem is always time, and the solution is always time. There's never enough time, unless there's suddenly too much time. Whenever Uncle Dan got tired of doing his job, he used to say, 'My problem is I waste too much time not wasting time.'"

She laughed. But then she paused with her hand on the door handle and said in a serious tone, "'I wasted time, and now doth time waste me.' Only I suppose I helped lay waste to time, which is a rather graver offense." She opened the door and gestured for Mick to go ahead of her. "In the coming perils, do take the utmost care. I don't wish to add any more graves to the list of my offenses."

Compared to all the fake Gunners and fake Catherine Collinses whom Chris had sent throughout London, Mick and his sister had an easy job in terms of getting around. To deceive and confuse the shifty and shifting sets of spies watching them, their doubles had to sneak, skulk, and impersonate. Catherine Collins and Mick simply had to walk three-quarters of a mile while pretending to be a governess and her pupil enjoying an unhurried stroll as a mild April evening glided into twilight. Of course, they had to keep alert, but Chris, Mr. Ferness, Mr. Victor, the young Mr. Davies, and several others were arrayed around them to deal with spies and thugs. Their protectors flickered in and out of sight occasionally, but always at a distance and always without giving any sign that they were aware of Mick and Catherine Collins.

As they walked, Catherine Collins went over the plan yet again. They would enter the recently closed Granville Square alley and anchor it to March 1, 1853 or a bit earlier, giving themselves at least a week's cushion until Mick's original drop alley appeared on March 8. After dropper Mick exited the March 8 alley, they would sneak into it and follow it all the way to 2024. Then, they would stick their hands or feet or something into the real world, doing the time-travel hokey pokey until they generated enough birth flame to destroy the toils and stop Lady Penbrook from starting the Summons. Then he and Catherine Collins would retrace their steps in the alley realm, returning to the real world as close as possible to the same day they were leaving 1854 by doing the alley rat equivalent of jumping out of a moving car and hoping the shoulder of the road was soft.

You know, Mick thought, *the usual.*

He must have had a distracted look on his face. "Mr. Gunn," she asked with a faint note of exasperation, "are you quite sure you understand what you must do?"

Mick laughed.

"This is no time for levity. We are—"

"I'm about to travel in time," he said in what he hoped was a calm tone. "My time-travel babysitter is my twenty-one-year-old sister, who I used to babysit back when she was way younger than me. Which was when we were both younger, and that was about a hundred and seventy years in the future. So, nope, I don't understand what I'm supposed to do. I *know* what I'm supposed to do, and I'll do it. But I don't *understand* it. I still mostly can't do the formulas in the first chapter of the book on apertures. I'm not trying to be funny or," he dug up a good Victorian word, "impertinent. I'm just being honest."

She gazed at him for a moment and then smiled faintly. "Very well."

Not long after that, despite their gentle pace, they had almost reached their destination. Without warning, Catherine Collins shoulder-checked him into a side street. She grabbed his sleeve to halt him and then shushed him before he could ask what was going on.

They stood still and silent for a while until a young woman carrying a basketful of vegetables approached from the opposite direction. Mick only realized it was Chris when she winked at him.

"Was that Lady Penbrook's spy in the yard ahead?" Catherine Collins asked.

Chris nodded. "Two spies. Precisely where the time alley is."

"Only two?" Catherine Collins asked.

Chris nodded.

"Lady Penbrook is being cautious because she knows there is an aperture here," Catherine Collins said musingly, "but she cannot have any serious thought of our using it in the manner we intend, otherwise she would have far more people guarding it. And not just spies. Thugs. Counterfeit police. Real police."

Chris and Mick nodded.

"One assumes you are taking measures?" Catherine Collins asked Chris.

Chris grinned broadly. "Indeed. Mr. Davies will signal when you may proceed. You may safely watch from the far end of that passageway there." She gave a slight curtsey and walked away.

Catherine Collins and Mick crossed the square in the direction that Chris had indicated. She then led him cautiously down the arched passageway until they had a view of the yard.

Mick did a double-take when he recognized the gentleman in the beautiful frock coat who lurked outside Lady Penbrook's townhouse twice each day. He was leaning against a building with his back mostly to them. He was obviously keeping watch despite smoking his pipe and pretending to take the air.

"Definitely one of Mr. Harris' creatures," Catherine Collins whispered. "Too vain to change his attire, even though it makes him easy to recognize." After a pause, she added, "Still, if I owned that coat, I too would be reluctant to wear anything else."

They waited nervously for a few minutes until a handsome carriage rolled to a halt where the yard met the street. The carriage had no obvious markings, and its window shades were pulled down. Its occupant's voice carried clearly across the empty yard. "Mr. Griggs, you and your associates are required at Montague Square."

Lady Penbrook.

"Ah, of course, my lady," the man in the frock coat said, removing his hat and bowing toward the carriage. "Though, begging your pardon, Mr. Harris instructed me—"

"Mr. Harris," Lady Penbrook said, "is invaluable to me because he so often anticipates my wishes. That being said, Mr. Griggs," she added, the edge to her voice clear even at a distance, "I am quite capable of knowing my own wishes. And I wish for you and any and all associates here with you to present yourselves to Mr. Harris at the southern tip of Montague Square. At once, Mr. Griggs."

"Of course, my lady," Mr. Griggs said, bowing.

Without further word from its occupant, the carriage pulled back onto the street and disappeared from view. Mr. Griggs gave a long whistle followed by three sharp ones before also exiting the yard.

Catherine Collins squeezed Mick's upper arm to let him know to wait. After a few minutes dragged painfully past, the young Mr. Davies stepped into the yard. For twenty paces or so, with a deadpan expression, he spun his walking stick in front of him like he was twirling a fire baton in the Chicago Thanksgiving parade. It was such a surreal sight that Mick almost didn't realize that it was the all-clear signal.

Catherine Collins led Mick halfway across the yard and then halted. There seemed to be a faint orange glow where they were standing, something distinct from the soft hues of early twilight, so he assumed they were on top of the now-closed time alley.

"We're lucky Lady Penbrook came along when—" Mick started to say before realizing what had actually happened. "That wasn't Lady Penbrook. It was Miss Richardson."

"I'd assume it was something devious, at any rate," Catherine Collins said. "Chris seemed quite pleased with herself."

Mick smiled. That was exactly the sort of thing that Chris would be smug about for a long time. Miss Richardson too, probably.

Looking like she was having a mild seizure, Catherine

Collins felt the air around her with gloved hands. Eventually, she gave a satisfied grunt and she extended her hand as far as it would go, wiggling it about for a moment.

"If you please, Mr. Gunn?"

Mick pulled a rope harness from his satchel, tying one end around his waist the way Chris had made him practice. As he did that, Catherine Collins tied the rope around her waist, checking the knots and tugging at the six or so feet of rope connecting them.

Then she pushed her hand back into the alley and, like a gentleman opening the door for a lady, pulled her hand back toward herself. The orange glow grew brighter, and the alluring sounds of alley song reached Mick's ears.

Catherine Collins gestured Mick forward.

Tensing himself against the disorientation and misery that he remembered from his first time alley, he forced himself to step forward into...

... into...

What?

Nothing.

Or that's how it seemed, anyway. Forgotten memories of his time alley returned. Once again, he was in a world without light or dimension but still able to do something like see. But what he saw was impossible, and what he felt was unreliable. His body felt as if it were the wrong shape, and when he could see its outline, it looked different than it felt and different than it should look. But so far, at least, Catherine Collins had been right that he wouldn't get the nauseating tearing sensation that he'd suffered in his first time alley, like his body was being hurled in a hundred directions and his mind in a hundred different ones.

—*You're doing well,* Catherine Collins said from somewhere nearby. *The key is to keep calm.*

Only, she wasn't exactly speaking. What he heard didn't really sound like her voice, or a voice at all. It sounded like something his brain was translating into sound from something else.

He tried to remember what to do next. Something about the tug. Right, he was supposed to be feeling the tug of his drop point.

—*I don't feel a tug,* he said.

But then he did. It was subtle but clear, like a gentle pull on a leash fastened to his ribcage.

—*I feel it now,* he said. *I just let it pull me, right?*

—*Yes,* she said. *Please be silent a moment while I explain matters to the alley. She's a bit moody and doesn't wish to converse.*

Talking to the alley meant getting a read on how much chronal energy there was left, which way was future, which way was past. When they'd been trying to stop the Realignment, Mrs. Cutter, Mr. Yardley, and the other fancy math people had described the inside of time alleys as threads, wires, corridors, or train tracks—long, narrow things that existed in real space. Mick was realizing now that wasn't at all how they actually were. Or at least it wasn't how they felt. It felt like he was in a room so big that, if he could make a real sound, the echo would take lifetimes to bounce back, but also so small that he was constantly brushing against the walls.

In a way, he supposed, Catherine Collins really was touching the alley's walls, sensing how to move herself and Mick through the alley in a way that let them un-anchor the thread and take the right end of the thread to the past. He could fake-hear a murmur that might have been a conversation between

Catherine Collins and the alley. She had explained this all to him already, of course. But the explanations only went so far. The language of the regular world was inadequate to the alley realm. Saying "wall" or "move" or whatever to describe a thing or an action in the alley realm was like trying to paint a scent. Even if you could finally get to where you used the right shape and color to depict "dirt road after rain" or "cesspit at midafternoon," they meant nothing unless you already knew those smells.

Fortunately, Catherine Collins did know. Talking to the alleys was her job, and he had to trust her to take care of it. His job was just to feel the tug of his drop point so that she had a fighting chance to anchor the far end of the alley to the right time, even though the right time was at the edge of the desert zone of the Collapse.

—*That's a strong tug,* she told him. *This may actually succeed. Call out when you feel the tugging cease. That will place us at your drop date. And then I shall try to take us a week beyond.*

They continued on for some time in that world without time, and Mick was proud of himself for not screaming like a cat in a bath whenever the alley changed his size and shape.

Then the tugging stopped. He told Catherine Collins. The murmur of her communion with the alley seemed to change.

—*Take my hand,* she said.

He did, and there was a faint sensation of motion, as if the alley were twisting and rotating around them while they floated motionless except for a strange, subtle vibration from the inside. Then the alley suddenly bounced to and fro, like a jet plane landing on a dirt road.

Catherine Collins tightened her grip on his hand.

—*Come with me.*

And suddenly they were back in the regular world.

Mick found himself lying on a patch of grass after being flung out of the alley. He stood up carefully, making sure nothing was too badly hurt. Catherine Collins had kept her feet.

Even the overcast sunlight was far brighter than the alley realm had been, so Mick found himself squinting as he surveyed the yard they'd dropped into. For a moment, he wondered if they'd actually traveled in time at all. Then he remembered that when they'd stepped into the alley, the sun had already dropped below the buildings. But it was now much higher in the sky, lurking behind a gray mass of clouds.

"By the end, our thread was sleepy and sullen," Catherine Collins said. "I misdoubt the perfection of our timing." She paused. "Are we presentable?"

Mick looked her over. "You are." As far as he could tell, she looked exactly the same as when they'd stepped into the alley, her simple dress still clean and crisp, her hair still held in place by her white silk ribbons. Dolly had been right about all-natural fabrics.

"You too, if you can clean off that dirt."

Mick brushed the dirt from his trousers and jacket sleeves.

"We have lost our harness," Catherine Collins noted.

Mick looked down. The rope they had so carefully secured to themselves had vanished. Possibly the alley had rejected it. Possibly it had simply come loose in the strange geometries of the alley realm.

From somewhere to the west came a confusion of competing bells, like crows threatening each other from nearby branches. Then a laggard, lonely bell rang out a few times.

"Three o'clock?" Mick asked.

"Indeed," Catherine Collins said. "Now for the mere detail of the date," she said, starting toward their destination.

Crossing Pentonville Road, they spotted a teenage boy in scruffy but respectable clothing, and Catherine Collins asked him the date.

"Eighth of March," the teenager said.

Catherine Collins and Mick looked at one another.

"Year of our Lord eighteen hundred and fifty-three?" she asked the teenager.

The teenager looked at her skeptically.

Deadpan, she explained, "We're only just arrived from Wales."

If sense of humor was genetic, Mick thought, Catherine Collins had obviously gotten hers from their mom.

The teenager looked at her as if she were a madwoman but eventually conceded that it was indeed 1853.

Catherine thanked the teenager and raised her eyebrows at Mick. They had arrived far later than planned, and Mick's drop alley would open in an hour. They started hustling.

As they went, they debated whether heading to Mick's drop alley was actually the right call. Their other option would be to try to use the Granville Square time alley for a re-do. But Catherine Collins was worried that the thread of that alley wouldn't be reliable because its low chronal charge had made it difficult to anchor and manipulate on the first trip.

"The Collapse would make things difficult even for a thread with more energy remaining, of course, and that thread has turned her face to the wall, poor thing," Catherine Collins said.

So they decided to keep heading to Mick's drop alley. The good news was they didn't need to run. It was only about a mile and a half from where they had started. Besides, running would probably be slower. A woman and a boy pelting down the streets would invite questions, and interference, from good Samaritans or even the police.

So they briskly walked the streets of London, which soon became slick and muddy with the rain that had begun to fall.

Mick tried hard to keep alert to London's usual perils—pickpockets, puddles deep enough to swim in, carriage horses with murder in their hearts. But all he could think about was time travel. First, he had traveled in time *again*. On purpose, this time. He was back where—when—all the insanity had begun for him. Second, and more important, if he could get back to 2024 and prevent his younger self from getting into the alley, maybe he could stop it all from happening.

No, he told himself, again. He'd been over this. If he could get into the alley at all, it was because the alley existed. That meant, at least in the alley realm, the alley had already taken him from 2024 to 1853. Trying to undo what couldn't be undone would have nasty consequences. For all he knew, it could trigger some temporal apocalypse that killed countless people and made him time travel's greatest villain.

Which didn't seem like, you know, a *great* plan.

When they were almost where they needed to be, they asked a passing gentleman for the time and learned they had nearly half an hour.

"One of the more noxious ironies of time travel," Catherine Collins muttered irritably, "is that it's impossible to carry a watch."

After a second gentleman confirmed the time, they stopped in a spot on Parker's Lane not easily seen from either end of the lane. Although the Squad hadn't been able to remember exactly where they'd gone the afternoon before Mick's drop alley, they were confident that they hadn't set foot in Parker's Lane. So Catherine Collins and Mick were safe to stand where they were until the Squad was heading toward Mick's drop alley from the south. Then it would be safe for Mick and Catherine Collins to approach Mick's alley from the north.

With only fifteen minutes remaining until they needed to be at Mick's drop alley, they sauntered in that direction. At t-minus ten, they were standing on a narrow side street, sneaking an occasional peek around the corner at Mick's drop alley, which was on schedule and as expected: a glow-orb Eight shimmering with mixed blues. It had already framed up with bright rings the color of stainless steel. Mick was irrationally proud of how beautiful his alley was.

The alley was also, of course, singing its siren song to him, trying to lure him in, and he was grasping a row of protruding bricks like a rock-climber relying on finger holds to keep himself from falling off a cliff.

He looked down and realized that Catherine Collins was doing much the same. "No Covent Garden street-walker has ever been so insistent and so brazen as a time alley," she said with a tight grin.

Carefully, Catherine Collins poked her head around the corner, holding up a finger to let him know to wait. After an agonizing pause, the warning finger turned into a hand patting him urgently on the shoulder. Moving quietly, she went around the corner, and Mick followed. Keeping one eye closed and the other eye open just a slit, he followed Catherine Collins into the fireworks show of an aperture about to close.

Wow, that's weird, Mick thought, as he saw his dropper self lying face down and motionless, brightly lit in a kaleidoscope of colors. Also embarrassing. Why hadn't anybody told him his naked butt had been sticking out of his tattered shorts like an unfrosted cupcake rising from a cupcake tray?

"I gather your clothing from 2024 was not altogether natural," Catherine Collins said with a tiny smile.

As the time alley's light show continued to intensify, he raised a hand to cover his eyes and accidentally knocked over a broken plank that had been leaning against an ash bin.

Catherine Collins grabbed his hand and pulled him into the alley's aperture. As the outside world disappeared, Mick irrationally hoped his dropper self would be okay. And that he'd find some damn trousers.

Mick had been floating in the alley realm's dark and eerie nonsense space for what felt like a long time. Still holding his hand lightly, Catherine Collins continued to hum-mutter happily with the alley.

—*This one is full of life,* she told him after a while. *And she has so much to sing.*

Mick wondered if Catherine Collins was insane. Then he wondered if there was any such thing as sanity among people who spent their entire lives a century or two before they were born, studying time travel and fighting sinister conspiracies.

Maybe he was the crazy one. Or maybe he'd eaten some bad barbecue at the family picnic and was still in 2024, passed out in the grass near the lake, having a vivid food poisoning dream. His cousin Mateo *had* been handling the burgers, and Mateo *did* get distracted whenever women in sundresses walked by.

Mick sighed as best he could with lungs that felt ten percent too big for his chest and also possibly strapped to his shoulder blades. Nope, this was real. Well, the alley realm wasn't real, exactly. But it existed. And what happened in it, really did happen.

He started to feel uncomfortable, like his stomach was full of bees trying to sting his oversized and wandering lungs. He realized that at least part of the sensation was the tug of his late point.

—*What's going on?* he asked. *I feel weird. It's the tug, I think, but weird.*

—*You are in the thread of your own drop alley, traveling away from your own drop point. The tug is being thwarted, which I imagine could cause an uncomfortable sensa—*

She broke off, and Mick could hear more hum-muttering. He was almost starting to make sense of some of it. Not of the words, if there were words. More like the tone of voice. She was right—the thread did sound a little excited.

—*Is something wrong?* he asked.

The hum-muttering continued for a while.

—*Nothing is amiss, precisely. But the thread is qualming.*

—*Qualming?*

—*Vibrating with energy and uncertainty,* she said. *Unsurprising, given all the complications, actual and potential, woven into this particular thread. It likely is not a reason for concern.*

"Likely." Mick tried to sigh, triggering protests from his backpack lungs and his belly bees.

For an immeasurable while, Mick half-listened to the mostly cheerful hum-mutter between Catherine Collins and the alley while his body complained and his brain played stupid word games. Was time passing? Were they passing time? Had all the time passed, and were they now past time? If, like Catherine

Collins, passing time was your job, did that mean you couldn't have a pastime?

He was starting to get annoyed with his own thoughts when he realized that he felt too terrible to focus on them, anyway. For a while, the nausea and stinging had come in waves, but then the waves had merged into a tsunami of misery that was growing more powerful every whatever passed for a minute in the alley realm. It wasn't just his lungs or his stomach any more. Every muscle was contracting as hard and as suddenly as it could, at random times, in random order, and what wasn't contracting felt like it was dissolving in acid.

He tried to tell Catherine Collins that something was wrong, but he couldn't assemble the words. He tried to squeeze her hand harder, but he couldn't even tell whether his hand was still touching hers.

Several lifetimes earlier, right after Mick had stepped into the time alley in 2024, the alley had tried to pull him in a hundred directions. Now, though, it seemed to be pressing in on him from a hundred directions, trying to compact him into the head of a pin so that wrathful angels could tap dance on him. He wasn't going to fit. He was pretty sure he wasn't going to survive. But the pain burned away any terror he might have felt.

And then even the pain disappeared as the world went blindingly, searingly white before plunging into darkness.

14

THE SHROUD FALLS

—*Well, that was disagreeable,* Catherine Collins said somewhere inside Mick's skull.

Mick tried to open his eyes and realized they were already open. The thread was dark.

—*We are in the vestibule to the tenth of August, 2024,* she said.

That was good news, he thought. Also, he was delighted to discover that his lungs were in almost the right place and the bees had left his stomach.

—*Has Lady Penbrook started the Summons?* he asked.

—*Well, starting and stopping are not the same in here as they are in the tritical, of course,* she said.

He could feel the slight mischief in her thought, and he knew he was being trolled.

—*But there is no sign that the waiting alleys have begun to gain chronal charge,* she said. *Still, there is something happening at the other end of the alley.*

—*Lady Penbrook?* Mick asked, alarmed.

There was more hum-muttering between Catherine Collins and the alley.

—*Perhaps,* Catherine Collins said at last. *But I rather suspect it's alerting me that you and I have entered the 1853 vestibule.*

—*But it brought us here from there,* Mick said. *Why would it alert—*

—*Starting and stopping are not the same here as in the tritical,* she said.

She and the alley hum-muttered at one another.

—*In any case,* she told Mick, *I must now find the vestibule of Lady Penbrook's alley and re-anchor it to this alley. That shunt absolutely must be in place before we can use the birth flame. And we must use the birth flame before Lady Penbrook has a chance to begin the Summons. Wait here. And you do remember that you mustn't move, yes?*

—*Yes,* Mick said. *Wait, though, should—*

But she was already drifting away, or at least growing smaller. Soon, he lost the sense of her presence. He did his best not to move, though he wasn't sure how he'd know whether he was moving.

And he kept doing that.

Forever.

Or it felt like forever. Yes, yes, he thought, time doesn't move the same in the alley realm as the regular world, so who was to say how long he was floating in the empty dark, his body subtly changing shape on him, hoping he wasn't drifting away from the vestibule.

He hoped Catherine Collins was okay.

He hoped she was coming back for him.

Seconds and eternities passed, leaving Mick ever more

certain that she wasn't coming back. He became convinced that Lady Penbrook had killed her. Or that she'd been working for Lady Penbrook all along, and the two of them were off in a different alley, beginning the Summons and laughing that he had trusted Catherine Collins, laughing that he would die frozen and forgotten as his thread slowly lost its charge.

Then, he felt a distant lurch, like he was on a long train and one of its cars had hit a rock. There was a burst of hum-muttering, closer and louder than usual. Then another. Then several more, all of them loud and insistent. It was like an ugly version of the siren song, except closer to speech than music.

No, not *closer to* speech. Speech.

—*Mr. Gunn? Mr. Gunn? Oh, do answer.*

It was distorted and full of echoes, like the kidnapper's disguised voice in action movies, but it felt like Catherine Collins.

—*Hello?* he replied.

—*Mr. Gunn?*

—*Who is this?* he asked, being cautious, in case it was Lady Penbrook.

—*The woman with the lumpy poppet,* the voice said.

It had to be Catherine Collins. And the voice was sounding more and more like hers anyway.

—*Hello,* he said. *Um, how's it going?*

She responded with the hum-mutter equivalent of bitter laughter.

—*Well enough, I suppose,* she said. *I've completed the shunt. Successfully, I believe.*

—*That's great.*

It was great. The 2024 vestibule of Lady Penbrook's alley was now anchored to Mick's and Catherine Collins' alley, not to the real world. So Lady Penbrook couldn't use her alley to start the Summons without re-anchoring that vestibule to the real world, if she even knew how.

Even more importantly, it meant that all of the waiting alleys that Mr. Ambrose's minions had knitted into the toils were now also attached to Mick's and Catherine Collins' alley, which meant that Mick and Catherine Collins could use the birth flame to destroy them.

Mick realized he hadn't gotten a reply from Catherine Collins.

—*It is great, isn't it?* he asked.

There was a long silence.

—*In itself,* she answered at last, *yes. However, it would appear Lady Penbrook entered her alley before I finished the shunt.*

A surge of panic ran through Mick's slightly unstable form.

—*What does that mean?* he asked.

—*It means you must immediately open the vestibule enough to reach into the tritical to initiate the birth flame.*

—*But*—

—*No time for argument. I must remain here at the shunt to stop Lady Penbrook. And you must initiate the birth flame.*

The panic continued to sweep over him, flowing in all directions like a confused whitewater current. He breathed as deeply as his alley-addled lungs would let him.

—*What do I do?* he asked.

—*Ask the alley for its attention.*

—*What?* he asked.

—*Imagine calling a beloved child or pet.*

Feeling like a fool, he imagined calling Scootie, one of those times Scootie had gone off to snooze on the cool tiles of the laundry room and was pretending not to hear him.

—Here, time alley. That's a good impossible entity. Who's a good impossible entity? Does impossible entity want to go for an impossible walk in a place without physical dimensions?

Weirdly, it worked. He could feel the alley paying attention to him.

—Tell it you would like to reach into the tritical.

This part was tricky. When they'd been preparing, Catherine Collins had told him that, normally, alley rats just told alleys that they wanted to leave. She did it by picturing herself opening a door handle. Mr. Ambrose apparently had pictured a butler turning the handle. But Mick didn't want to leave, not entirely. He wasn't asking for a door, exactly. He found himself picturing a drive-through window, open just wide enough to hand out a bag of burgers.

Improbably, it worked. The air around him somehow became tangible, like a frothy gelatin. He focused on really seeing the drive-through window, and the air grew more substantial, almost watery. Holding his breath, he pulled the window sideways to open it.

The window didn't budge.

—Again, Catherine Collins told him.

Mick tried again, and then again, trying to make the window as real in his mind as possible. After maybe the tenth try, it worked. Through the open window, he could see the bedroom he'd shared with Emilia at Uncle Dan's. The big, ratty yellow chair under the window and next to the radiator. The single bed that always wobbled a little bit no matter how many scraps of cardboard he wedged under its legs. The crib that his cousin Gabriela had given his Uncle Dan when it became obvious that Mick's dad wasn't coming to get them anytime soon. It still had pink paint flaking off where Mick had tried to paint over the original blue.

He realized that looking at the bedroom from within the vestibule didn't feel quite like seeing things in the real world—it felt more like a vivid memory. Even so, he was sure that what he was seeing was actually happening. For one thing, there was baby Emilia, wide-eyed and wide awake. It was hard to be sure what she was doing because, seen from the vestibule, time in the real world appeared to move in ultra-slow motion. But his sister had her arms out and seemed to be trying to pull the glow-orb toward her. Her face was nearly frozen in a broad, giggling grin rather than twisted into the surly frown she usually got right after being woken from sleep.

If there had been an up or a down in alley space, Mick would have needed to sit down. It was all there, everything he'd lost to the time alley.

—*Good*, Catherine Collins said. *But I can feel Lady Penbrook drawing near. I may not be able to explain much more to you. Now is the time to put your hand through the opening to trigger the birth flame.*

Remembering the disgusting death of Cassandra Halliwell, Mick gently poked the fingertips of his left hand through the imaginary window. Immediately, his hand began to tingle and pulse. He jerked it back reflexively.

—*Keep on*, Catherine Collins instructed him sternly. *From now onward, keep on even if I can no longer remind you.*

Mick slowly returned his hand through the imaginary window, knuckle by nervous knuckle. The tingling and pulsing returned, but they weren't painful. It felt almost like circulation returning to his hand after it fell asleep. Except warmer. It was definitely warm, though more relaxing-shower warm than all-consuming-flames-of-death warm.

—*Good*, Catherine Collins said. *Now tell the alley you have a gift for it. We must begin the burn. I have been explaining to the alley what must be done, and I shall continue to do so as long as possible. I believe it understands, but I cannot be sure.*

—*Here, imaginary entity*, Mick said to the alley. *I've got treatos.*

—*Give the alley the birth flame. With your other hand*, she said sharply, as he started to pull his left hand out of the imaginary window.

Mick reached out his right hand and felt it sinking into frothy gelatin that also solidified into something like water.

—*Here you go*, he told the alley.

Like electrical current arcing between two wires, the tingling and pulsing leaped from Mick's left hand to his right hand, apparently not passing through the rest of him at all.

The alley itself began to glow, like a faint white LED in a translucent bottle.

—*Good*, Catherine Collins said.

There was a moment of silence as Mick watched the current spark and pulse from his one hand to the other.

—*Lady Penbrook is here*, Catherine Collins said. *Keep on, whatever happens. Even if you must step further into the tritical for the birth flame to burn hot enough. Keep on and do not falter.*

Mick heard hum-muttering between Catherine Collins and the alley, and then there was another hum-muttering, angry and new. There was a violent lurch, then another. The lurches weakened slightly but continued.

He hoped Catherine Collins was okay.

Through the window he had opened into 2024, came a noise blending alley song with the buzz of massive overhead power lines. It almost but not entirely drowned out the distant, angry hum-muttering that he now realized was whatever Catherine

Collins and Lady Penbrook were saying to—screaming at—one another.

—*More, Mr. Gunn*, came Catherine Collins' voice.

She sounded tired and angry.

Mick extended his arm through the imaginary window. If he'd been working at an actual fast-food place, his arm would now be hanging out to mid-bicep. The tingling and pulsing intensified. It felt like it was starting to pass through his entire body. The alley got brighter, almost bright enough to read by.

Still, in his gut, Mick sensed it wasn't enough. He waited a moment to see if Catherine Collins would give him more guidance. But if she was saying anything to him, it was lost in the loud drone of the birth flame and the angry buzzing between her and Lady Penbrook.

Mick mentally transformed the sliding drive-through window into a door. What popped into his mind was the sliding glass door at the back of his family's little brick house in Logan Square. He remembered pushing hard one morning to open the sticky door and setting one foot down onto the cement block patio, where his mom and dad were sitting across from each other at the white metal table. They were smiling at each other like they'd won the lottery, and when they heard Mick at the door, they looked at him, including him in their smiles.

Pain and longing jolted through Mick, weaving themselves into the tingling, pulsing currents of birth flame. He realized he was standing with one foot in the vestibule and one foot in his 2024 bedroom.

His baby sister slowly turned her face to him and smiled with recognition. She seemed to be moving faster now, though not full speed. By habit, Mick started to step over to get in a better position to pick her up but realized that would get him burnt alive. He froze in place.

That was the right choice. He couldn't think and move at the same time. Even standing still, it was almost impossible to concentrate. His ears were overwhelmed. The birth flame was screaming at him. Catherine Collins and Lady Penbrook were screaming at each other, or their alleys, or both, their voices almost sounding like words. The alley was humming like every buzzing insect in the world had found a kazoo and joined a demented jug band.

And his eyes were no better. In his peripheral vision, the thread was a painfully bright white. In front of him, he was seeing Emilia and their bedroom both through the imaginary sliding door and through his regular, everyday eyes, which gave him a dizzying double vision, like looking through binoculars with two very different sets of lenses.

—*Stop, Mr. Gunn*, a voice said.

He almost stopped before realizing that the voice was Lady Penbrook's. It was distorted and distant, but he recognized the firmness of will and note of command.

—*You must stop*, she said.

—*Ignore her*, Catherine Collins said.

—*Miss Collins' worries are misplaced*, Lady Penbrook said. *And even if they were not, she would have you doom millions of people in order to save dozens. Ruthlessness in the service of justice is a virtue, and sentimentality at the expense of justice is a sin.*

Despite himself, Mick hesitated.

—*The dozens are real alley rats*, Catherine Collins said. *Real children who will live or die depending on the choices we make. The so-called millions are phantoms, the imaginary cries of her ambition echoing upon themselves throughout the mausoleums of her victims.*

—*You must stop, Mr. Gunn,* Lady Penbrook said, a desperate edge to her uncanny voice.

—*Do not flinch from what must be done, Mick,* Catherine Collins told him. *My lady, you do not command in this place. Your way is barred. Leave here, or perish here.*

There was more loud, angry hum-muttering. The alley lurched again, slightly.

—*She is gone,* Catherine Collins said. *For now, at least. Keep on, and I shall rejoin you shortly.*

The pulsing, surging sensation of the birth flame being transformed into chronal energy was all Mick could feel, and the humming from inside and outside the alley was all he could hear. He wasn't in pain, but his body was increasingly warm and weary, as if he were sprinting on an ever-accelerating treadmill. He was afraid he wouldn't be able to hold on much longer.

Then, blessedly, he felt Catherine Collins beside him.

—*I shall have to join you in the tritical,* she said.

In the real world, in 2024, he felt her actual hand clasp his.

There was a long pause.

—*Yes,* she said, speaking to herself or possibly the alley. *Yes, that would serve.* To Mick, she said, *I shall now very cautiously step into the tritical, all but my left foot and whatever length of leg I can spare. Please do not jostle me, especially my left foot.*

—*What?* Mick protested. *You'll get fried.*

—*I think not,* she said. *But if I do burst into flames like a pagan Norseman at his funeral, do try not to catch fire yourself.*

She inched forward or, perhaps, the alley vestibule retracted slightly until nearly all of her body was in the regular world. Mick's double sight saw both versions, which made him a little nauseous, as did watching the parts of Catherine Collins inside the vestibule appear to move faster than the parts in the real world.

For a moment, in double vision and at competing speeds, Catherine Collins stood like a contemplative ballerina, her right leg bent, her left leg extended straight with its foot pointed into the vestibule, as she gazed down at the Emilia, at herself, moving in cheerful slow motion.

"There you are," she said to Emilia, her voice sounding in the real world.

She scanned the room, her gaze falling on the small dresser between Emilia's crib and Mick's bed. "Oh, I am relieved," she said.

Mick realized that she was looking at the two pictures Mick kept there: one of him and Scootie and one of Mick's parents not long after they'd met. Despite the double lens of alley sight and regular sight, their photos were clear in the light of the glow orb, which was now mostly white with blue and silver flickers.

He'd been right. Catherine Collins really did look like their mother.

Seeing the photo of his parents hit hard, a breath-stealing gut punch telling him that he was a half-step from home.

He wanted to stay home with his baby sister.

But he couldn't. He'd die in the birth flame. And even if he didn't, keeping Emilia with him in 2024 would kill Catherine Collins, who only existed because Emilia had traveled backward in time. No, it would do worse than kill her. Killing somebody ended their life early, but at least that life had existed. The dead person got to live it, and the living got to remember it. Erasing a person didn't even leave that. If he kept Emilia in 2024, he would be not just a murderer but a monster.

So he would do the right thing, as best he could figure it out. Lady Penbrook was right that sometimes you had to be ruthless. But she didn't seem to understand that sometimes you had to be ruthless with yourself.

He stood shoulder to shoulder with Catherine Collins. By now, he was in pain, some of it from his muscles straining to hold himself steady, some of it from the growing heat of the birth flame. His eyes stung with sweat, and his legs trembled. He held on grimly, gritting his teeth and lying to himself that it wasn't any harder than running course with the dons.

Just when his legs and his denial were going to collapse, Catherine Collins said, "That will more than suffice. You may return to the vestibule."

She reached her right hand into her left sleeve and then extended both hands into the crib. She lifted Emilia from the crib and, her face unreadable, stared for a moment at the baby.

Shifting Emilia to one arm, she said, "And you, of course." She picked up Swaggy Bear with her free hand and pressed it into Emilia's waiting grasp. Cradling her infant self while her infant self clutched her teddy bear, Catherine Collins leaned back into the vestibule, which reached out to cover her over again.

Still seeing with double vision, Mick silently said farewell to the empty little room that he had spent the last year considering his home and salvation.

He pulled himself back into the vestibule, which was still bright white but not as blinding as it had been. The overwhelming humming had faded to a distant murmur.

Mick floated in the featureless white nothingness, somehow sore and hollow at once. Catherine Collins' alley self was floating there with him, Emilia nestled in her arms.

He once again heard the hum-mutter of Catherine Collins communing with the alley. Something on her side of the exchange felt solemn, even sorrowful. It went on a long time before falling silent.

—*Is that it?* he asked. *Did we do it?*

—*We did.*

Her tone was heavy with something—exhaustion, maybe, or regret.

—*Can Lady Penbrook undo it somehow?* he asked.

—*No. We needn't concern ourselves with her at present.*

—*But what if she—?* Mick started to ask.

—*This alley is exhausted,* Catherine Collins said. *We must return to the past swiftly, while there is yet life in her.*

As the light continued to dim, Catherine Collins and the alley hum-muttered to one another for a while. At some point, Mick began to feel his heavy bones being tugged toward his drop point in 1853. They were moving again.

They hadn't been moving very long before they drew near a patch of the alley that hissed like a frightened cat. In the dim light, the patch felt darker and blanker than the rest of the alley.

—*Where I shunted Lady Penbrook's thread to this one,* Catherine Collins explained.

Mick waited for a fuller explanation but got none.

Except for the fading background hum presumably left over from the birth flame, their trip was quiet. The light faded along with the hum.

Though quiet, the trip was not smooth. At random intervals, Mick was jolted about, sometimes in several directions at once. It was like being on a small plane during bad turbulence, except that he had no idea which way was up.

—*Why are we getting bounced around so much?* he asked.

—*My best hypothesis,* she said, *is that it's a combination of the chronal energy overcharge and possibly the attaching and detaching of the waiting alleys.*

—*But the waiting alleys were attached to Lady Penbrook's alley, not ours.*

—*Her alley was attached to ours by the shunt, and the sympathies between alleys so attached can be profound.*

—*How does that work?*

—*Mysteriously.*

Mick let a slow sigh build and escape through his uneven and uneasy lungs. Then a thought occurred to him.

—*When an alley's damaged like that, can a rat in the alley sort of fall in and out of way-worlds?* he asked.

There was a surprised silence.

—*A clever hypothesis. And likely a correct one.*

Mick nodded. That could explain all the way-worlds he'd gotten pulled into his original time through the alley. But, wait —younger Mick had already gone through the alley and dropped in 1853. So, actually, that couldn't explain all the way-wor—

He broke off when he felt someone else in the alley. Someone getting closer.

—*Is it Lady Penbrook?* he asked fearfully.

She gave him the alley-space equivalent of a laugh.

—*No. There is a fourth person sensible to us, yes. But that person is not Lady Penbrook. And is not here, precisely.*

Mick was grouchy about the non-answer until the fourth presence drew close enough that he got a clearer impression of it. It was still oddly fuzzy, but he knew who it had to be.

—*It's me, isn't it?* he asked. *Dropper me traveling back to 1853 for the first time.*

—*Unless I very much miss my guess, yes.*

Dropper Mick disappeared suddenly in a puff of light and then reappeared a few seconds later the same way. That happened a few more times in short succession.

—*Way-worlds?* Mick asked.

—*One would imagine.*

—*Why aren't we falling into the way-worlds like that poor guy?* he asked.

—*I explained to the alley that it would be most inconvenient.*

They hit another patch of turbulence, rattling Mick's teeth.

—*Alas, she cannot spare us from the buffeting,* Catherine Collins said.

Now a good way off, dropper Mick disappeared from view and didn't reappear.

After more turbulent drifting, Mick felt a slight change in the tug of his drop date and alerted Catherine Collins.

She communed with the alley and said that they were close enough to 1853 that they needed to get ready to exit the alley in 1854.

—*What about Emilia?* Mick asked.

—*The alley will see to her safety. To my safety.*

—*But the turbulence. The way-worlds. She could be hurt or—*

—*This alley branches not long before your drop date in 1853. In the branch that leads to her—my—drop date in 1833, the buffeting and the way-worlds will not be a concern.*

They had discussed most of this already. But he hadn't really understood it then, and he was worried about Emilia now that it was actually happening.

—*But—*

—*I promise you that I consider Emilia's safety every bit as important as my own,* she said in an amused tone.

Oh, Mick thought. Right.

—*The alley assures me*, she said, *that the 1833 branch is in good health. The babe will arrive unscathed. After all, I already did.*

Mick nodded. He supposed Emilia would be okay. But he wouldn't see her for another twenty years, when she would no longer be Emilia.

—*Can I hold her?* he asked.

Catherine Collins handed over her younger self, whom Mick took carefully in his arms. It wasn't possible to drop her, not in a place with no up or down. But it still felt important to be careful.

Holding her brought back floods of memories, of his mom, his dad, his loneliness, his sometimes tired, sometimes surly, always profound love for his baby sister, his warm, squirmy little source of joy and ill-timed poop.

The bones of his body bent with changes to the tug of his drop point. They were starting to get close.

—*Not long now*, Catherine Collins said. *Please say your farewells.*

Mick nodded. Unsure what to say to this baby sister whom he had already lost and only just found again, he kept it simple:

—*I love you very much, Emilia. We all did. Be brave. Be good. Be tough. And you're from 2024, so you can say "okay" sometimes if you want.*

—*You will need to let her float freely now*, Catherine Collins said. *There can be no physical contact between her and either of us when you and I step into 1854.*

Gently, hesitantly, Mick let Emilia go, giving her a nudge so that she began to drift away from them both. He looked for signs of distress, but Emilia remained as improbably good-humored as she had been since the alley had appeared in their bedroom in 2024.

—*Goodbye, Emilia,* Mick said.

—*It's been a pleasure to make your acquaintance,* Catherine Collins told her infant self.

A long, eerily quiet moment passed. Then there was a hum-mutter between Catherine Collins and the alley.

—*It's time,* she said, taking Mick's hand.

After one last look at the shadowy outline of his baby sister, Mick took a deep breath and closed his eyes, ready to sneak back into the real world.

15

THE SIGHT OF HOME

Mick tumbled halfway to Edinburgh before coming to rest with cobblestones wedged between his ribs. He lay there long enough to take a few deep breaths and decide that he had landed in the same alleyway where he and Catherine Collins had entered his drop alley and that nothing significant was broken. Still, he felt like he'd been run over by a carriage and six and was pretty sure he'd be nothing but bruises the next day, whenever day that turned out to be.

After much struggle, he got to one knee. A few paces away, his sister was also struggling upright. In the slightly overcast sunlight, she looked frazzled and frayed, her hair half-escaped from its ribbons, her dress smudged and torn. Mick assumed he looked at least as bad.

He patted his butt and was relieved that his trousers were still covering it.

"Are you quite well?" he asked her.

"I'm okay," she said, deadpan.

He laughed more than the joke deserved.

She beckoned him toward her. They trudged down the side street and then turned toward Castle Street, where his sister spotted a boy about Mick's age twenty paces distant.

"You there," she called to the boy with a mischievous smile, "what's today, my fine fellow?"

The boy looked at her suspiciously before answering. "Tuesday, miss."

"And the date, if you'll be so obliging, young sir?"

"May the ninth," the boy said.

So far so good, Mick thought.

"Year of our Lord eighteen hundred and fifty-four?" she asked.

Mick held his breath.

"And what else would it be?" the boy asked sharply, clearly worried that he was being mocked or gulled.

"One never knows," she said in her most aristocratic accent, which made the boy snap to attention despite himself. "One encounters so many years, after all," she said, waving a hand airily.

The boy waited a moment in case she tossed him a coin. When no coin winged its way toward him, he turned abruptly and disappeared down the next street over, plainly eager to escape something, possibly an ambush organized by this inexplicable woman with a queen's pure voice and a governess' soiled dress.

Mick and his sister looked at one another, smiling broadly. "Sloughing off within three weeks of our target from a qualming alley scorched by birth flame," she said. "I should put that against any feat of the shuttlers, including any feat of Mr. Ambrose's."

Mick nodded. He was definitely impressed.

"Still, though," she said, "three weeks will seem rather a long time to your friends and companions, who likely fear you dead."

"Not for long," Mick said. An Eye stationed across the street had scampered away soon after they had emerged from the alley. Someone from the Institute should picking them up soon. Quite soon if a telegraph was involved.

"Yes, the girl with the unfortunate bonnet and the swift feet," she agreed. "Well, I shall take my temporary leave of you, Mr. Gunn. Your friends are charming people, but I fear that quite a few other, less than charming people will also wish to speak with me."

"Are you sure you'll be all right alone?" Mick asked. "If Lady Penbrook or her thugs find out you're back—"

"I suspect Lady Penbrook's thugs, at least in the main, continue to believe me her devoted servant," she replied. "The lady herself, I'm afraid, is dead."

"Dead?" Mick asked. "Really?"

"As the alley described it, it would seem that in the end, Lady Penbrook was able to reclaim her alley and reconnect it to the future. But by then she had lost the waiting alleys, and it appears she made some fatal miscalculations involving the birth flame."

Mick had a lot of questions about that, but didn't get a chance to ask them because his sister was already jogging away. By the time his brain realized it might be a good idea to follow her, she had turned out of sight. Also, everything hurt, and he didn't want to move anyway.

So he let her go, leaned against the nearest wall, and waited for someone from the Institute.

. . .

Fewer than ten minutes later, alley rats came at him from
several directions. He was starting to feel like a hunted fox
when he gratefully spotted the Squad.

Leech reached him first, clasping his hand and then pulling
him in for a hug. Alison and Dolly joined in. Dolly might have
caused some internal bleeding.

Eventually they all let go and stepped back enough to let
him breathe.

"Miss Collins?" Alison asked.

"Gone." Mick pointed back down the alley. "A little while
ago."

"Can you walk?" Alison asked him.

"Must I?" Mick asked.

His dismay made them all smile.

"Don't worry," Alison said. "We shall hail a cab."

Mick laughed loudly. Based on the looks they gave him, his
laugh must have sounded a little crazy. "Sorry," he said. He
gestured around at the alley and the street. "This is where I got
into my first cab in London. With you. After I dropped and was
hurt and tired and could barely walk. So, here we are again, I
guess."

Leech hailed a hackney that took them back to the Institute.
The warden said they were all supposed to present themselves
at the solarium in an hour. Mick decided he needed to shower
first.

Alison and Dolly went to find Miss Emmet, and Mick waited
in the warden's nook while Leech fetched him a clean instisuit.
After that, Leech insisted on escorting him to the gym. At first,
Mick couldn't understand why Leech was sticking with him so

closely. But by the time he'd crossed the Great Hall, he realized that Leech was serving as his bodyguard, invoking the Vicar's authority to shoo away several people who wanted to talk to Mick. Even among those who didn't try to talk to him, Mick was getting a lot of weird looks, including from professors.

"There have been rumors about your fate," Leech said. "People are shocked to see you returned from the dead."

Mick showered as quickly as possible because it was plenty weird enough to get stared at when he had clothes on. He then climbed wearily up the stairs to the solarium, letting Leech fill him in on what the Squad and others had done during the three weeks Mick had been in the alley realm with Catherine Collins. It all sounded pretty impressive.

Alison, Dolly, and Miss Emmet awaited them at the top of the stairs. Miss Emmet led them to the antechamber that joined the Vicar's office to the solarium.

After gesturing that they should all crowd into the small room, Miss Emmet held a finger to her lips for silence. In a whisper, she said, "They are in private discussion within, and you will be summoned to join them in due course. Not all present are Palladians, or even members of the Undertaking. Two of them have just arrived from the Seat. I do not think any of them are hostile to the Palladians' goals at the moment, but I cannot be certain, especially not about the gentlemen from the Seat. So, when summoned, speak only when absolutely necessary. When speech is necessary, be cautious. And be slow to begin, so that one of us will have the opportunity to intervene."

She looked each of them in the eyes in turn. "Understood?" she asked, still whispering.

They all nodded, and she nodded in satisfaction.

"Now, Mr. Gunn," she said even more quietly, "many of their

questions will be for you. If you must answer, say nothing flatly untrue but do say as little as possible. If necessary, pretend to be exhausted or injured by your ordeal—"

"I *am* exhausted and injured," he pointed out.

"That should improve the quality of your play-acting, I should think," she whispered approvingly. "Also, it is entirely possible that a child such as yourself, when exposed to the madness of the alley realm in an aforementioned exhausting and injurious ordeal, might find that he suffers from fogginess of his faculties of memory. Might you suffer from such fogginess, Mr. Gunn?"

"I fear that I do," he said, with a small smile.

"I am exceedingly sorry to hear it. Let us hope it will be speedily remedied, perhaps shortly after you finish answering this afternoon's questioning."

She pointed to the door that they had just come through and said to them all, "Go back to the main door and wait to be summoned. I shall join you as soon as I may."

Mick was the last to reach the door.

"Mr. Gunn," Miss Emmet whispered.

He turned to look at her.

"Thank you for coming back alive," she said. "I'm detectably fond of you."

They were called in after a quarter hour's wait. The solarium's table was crowded and the conversation was confusing. Mick was pretty sure the confusion was deliberate. Any time the questions got into dangerous areas, a Palladian adult would intervene and say something to push the conversation in a new direction.

Alison, Leech, and Dolly were sitting in the chairs and sofas by the fire on the far side of the room, and the adults were sitting around the big table near the main bank of windows. Mick knew many of the adults: the Vicar, Miss North, Mr. Victor, Mrs. Cutter, Mr. Hartnell from the Scriptorium, and eventually Miss Emmet, after she entered through the antechamber door bearing tea as if she'd popped down to the kitchens for it herself. Mick recognized a couple other professors from the interrogation of Cassandra Halliwell. There were also two unfamiliar men with expensive clothes, grim expressions, and brighter than average alley rat eyes. They were about the Vicar's age, one slight and dark-haired, the other stocky and with hair mixing blond and gray. The Vicar had introduced them as "gentlemen from the Seat" but given no names.

The Vicar was at the head of the table with the gentlemen from the Seat directly to his left. The foot of the table was empty, without even a chair, so that Mick could stand there.

At one point, probably to disrupt some questions from the stocky gentleman, Miss Emmet insisted that Mick be brought a chair so that he could "rest his hattered and battered bones." Ruse or not, Mick was deeply grateful for the plain oak chair that eventually appeared. In that moment, it felt as luxurious as any overstuffed recliner.

The gentlemen from the Seat did not seem worried about his battered bones, except possibly as something to gnaw on. They asked him dozens of questions, often the same ones from different angles. He was too tired and sore and ignorant to really understand what they wanted, but they mostly seemed interested in Lady Penbrook's political and financial affairs, which Mick didn't know much about. They hardly asked about what he and Catherine Collins had accomplished in the alley realm.

When the bells at All Souls rang half-four, the gentlemen from the Seat brusquely announced that they really must be going, almost as if it had been rude of Mick to make them ask him so many questions.

The Vicar instructed Alison to see the gentlemen out and told Dolly and Leech to escort Mick to Dr. Quinn for an examination.

Mick was pretty sure that Alison made it up to the infirmary before Miss Weathers and Dr. Quinn finished poking at him and pronounced him healthy but exhausted. He was also pretty sure that she helped Leech, Dolly, and maybe a few others drag him back to Tory Six. After that, he wasn't sure about anything until he woke up late the next morning.

When he woke, Mick was still wearing the instisuit he'd donned the day before. He was also wearing an extensive array of bruises everywhere he could see and surely many places he couldn't. But, he discovered as he stood up, moving didn't hurt much worse than lying still. And he was starving. Although it was too late for breakfast, he still had much of Lady Penbrook's half-sovereign in his satchel, so he decided to PV himself out with the warden and buy a baked potato from the vendor beside the county court on Berners.

The warden refused to PV him, informing him that he was to report to the garden gate immediately.

Mick carried his whining belly and grumbling bones through the corridors and across the garden. The coal man was at the garden gate, making a delivery, but just beyond him, in the alley, was the elder Mr. Davies and his pair of ancient mares hitched to their sturdy wagon. Mick paused at the rungs leading up to the wagon bed.

"Are you waiting for me, Mr. Davies?"

"No longer," the waggoner said, unhitching the reins and urging the mares into motion as Mick clambered painfully into the bed of the wagon and settled into a small pile of hay.

The wagon thudded north for a little while before Mr. Davies reined in the mares. At that point, Chris vaulted up into the wagon bed, hauled Mick to his feet, and caught him in a bear hug. He was tough about it for a few seconds but then started whimpering.

Chris let go and took a step back, taking in the bruises on Mick's face. "My apologies, Gunner. But you know how we fine ladies are," she said, gesturing at what might have been a black-smith's apprentice's Sunday clothes. "We're simply driven by vapors and sentiment."

"Blarney and Cornish steam engines, more like," Mr. Davies said quietly.

"I heard that, Mr. Davies," Chris said. "Do sit, Gunner," she said, plopping herself down in the wagon bed.

"Often heard, seldom heeded," Mr. Davies said, "'tis me lot in life." He flicked the reins at the mares until they resumed their slow northerly route.

From her cloth bag, Chris extracted a parcel wrapped in newspaper and bound with twine. Opening it, Mick found a pair of large sandwiches.

"I suspected you would be famished," she said.

"You're a star," he told her, digging in. Brown bread and chicken. Good chicken, not gizzards and feet.

He wolfed down the first sandwich in half a block but made

himself eat the second more slowly. Even so, he had licked the last crumbs off his fingers before Mr. Davies stopped the horses again.

Mick wasn't especially surprised to see Miss Emmet waiting for them, but he was surprised to see Miss North standing beside her.

Chris hopped to the ground, and Mick eased himself gingerly down. He noticed that Chris had left her bag in the wagon bed. There was probably something top secret in it for Mr. Davies to deliver. The wagon started rolling away as soon as Mick had both feet on the ground.

It was a pleasant day, and Chris, Miss Emmet, and Miss North all seemed cheerful and calm as they greeted him and proposed a stroll along Regents Park. But this was an unusual situation, and Mick couldn't remember the last time something unusual had turned out to be something good. "Please tell me there isn't some alley emergency," he said as they began to walk to the park.

"Not to my knowledge," Miss Emmet said. "Ladies?"

The other two shook their heads.

"Lady Penbrook is still dead?" he asked.

"If Miss Collins is to be believed," Chris said. "And we have no evidence to gainsay her."

"The Summons definitely failed?" he asked.

"Same answer," Chris said.

"There are no weird new alley phenomena?" he asked. "No excess fawkeses, no time lighting, no incorrect coloration?"

"Indeed not," Miss North said.

Mick paused, thinking. "Cassandra Halliwell and Lord Harrowgrave are still dead?"

"There were rumors," Chris said in a grim tone of voice,

"that they had been raised from the grave by a mad acolyte of Victor Frankenstein, and that a dozen priests witnessed them dancing an unholy tarantella at midnight." She grinned at him. "But it turned out merely to be Miss Emmet and Miss North shouting drunken vulgarities at the young men of the Royal Polytechnic during a magic lantern ghost show."

Miss Emmet hooted with laughter, and even Miss North grinned.

When she stopped laughing, Miss Emmet said, "Please don't tease the poor boy with nonsense and slanders." She told Mick, "I am unaware of any urgent time alley situations. Apparently, Chris also knows of none."

Mick smiled gratefully, but a doubt still nagged at him. "Lady Penbrook really is dead, though? Not coming after us? Or my— Or Miss Collins?"

"So far as we know," Miss North said. "We must draw inferences, but the available facts do indeed point to Lady Penbrook's making a fatal error involving birth flame after her plans went awry."

"There has been no sign of her since she stepped into that alley three weeks prior," Chris said. "That to me is proof enough. Her empire was at a crucial moment, on the knife's edge between rising and falling. In her absence, it is falling, and I cannot conceive that she would permit that to happen if she had a single breath left in her."

"Nor I," Miss North said.

It wasn't slam-dunk proof, but Mick did find it persuasive.

"So," Mick said as they turned north at Cumberland Terrace, "if there aren't any emergencies...?"

"Ah, well," Miss Emmet said. "There are always emergencies. You asked about *alley* emergencies."

She chuckled at Mick's worried expression.

"The emergencies are of interest to the three of us," Miss Emmet said, indicating herself, Miss North, and Chris, "but they are not presently your concern. And one hopes they never will be. However—"

"However," Miss North interrupted, "emergencies are like a pestilence. They spread in surprising directions, especially among the ill-prepared."

"So we're here to keep you from getting the plague," Chris said.

"In a very imprecise manner of speaking," Miss North said, with a sharp glance at Chris, who smiled back cheerfully.

Miss North sighed, took a deep breath, and continued. "As Chris alluded to earlier, Lady Penbrook's star was ascendant in the Project. With her death comes great uncertainty and much jostling for eminence. Especially since it was only her clever maneuvering that resolved the uncertainty and jostling after Lord Harrowgrave's recent death."

"There are a great many hogs at the trough," Miss Emmet said. "Many are hungry. Many are angry."

Miss North made a pinched face, but that might have been in response to the pungent smell wafting from the stables of the nearby cavalry barracks.

"In any case, as faction and Napoleonic urges and even idealism all compete to gain followers, the Palladians and, indeed, the entire Undertaking must also be part of the distasteful process," Miss North said. "At the same time, and inseparably from that mêlée, we are also endeavoring to understand how far Lady Penbrook's reach extended into particularly important parts of the Project."

"Such as the Eyes," Chris said.

"And," Miss North said, "the Undertaking itself. It is still extraordinarily hard to know whom to trust."

Mick nodded. That all made sense. But they were right that it didn't seem like his problem.

As she often did, Miss Emmet read his mind. "In all of that, what may become relevant to you is what the various factions and would-be conquerors know of you."

"Me?" Mick asked.

"We have done all that we can to conceal the true extent of your talent for the alleys," Miss North said. "But you are now closely associated with all of the most spectacular and consequential alley phenomena of the past year or so, which likely are the most spectacular and consequential alley phenomena since 1767. You will excite curiosity. And perhaps intrigue."

Following Miss North's lead, they turned onto the circular, tree-lined drive surrounding St. Katharine's Hospital, strolling through its dappled light.

Mick was suddenly glad to be away from potential eavesdroppers, "What should I do?" he asked.

"In the immediate future," Miss North said, "alert us immediately if anyone not known to you as a Palladian seeks to discuss with you Lady Penbrook, the Project, the Seat, or any other such topics."

"Like the gentlemen from the Seat did?" Mick asked, thinking back to the previous afternoon's interrogation.

Miss Emmet said, "I am hoping those particular gentlemen departed not thinking you an exceptional child. Still, it is significant that they questioned you in person."

"And if you must converse with such people," Chris said, "pretend to be foolish whenever possible. It is difficult for one's pride, at first, but a counterfeit fool can often learn more than an honest sage."

"That is how many women become learnèd," Miss Emmet said.

"Including Lady Penbrook, especially before she was widowed," Miss North said. "And her erstwhile protegee, Miss Collins, who for many years had us all convinced that she was far less capable and determined than she is." Miss North checked her pocket watch. "The hour is nearly upon us, I believe."

"Indeed," Miss Emmet said.

When they had completed a circuit of the hospital drive and returned to Cumberland Terrace, Miss North said, "We shall leave you here, Mr. Gunn. You should consider yourself at your ease. Your team is excused from patrols until next week, and you are excused from tutorials until then as well."

"Really?" Mick asked before he could stop himself.

Miss North's lips twitched with amusement. "Miss Emmet, of course, thought you should be required to resume your studies immediately, with extra work as punishment for missing tutorials these past weeks, but I prevailed upon her to be more forgiving."

Miss Emmet grinned. Mick looked back and forth between her and Miss North. Miss North had just made a joke. Mick wondered if Catherine Collins had brought him back to an alternate timeline.

"And while you are at your ease, Mr. Gunn," Miss Emmet said, "do be sure actually to take your ease. Dr. Quinn was most emphatic that you are to avoid straining your body or your mind."

Mick nodded and then winced from the pain in his neck. Yeah, he was fine with not doing anything for a while.

After they said their goodbyes, he watched them until they turned from sight. He was ninety-nine percent sure they weren't simply taking a stroll, but he couldn't guess what they might be up to. Taking a train from Euston Station to see the sights? Taking a canal boat to the Thames to catch a tall ship to explore the time alleys of Bombay? Stealing the silverware from Lady Penbrook's townhouse?

Well, if they had wanted him to know, they would have told him. He thought about walking to the Coliseum to see a panorama, but he hadn't even reached the drive to the Botanic Gardens before his legs informed him that his money would be better spent on a cab back to the Institute.

For the next few days, Mick did indeed take his leisure. Mostly, he slept and ate. He spent much of the remaining time in the tory common room or, in tolerable weather, on a bench in the garden. One afternoon, the Squad found him on a garden bench enjoying the moist, cool air that was making vague gestures toward storming.

Dolly was smiling gently, her equivalent of dancing with glee. "We've found them," she announced. "Well, Chris found them."

"Who?" Mick asked.

"The Collapsers," Dolly said.

Mick tried to make sense of that. "But they're not..."

"Alive?" Leech asked. "No."

"Their graves," Dolly explained. "These past weeks, while we were waiting for you to..."

"Stop playing truant," Leech said.

"Return safely," Alison said, swatting Leech's arm.

"Miss Mitchell and I," Dolly continued, "began to look for the Collapsers' graves. We thought that they might be buried near one another."

"And Chris told us that different arms of Project often pay for gravestones for alley rats," Alison said.

"The Institute paid for Owl's headstone in the Marleybone cemetery," Leech said.

"So we started our search there," Dolly said. "Chris' associates at the Seat pointed us towards several sets of plots from approximately the right dates. Whenever time has permitted, we have been looking at the headstones. And today we found the Collapsers," she said proudly. "All eight. We've just told Miss Mitchell."

Mick was going to ask if they were sure they'd found the right graves but realized what a dumb question that would be. Dolly wouldn't have mentioned it, especially not to Miss Mitchell, if she wasn't absolutely sure.

Alison apparently spotted the stifled question on his face, however. "It seems quite inarguable," she said. "All the headstones bear the date of the Collapse, in the same code you found at the Foundation."

"The oldest headstone is for a Reginald Bateman, from 1770," Dolly said.

"Mr. Bateson not having strained himself overmuch when choosing a new name," Leech observed.

"The most recent is from 1837," Dolly said.

"Can you tell which one—" Mick broke off, realizing that it might make Dolly sad to ask if she knew which headstone was Miss Jennings'.

Dolly nodded. "Jennifer Matthews. She died in 1831. Miss Mitchell says that would have made her about eighty-four at the time of her death. A long life and, I trust, a good one." She wiped a tear from her eye.

"Miss Mitchell says that she believes the Institute may wish to hold a memorial for the Collapsers," Alison said. "In the meantime, a few Palladians will visit their graves tomorrow evening. We shall attend."

Her tone didn't leave room for disagreement, not that Mick would have disagreed anyway.

The next evening was beautiful and clear as Mick and the rest of the Squad walked to the Marylebone cemetery. Along the way, when they couldn't be overheard, Mick explained some of what he and Catherine Collins had done. His friends let a lot of the insane and impossible stuff pass without a word, but Leech and Alison, especially Leech, thought imagining a drive-through window was hilarious. Dolly hadn't even heard of drive-through windows. Mick could see Leech getting ready to tease Dolly but then stopping when he remembered why they were going to the cemetery.

At the cemetery, they joined Miss Emmet, Miss North, Mr. Victor, the Vicar, Mrs. Cutter, Chris, Gail, and Miss Mitchell. Mick raised his eyebrows at Chris when he realized that the Collapsers' worn, mossy headstones were the same set of head-stones where Chris had recently asked him to review photographs of people who worked for Lady Penbrook. She shrugged to indicate that she hadn't known.

At Miss Mitchell's request, the Vicar said a few words, beginning by reading from a battered King James. "'For we know in part, and we prophesy in part. But when that which is perfect is come, then that which is in part shall be done away.'" The Vicar closed the Bible and took a deep breath. Seeing that the Palladians were safely alone on the hill, he added, "We are all of us parts, and even bound together in love and purpose, we are but part of a greater whole that we cannot know in this life. But though we must look through a glass darkly, though we must rely on hope and imperfect prophecy, yet good souls and good deeds shine in the darkness. And the eight people buried here, whom we knew as youths with their lives ahead of them, their good souls and good deeds shine across the decades, and in our memories."

They stood quietly for a while, chatting softly, crying, and listening to birds sing as the sun began to contemplate twilight. Eventually, people took their leave until only Miss Emmet, Miss Mitchell, Gail, and the Squad remained.

Miss Emmet said to Dolly, "Miss Tee, I thought you might wish to know that you were correct that the message Mr. Gunn found in the Foundation was indeed not the only one the Collapsers left. This morning, tormented by something half-remembered, I visited the approaches to the Vault and found an essentially identical message chiseled into a wall there. I feel a bit foolish for never having given it any thought, at least not after the events on the Hungerford Bridge."

"Well done, Dolly," Alison said as Miss Emmet took her leave.

"Despite our long months of thinking the Collapsers silent," Miss Mitchell said, patting Dolly on the shoulder, "it would actually seem they did their utmost to send us messages. That includes Matilda." She paused for a moment. "I wrote her a poem once, and she quoted a stanza in the message you found at the Foundation, Mr. Gunn. 'The willow dances in the storms / that split the thicker oak. / So must my heart bear seeing you / and when that sight be cloaked.'" She paused again. "Nor is that the only place she quoted it."

Miss Mitchell pointed to the inscription on the headstone in front of her. Below Miss Jennings' new name—Jennifer Matthews—was the phrase "She danced in the storms."

"I worked through the night," Miss Mitchell said, keeping her voice level, "to begin to learn about Miss Jennifer Matthews. And I discovered the most remarkable thing. She was apparently one of the founders of the Society for Chronal Fancy. She and Mr. Yardley both."

"What?" Dolly asked incredulously.

"But Miss Jennings hated the Society for Chronal Fancy," Mick said.

"With a deep and eloquent passion," Miss Mitchell agreed, grinning. "But apparently she and Mr. Yardley nonetheless concluded that the Society would serve vital ends."

"Such as publishing the cipher texts for the Collapsers' message to us," Dolly said, wiping her eyes and smiling slightly.

"Indeed," Miss Mitchell said. "Can you imagine her face when she realized that she would have to found the Society for Chronal Fancy?" She laughed, which set them all off, even Dolly.

After recovering from their laughter, the Squad left Miss Mitchell in Gail's care and went to visit Owl's grave.

"Gunner," Leech said as they all contemplated Owl's clean, bright gravestone, "while you were playing truant, we learned that the new edition of *Hyde's* will add the Thames cluster to the list of alley clusters. Its official name will be 'Hungerford Cluster,' but *Hyde's* will note that it is also referred to as 'Owl's Rest.' Some of us are already calling it that."

That caught Mick off-guard, and his eyes welled up with tears.

Everyone spent a moment discreetly wiping their eyes.

"He was a good lad," Leech said. "I wish I'd known him better."

They all nodded.

"And I'm glad I know you all as well as I do," Leech added.

"Even less than the common run of man," Dolly said, "none of us chose to be in this place and time. But even if I could have chosen everything, I could not have chosen better companions."

That also caught Mick off-guard, and he welled up again.

The first time he had dropped here, it had not been his choice. But the second time, in many ways it had. And he would make the same choice again. He would miss a lot about the future. He'd had a good family, all in all—people who had loved him and looked after him. And maybe someday his dad would even have remembered how to be a parent. But the future was no longer his home. His friends were his home. His sister was his home. A world where his abilities allowed him to help people who needed help was his home.

For a moment, the sunlight sparkled in his tears like twilight on the Thames—a mirror of sunshine, a shroud over graves. Then he wiped his eyes and savored the sight of home.

EPILOGUE
THE TIME BEFORE THEM

The two very somber and respectable solicitors exchanged somber and respectable glances and made somber and respectable bows to the company before withdrawing from Demeter Manor's formal parlor. Mick could hear their footsteps in the front hall, followed by the sounds of Mr. Anderson opening and closing the front door. Through a parlor window left open to exchange the stuffy air inside with the soothing, post-rainfall autumn air outside came the sound of horses nickering, carriage doors thudding, and the crunching of hooves and wheels on gravel as the solicitors' growler rolled away.

The snooty butler returned to the parlor and announced in his sonorous voice, "The gentlemen have departed, my lady," he said.

"Thank you, Mr. Anderson," Catherine Collins said. "We shall be adjourning to the Refuge."

"Very good, my lady. Will your ladyship require assistance with the hamper?"

"Generously though Cook has laden the hamper, I should think this strapping young fellow here"—she nodded at Mick—"will be equal to the task."

The hamper was so full because Mick's sister, as the new Lady Penbrook, was hosting a meeting of the Palladians in the Refuge, and the turnout would include the Squad, Gail, Miss Mitchell, Miss North, Miss Emmet, Mr. Victor, Mrs. Cutter, and even the Vicar. For discretion's sake, only a few of them would dine at the house afterward, meaning that the rest would have to be fed in the Refuge.

Catherine continued, "Mr. Anderson, if you think it consistent with the orderly operations of the household, please take your leisure now and extend leisure to the staff through the end of the coming weekend. There will be a great deal of work to be done come Monday, and I should very much like everyone to begin with rested arms and ready spirits."

"Very good, my lady."

"Oh, and Mr. Anderson," Catherine said, "after tonight's dinner, I should like that leisure extended to the kitchen staff. If necessary, you are permitted to make a reasonable draw upon the household account to purchase food from The Globe or otherwise, as you see fit."

"Very good, my lady," Mr. Anderson said.

Mick got the sense that Mr. Anderson didn't actually think it was very good, but Mick wasn't going to trouble himself too much about Mr. Anderson's happiness. In fact, that afternoon, he had gotten to live out a long-held, petty revenge fantasy by showing up to the Manor in a fancy carriage and a fancy suit and getting to watch the snooty butler be obliged to suck up to him.

"Dear brother," Catherine said, "if you would be so kind as to carry the hamper?"

"Of course, dear sister," Mick said.

He said it in a flippant tone that matched hers, but it was an enormous pleasure to be able to call her his sister, in part because deep down he had never totally been able to make himself stop thinking of her as his sister, even if it no longer made sense to think of her as Emilia. Of course, the public version of their brother-sister relationship was largely invented, part of a pack of lies that had allowed her to become Lady Penbrook and heir to most of the Penbrook estate.

Like the late Lord Harrowgrave, the late Lady Penbrook of course had been a fiction. The woman whom they had known as Lady Penbrook had been an alley rat smuggled into a position of power with the aid of forged documents, invented backstories, and rather good play-acting. So nobody at the Undertaking, especially the Palladians, had any scruples about executing similar deceptions to do the same for Catherine Collins. Miss Emmet had been a driving force, as had the Vicar. As Miss Emmet told it, at the Seat there had been a lot of bickering, making and breaking alliances, genteelly threatening blackmail, and haggling like hungry costermongers until two main factions emerged. One was led (secretly) by the Palladians, and the other was led by a coalition ranging from creepy megalomaniacs to well-intentioned reformers. In the end, the two factions had agreed that Catherine Collins would become the new Lady Penbrook and that the coalition's candidate, Mr. Vossington, would become the new Lord Harrowgrave. Some of the late Lady Penbrook's valuables and an estate in Kent had gone to various parties to seal the deal.

"Do keep up, brother dear," Catherine called. She had reached the chicken coop.

Mick was ten or fifteen yards back, struggling with the heavy hamper. "Yes, my lady," he called back snarkily. He wished Ward were there to help him, but Ward probably shouldn't be involved with the Palladians, even just to carry their hamper. Besides, it was one of Ward's days to go looking for street kids to rescue.

As to replacing the late Lady Penbrook, after the spoils had been divided in back rooms, old dusty documents had been "found" showing that Catherine Collins was the daughter of the late Lady Penbrook's only sibling, an estranged younger brother, now deceased. There was a complicated story about her concealing her true identity from the late Lady Penbrook out of loyalty to her father. That was designed to explain why she had never mentioned being the late Lady Penbrook's niece even though the two women had known each other for years. Similarly fraudulent documents showed that Mick was her half-brother, born to the same Italian countess mother.

Mick thought it all sounded like a bad telenovela, but Chris and Miss Emmet assured him that it would work. The trick, they said, was to pretend that you were trying to cover up some shameful secret. That way, everybody focused on trying to uncover the secret rather than thinking about why important parts of the story out in the open didn't make much sense.

And, as Miss Emmet pointed out, anybody who really had a problem with the story would be up against a beautiful, clever, wealthy woman who had been named as the late Lady Penbrook's devisee in an impeccably forged will—a woman admired by fashionable society, schooled in ruthless intrigue, and guarded by a regiment of somber and respectable solicitors in very expensive suits like the gentlemen who had just left the Manor.

Catherine took pity on him and waited for him at the far edge of the cow paddock, where the path to the Refuge turned to dirt and cut across the north pasture.

"Your legacy will soon be ripe," she told him, staring over his shoulder.

It sounded like a metaphor, so it took him a moment to realize she was saying that the farm's grapes were getting close to harvest. Lady Penbrook's forged will had included a few fun flourishes, such as giving Mick a life tenancy in a "reasonable share in the harvest of grapes on the Demeter farm for howsoever long grapes may there be cultivated." Mick was pretty sure whoever had forged that clause had heard the late Lady Penbrook's grapes speech at some point.

The thing was, Mick thought, it had been a really good speech. He still mostly believed it. You should sow now whatever you want to reap later, even if no one around you has ever tried to grow it before. The problem was that the late Lady Penbrook had started watering everything with blood without realizing it would hurt the harvest.

"The grapes were a nice touch," Mick said. Since his sister was standing still, he set down the hamper and rubbed his shoulder. To his relief, the Refuge wasn't too much farther. He could see patches of its stone walls and slate roof through the bushes, birch, and London planes at the far edge of the pasture.

"Whoever conceived and forged all those documents was an artist possessed of a rare genius," Catherine said. "It makes me all the more embarrassed by my clumsy efforts."

Mick laughed. Not long after Miss North, Miss Emmet, Chris, and Catherine had held their first summit about

Catherine taking over as Lady Penbrook, Catherine had confessed to him that, after she and Mick had discussed Mr. Ambrose's desire for his own father to be hanged for murder, she had started to worry about Uncle Dan. After all, both baby Emilia and Mick had disappeared from Uncle Dan's apartment in the middle of the night without any signs of a break-in, so Uncle Dan was the obvious suspect in their disappearance. So she had written a note reading, "Your children have been taken to serve justice. None may stand against our cause!" Just after they'd finished with the birth flame, she'd left the note in Emilia's empty cradle before stepping back into the time alley.

Mick had surprised her by breaking out laughing. He'd had to explain what he'd learned from watching cop shows with Uncle Dan. 2024 cops would be able to tell that the paper of her note was totally antique in terms of what it was made out of and how it was made. But it would also be brand new. Same for the ink. The handwriting would be archaic, especially because she'd written it with a dip pen. And her fingerprints would be all over it, and the cops would match those fingerprints to the ones that Tía Verónica had gotten taken as soon as Emilia had turned one. So his sister had left a kidnap note covered with adult-sized versions of the kidnapped baby's own fingerprints. It would melt the cops' brains.

But then they had realized all that would probably be a huge help to Uncle Dan precisely because it was so bizarre and impossible. Where would Uncle Dan get brand new 170-year-old paper? How could he leave a note that had adult Emilia's fingerprints on it? To do all that, you'd have to be a criminal mastermind with skilled minions. And a criminal mastermind would have come up with a way to kidnap his niece and nephew that didn't make him the prime suspect. Mick and Catherine were still trying to cook up plans to help Uncle Dan further, but so far none of them was half as good as that impossible note.

"I *can* help you with that," she said, nodding at the hamper.

"Chris would mock me the entire meeting," he said.

She smiled. "Onward then, brother of mine. The hour is nearly upon us, and there are a great many bad works to be undone before we can commence the good ones."

Mick hefted the hamper over his shoulder and smiled at her. "Don't fret, sister of mine. We have plenty of time before us."

www.ingramcontent.com/pod-product-compliance
Lightning Source LLC
Chambersburg PA
CBHW052019240626
47153CB00006B/1869